PEN

The L g

Libby Ashworth writes sagas set in Lancashire, England, where she was born and brought up.

Libby still lives in Lancashire and is passionate about its history. She can trace her direct ancestors back to the village of Whalley in the Middle Ages. Many of her ancestors worked in the cotton industry – first as home-based spinners and handloom weavers, and later in the mills of Blackburn. It is their lives Libby has drawn on to tell her stories.

Libby also writes under the name Elizabeth Ashworth.

The Rag Maiden

LIBBY ASHWORTH

PENGUIN BOOKS

PENGUIN BOOKS

UK | USA | Canada | Ireland | Australia
India | New Zealand | South Africa

Penguin Books is part of the Penguin Random House group of companies
whose addresses can be found at global.penguinrandomhouse.com.

First published 2024

001

Copyright © Libby Ashworth, 2024

The moral right of the author has been asserted

Set in 12.5/14.75pt Garamond MT Std
Typeset by Jouve (UK), Milton Keynes
Printed and bound in Great Britain by Clays Ltd, Elcograf S.p.A.

The authorized representative in the EEA is Penguin Random House Ireland,
Morrison Chambers, 32 Nassau Street, Dublin D02 YH68

A CIP catalogue record for this book is available from the British Library

ISBN: 978–1–405–96202–5

www.greenpenguin.co.uk

For Peter and Alice

1848

I

Kitty had vowed that she would not look back. But as they reached the brow of the hill she turned for one last glimpse. Clinging to the leeward slope of the valley, the walls of the cottage stood roofless, open to the rain that swept in from the sea. The thatch lay in ruins where the crowbar brigade, sent by the landlord, had wrenched it down as she'd pleaded with them not to destroy her home.

'Best look to the future,' Peter told her as he touched her arm to urge her on. 'The new world awaits,' he said, trying to make it sound as if it held the promise of a better life. It was what they'd told the children – that they were leaving the hunger behind and going to a land that was rich with food and opportunity. But what if the dream they had been sold was nothing more than the ones that dissolved into half-forgotten memories at the break of day? Times were hard. If Kitty had been given the choice, she would have preferred to stay in Ireland. But their potato crop had failed again and they were left with nothing, even though they'd had such hopes. The old folklore said that if the potatoes failed one year they would come back in abundance the next one, and when the first shoots had poked up from the soil and grown strong and sturdy through May and June, Kitty had been convinced that this time things would be better. Then the brown spots had appeared on the luxuriant leaves and within a day or two the bright green had given way to black. The plants had given off a sickening stench of decay. The stems had snapped. And when they'd dug the potatoes up they'd found the tubers were hard and withered.

Kitty had sat in the field and wept. She'd had no idea how they were to eat, never mind pay their rent. Peter had tried to find work, but there was none. They had begged for relief but none had been forthcoming. Then they'd received the letter telling them to leave their home. The landlord wanted to enclose his land to farm animals and now the smallholders and their families who had regularly paid their rent for generations were nothing more than a nuisance to him. The failure of their crop had given the landlord the excuse he needed to turn them out. And all he'd given them in recompense was a ticket for a ship to America.

Kitty turned away from her ruined home and began to follow her husband along the track that would eventually lead them north to Dublin. The eldest three followed their father in a line – Agnes, Timothy, Maria. They walked barefoot, the mud clinging to the soles of their feet, and each carried a small bundle of belongings that they had salvaged from the wreckage of the cottage. Her husband carried a pack on his back and held little Peter in his arms. Kitty carried the baby wrapped in the folds of her shawl. She prayed that the sickly boy she had given birth to only a few weeks previously would survive the long journey that lay ahead of them.

Ominous clouds gathered and Kitty felt the first spots of cold rain as the wind lashed them on to her face. Soon the downpour would begin in earnest, but it would make little difference. They were already wet and cold after a night spent sheltering against the walls of their roofless home, trying, and failing, to coax the turf into a blaze to warm themselves.

At dawn, she had given the children the remains of their food. She'd tried to feed the baby, but her own lack of nutrition had all but dried her milk and the child seemed too listless to suck anyway. Then they had left. The last of their family to go. And the only thing that Kitty knew for certain was that they would never come back.

They spent days on the road, begging for the odd handful of oatmeal or a drink of sweet milk for the baby as they travelled. The older children had complained of hunger and cold, but the baby rarely cried and seemed to be asleep most of the time. Kitty was relieved he was so still. It would have been hard to carry a wailing, threshing infant. He was a good baby, she thought, although she wished that he would feed more insistently whenever she did manage to sit down to suckle him.

People had been kind, even though they had little to spare, and although some nights had been spent sheltering in ditches, one night they'd been invited to sleep in a farmer's barn with some handfuls of straw for their mattresses. As they'd left the next morning, the farmer and his wife had blessed them and wished them well, but Kitty had seen the fear in their eyes that they might be next to be forced on to the road.

As they approached Dublin they fell in with others who had similar tales to tell of bailiffs who had turned them out of their homes. Some spoke with hope of the life that awaited them on the other side of the ocean. The dream of better things to come was the only reason they had kept walking through the rain and the chill, bellies growling with hunger and children whimpering with tiredness. But most were just weary and resigned to their fate, knowing that they had no option but to leave their homeland for an uncertain future.

Some of their fellow travellers were headed for the workhouse in the city. They had no money for the ships and Kitty was thankful that at least their landlord had given them tickets. If they had been forced to beg for relief at the workhouse, she thought that they would never have escaped from its dreary walls and they might as well have thrown themselves into a prison cell.

'It'll be all right. We're nearly there,' she told the children as she urged them on towards the port. 'Can you see the ships yet? Can you see the masts? One will be there to take us to our new home and we'll be well-fed and healthy, you'll see . . .'

She clung to her words even though she didn't truly believe them. How could any place be better than her home? She'd been born here, as had generations of her family going back to a past that was too distant to remember. She was a part of this land. The soil and the rain and the sun had nurtured her and her ancestors. They had farmed the land, raised a few animals, kept chickens, had spun and woven wool for their frocks and shawls – and although there had been little luxury, they'd been happy, and they had thought they were safe.

The dock at Dublin was a seething mass of people, cows, pigs and horses. Each waiting their turn to board the ships.

'Which one is for us?' asked Kitty, trying to keep hold of all her children and at the same time not lose sight of her husband as he forged a path ahead of them through the crowd. She could see three vessels tied up at the dockside. Two were paddle steamers with a tall chimney in the middle of their deck as well as masts with sails that were furled. None looked as big or as seaworthy as she had imagined.

Peter showed his tickets to a sailor who was holding the halter of a fractious horse that was rolling its eyes and tossing its head in alarm.

'Which ship?' he asked. The man shrugged.

'Take your pick,' he replied. 'But the animals go on first.'

Kitty watched as he swore at the horse and pulled it up the ramp on to the deck. There were pens of cattle too, and sheep, waiting to be loaded, and she wondered how there would ever be room for all the livestock and the people who swarmed the quayside.

She called to the children to stay close to her, terrified of taking her eyes off them. She moved her shawl aside to glance at the baby. He seemed to be asleep, but he looked pale and scarcely moved in her arms.

There was a sharp gust of wind and another lash of stinging rain was driven into their faces. She hoped that at least they would be able to take shelter once they were aboard.

Then suddenly, the crowd around her surged forward, almost knocking her from her feet. She reached out to grasp Maria and called to her husband to pick up little Peter to keep him from being trampled.

'Quickly!' urged her husband. 'We won't get on if we don't push forward!' And so they were swept along with the crowd, buffeted this way and that as people fought to reach the ship. Kitty caught a sharp elbow in her ribs and shouted at the man to mind her baby. He didn't even turn her way but hauled his own family ahead of her, determined to let no one get past him. Maria was sobbing beside her as the mass surrounded them and Kitty was terrified that she couldn't see Agnes. She shouted her daughter's name, trying to scan the faces around her, and it was only when she heard the small voice say 'I'm here' that she realized her eldest daughter had been clinging to her all the time.

As they reached the edge of the quayside she was afraid that they would be pushed aside and lose their footing. She could glimpse the water below, swelling on its rise and making the ramp to the ship unsteady. She was afraid of setting foot on it, thinking that she was sure to slip and fall.

'Keep moving!' someone shouted and Kitty pushed her children ahead of her, telling them to take care. She hardly dared to watch and it was only when she felt her husband take her arm that she set foot on the ramp herself and took the few steps that brought her to the deck of the *Sirius*.

'Deck passengers that way!' shouted a sailor. 'That means you!' he added, pushing Kitty roughly towards the cattle pens that were filled with wide-eyed cows, calling in terror.

She looked about her in horror. There was nowhere to sit and barely room to stand under the flimsy tarpaulin where the crowd of families was packed tightly together. She could feel the ship heaving beneath her feet as the wind increased. She knew that an autumn storm was brewing.

'We can't go like this!' she told her husband. 'We need to get below or somewhere where there's more shelter.'

'They want more money to let us go below,' her

husband told her after he'd been to enquire, 'and it's filled with animals down there as well. They offered the engine room but they want sixpence each. It's more than we can afford.' He put his arm around her and led her towards the paddle box where they would be shielded from the worst of the weather. 'We'll be all right here,' he said. 'It's only until we reach Liverpool. They said there'll be a bigger ship there to take us on to New York.'

Kitty wanted to get off the *Sirius* and feel the firm ground beneath her feet again, but the sailors were pulling the ramps away from the crowd of would-be passengers who were shouting and complaining on the quayside. It was clear that even if they had been able to disembark, there wasn't an inch to stand on and they would surely have been thrust into the ferocious water.

Steam began to pour from the chimney and Kitty felt a shudder as the paddles in the box she was wedged against began to turn. Her husband managed to elbow enough space around them to make room for her to sit down with her knees pulled up to her chin. Maria and little Peter crawled beneath her skirt to shield themselves and Kitty moved aside her shawl to check the baby. He was very still, and he felt cold. She wrapped him more tightly and held him close as her husband stood over them and Agnes and Timothy cuddled against her. Their faces were filled with fear and Kitty knew she must appear brave for the sake of her children.

2

When they got out into open water, the spray from the sea began to wash over them and the flimsy tarpaulin offered no protection. Within minutes they were soaked through and their ragged clothing clung to their bodies as they shivered in the cold wind. The salty tang of the sea spray mixed with the stench of urine and dung from the animals that was escaping the cattle pens and sliding across the slippery deck. Soon their clothing was not only saturated but befouled with the muck. Kitty thought it was intolerable, but whenever she lifted her head for a moment, all she could glimpse through the mass of dejected bodies surrounding her was an endless vista of grey where there was no clear definition between the heaving sea and the dark grey clouds that poured down rain on to them. There was no escape and the ordeal must be endured if they were to live.

The baby slept on in her arms and the children, exhausted from their long walk and lack of food, dozed as they were tossed up and down on the water. No one spoke. Every person seemed locked in their own hell – eyes blank in hollowed cheeks, wet and filthy and cold. Someone called out for water. Kitty was thirsty herself, but the pump was too far away and it would have been impossible to cross the mass of bodies to reach it.

A woman near her was violently sick and Kitty turned her head away as the sight made her retch herself.

'I'm sorry,' whispered the woman, and although her family was trying to comfort her in her distress, there were some nearby who complained and called her vile names. Kitty could see that the woman was hemmed in and could never have reached the side of the ship, and although she felt sorry for her she was glad that she, herself, was seated nearer to the rails.

Kitty lost track of time as they floundered on the water and it was only when she noticed the light fading that she became aware of the imminent nightfall.

'How much longer?' she asked her husband. 'Shouldn't we be there by now?'

'They told me ten hours,' he shouted over the noise of the howling gale. 'But I think the wind is holding us back. And they won't unfurl the sails in this storm.'

Kitty pulled her sodden shawl further over her head. Water dripped from it as she bent to check on the baby. She hadn't felt him move in a while and she was worried. She fumbled with her clothing to try to press him to her breast, but he wouldn't suckle and she wept as she held him close and rocked him in her weary arms.

After a while, she fell into an exhausted sleep and

woke much later with her neck aching. There was no steam coming from the ship's chimney and they seemed to be floating adrift, low in the water, at the mercy of the sea. But dawn was breaking and she could see the outline of distant buildings on the horizon. It gave her some hope. They were nearly there.

Beside her, her husband was still sleeping. He was soaked through, his fiery red hair plastered dark against his skull. She hoped the cold wouldn't settle on his chest. He'd been poorly enough the last winter with a pleurisy. Little Peter and Maria were still curled up below her skirt which was giving them some shelter, but they were lying in filth. Their scanty clothing was ruined and they had nothing else to wear. Kitty worried about how she would manage to get them clean, fed and clothed when they arrived. They couldn't continue their onward journey as they were.

Suddenly, a bell began to ring.

'What's happening?' asked Kitty, alarmed as she saw sailors running towards the engine house with buckets in their hands.

'Man the pumps!' went up the cry and the passengers began to wake from their sleep and try to get to their feet to see what was going on.

Kitty watched as someone opened the cattle pen and began to push the animals towards the side of the boat.

'No!' she cried as, to her horror, she heard them splash into the water below. 'What are they doing?'

'I think they're trying to lighten the load,' replied her husband quietly as he shielded Agnes's eyes from the sight.

Kitty didn't reply. She didn't need to ask if they were sinking. The panic all around her was enough to tell her that they were all in danger of following the animals to a watery grave – and the land was still far off.

'God preserve us!' she whispered in prayer. It would be too cruel to have come all this way only to die when they were within sight of Liverpool.

Another wave washed over them and Kitty found herself gasping for breath. Even with the deck cleared of cattle the ship was beginning to lean to one side. All around her she could hear the mounting panic as people began to pray out loud and implore God to help them. The alarm bell clanged on and Kitty wished it would stop. It was making her head hurt and now that the children were awake they were sobbing and clinging to her, asking if they were going to drown.

'There's a ship coming to help us!' cried someone and a mass of people moved to the side to watch it approach, making their own vessel list even more.

Kitty managed to get to her feet although her legs felt leaden. She clasped the baby close and held little Peter firmly by the hand to prevent him slipping away from her down the deck. 'Stay close,' she told her other children. She wasn't sure they could hear her above the tumult and her voice was hoarse and croaky when she tried to speak. She craved a drink of fresh water. They'd had nothing since they left Dublin.

Her husband put his arm around her and the children to protect them as best he could.

'Help is coming,' he told her. 'Hold on.' But no sooner had he spoken than there was a crack above them and the foremast shattered down on to the deck. There was a moment of stunned silence, followed by a woman's wail of anguish. 'Stay here,' said Kitty's husband. 'It looks like a lad is trapped. I must help.'

Kitty grasped his sleeve, not wanting him to leave her, but he made his way across the deck, still awash with filth and water, and joined the other men who were trying to heave the mast aside. Then she felt a bump and almost fell. She tried to grasp the slippery side of the paddle box. The water was up to her ankles now, freezing around her bare feet, and the children were sobbing even louder.

'Women and children first!' shouted someone. 'This way!'

Kitty was swept along in the rush. She tried to hold on to the children and look around for her husband, but it was impossible. One of the sailors grasped her arm and pushed her towards the edge of the deck. The ship that had come alongside was jolting and pushing the wooden hull of the *Sirius*, and with each collision there was the danger that it would break it completely. A man took hold of Maria and tossed her across the water into the arms of a waiting sailor on the deck of the rescue ship.

Kitty watched in horror as her daughter seemed suspended in the air for a long moment. But the sailor caught her and passed her to another. Agnes went next, then Timothy. Someone tried to pull Peter from the grip of her hand. She protested and tried to keep hold of him, but he was wrenched from her. 'Save the children!' someone cried.

'My baby!' cried Kitty as one of the sailors pushed her up on to the ship's edge.

'Give it to me and I'll toss it across.'

'No!' Kitty was horrified. What if he fell into the sea? She couldn't risk that. She wouldn't let him go.

'Jump, then!' shouted someone. Kitty hesitated. 'Jump, damn you!'

She closed her eyes and leapt from the sinking deck. But the rescue ship was suddenly swept further away on a huge wave and Kitty knew, before the swell of the sea came up to meet her, that she wasn't going to reach it. She plunged into the water. It was suddenly dark and cold and the shouting and the ringing of the bell was muffled. It seemed to last for ever and Kitty feared that she would drown. She struggled against the current, desperately trying to reach the air so she could breathe. Then finally, she saw bubbles and broke the surface, gasping and trying to wipe the seawater from her eyes. The baby. All she could think of was the baby. She grasped his little body against her as she tried desperately to stay afloat, but the next wave hit her with a force that knocked the breath from her feeble body and

the sea enveloped her once more. Then she felt someone pulling on her hair, hurting her. She tried to cry
out, but her mouth filled with the salty brine. She felt
her arms being grasped and she was lifted from the
waves. Soon she was lying on something solid, gasping
and breathless.

'My baby,' she croaked. But her arms were empty.

3

The lifeboat, which had come out from Liverpool, rowed Kitty to the bigger rescue ship and she was hauled up on to its deck with a rope tied around her waist. Someone wrapped a blanket around her, but she couldn't stop shivering. She vomited up seawater twice and her body was numb.

'Where is my baby?' she kept asking, but the sailors shrugged and moved on. She must have lost hold of him as they'd pulled her into the lifeboat. She was filled with horror at the thought. Why hadn't she held on to him more tightly? But surely somebody must have saved him? She couldn't bear to think of the alternative. She had to hold on to the belief that someone would bring him to her soon, and that her husband would come and that somehow everything would turn out well.

One by one, her older children crawled across the deck until they found her, but even their small, soaked bodies did nothing to warm her. As she sat, trembling, she watched the *Sirius* sink further and further under the sea until only the bow was visible. All around it, being tossed up and down on the grey waves, she could see people and animals trying to swim and keep afloat.

She searched desperately for sight of her husband, but she couldn't see him.

More vessels came out from the port to help them and the numbers thrashing in the sea grew fewer as the sailors tossed ropes from the steep sides of the bigger ships and the lifeboats plied their oars in the rough swell to reach others. Soon there were only cattle and horses left in the water, bellowing or neighing in terror as they swam for their lives. The lifeboats ignored them and Kitty wept as she watched them become exhausted and drown. She wished that they could be saved as well, but there was no room for them on the lifeboats and no way of getting them up on to the ships.

When there were no more people in the water, the lifeboats turned to row the last of the survivors to shore, and the ship that Kitty and her children were on set sail to take them into Liverpool. Her husband and the baby must be on one of the other boats. They would find them when they reached the shore, she told the children to reassure them.

Those who had been rescued were silent as they docked at Liverpool. The quayside was bustling with activity as ships were loaded and unloaded with cargo, and travellers with their meagre possessions piled on handcarts awaited their turn to board a steamer.

'Name?' asked a man. Kitty looked up miserably. He was silhouetted against the weak morning sun but she could see he was well-dressed and wore a tall hat.

'What's your name?' he asked again, crouching down so that she could see his face. He looked kind. 'I'm here to help,' he reassured her. 'I'm a doctor.'

'Kitty Cavanah,' she told him.

'Are these your children?'

'Yes. And there's my baby too,' she told him. 'I don't know where he is. I need to find him, and my husband.'

She heard the desperation in her own voice and the man frowned.

'Can you walk?' he asked.

Kitty attempted to get her feet, but her legs wouldn't hold her and she sank back down on to the deck. 'I need water,' she whispered, 'and food for the children.'

'Soon,' he replied. 'Do you have any fever?'

She shook her head. 'No.'

The doctor grasped her wrist to take her pulse and put his hand to her forehead. He seemed satisfied.

'Will you help me to find my family?' Kitty pleaded. She couldn't shake off the image of her husband as he'd crossed the deck to help free the trapped boy. She hoped he'd been successful and that they'd both been saved. There had been no one left in the water when they'd sailed away – he must have been brought ashore on another boat.

'We're going to America,' she explained to the doctor. 'My husband has the tickets.'

Kitty saw him frown again as someone brought a jug of water and cups for them to drink. She made sure the children drank first then put the cup to her swollen lips.

'Slowly,' said the doctor, staying her hand. 'Just a little at a time.'

'I need to find my husband,' she told him again. 'He has our money as well as our tickets. I have nothing to feed these children with.'

'You'll have to go to the parish office,' he told her kindly. 'They'll help you there. They'll give you food.'

'I'll not go in the workhouse!' Kitty protested, fear filling her at the prospect.

'You'd be better off there than on the streets,' replied the doctor. 'I'd send you to the hospital but it's crowded with typhus cases and you and the children seem well – apart from being undernourished and half drowned.' He got to his feet. 'The parish office will at least find you some dry clothes and give you a meal ticket.'

The doctor moved on to the next person and Kitty got slowly to her feet. She felt a little better now and she managed to lift Peter in her shaking arms even though he felt like a dead weight and she wasn't sure how far she could carry him. She told the other children to stay close and they made their way off the ship and began to follow the crowd of sorry survivors through the busy quayside to seek help. All the while Kitty looked amongst the milling crowds to try to catch sight of her husband, and although she saw several women with babies in their arms, not one of them was hers and she despaired of finding him amongst so many people.

There was a long queue of people outside the red brick building. Kitty doubted that she could stand for long enough to reach the front of the line, but she had nowhere else to go so she sat down on the wet pavement with her back against the wall to wait, with Peter in her lap and the other children sitting beside her. None of them spoke. They simply looked around at the unfamiliar surroundings.

Eventually, Kitty reached the front of the queue and was called inside the office and offered a chair to sit on. She accepted gratefully, staring at the two men sitting behind their wooden table. She was afraid, feeling that they were here to judge her.

She gave them her name and began to explain about the baby and her husband, but as she told her tale she was overwhelmed with tears.

'I've been searching for him,' she sobbed. 'The mast fell and trapped a boy. He went to help so we were separated. His name is Peter Cavanah.'

'Peter Cavanah?' repeated the man with a ledger open in front of him. He ran a finger down the page and shook his head. 'No one by that name has come today,' he said. Kitty's hopes waned.

'What ship were you on?' asked the second man. He sounded kinder than the first.

'The *Sirius*,' she replied.

'Many of the passengers on the *Sirius* were drowned,' he told her. 'I'm sorry, Mrs Cavanah.'

For a moment she considered with despair what her

fate might be if her husband didn't come – she would be alone and destitute in a strange city in a foreign country. She had no idea how she would find food and shelter for herself and her children. But she refused to contemplate such an outcome. She had to believe that her husband was alive.

'We have tickets to America,' she told the men. 'We're going to a new life. But I need some food for my children until my husband finds us.'

She saw the men exchange glances and although their expressions were not without compassion she could see their doubts.

'Do you have the tickets?' one asked her.

'My husband has them.'

There was a moment of silence before he spoke again.

'Do you have any money?'

'No. I wouldn't have come here if I had,' she protested. 'I just need to feed my children.'

The men sent them through to another room where a woman sat her down and tried to comfort her, but Kitty knew that she could only feel whole again when she had her baby in her arms and her husband at her side. Until then, all could she do was pray and hope.

'Pull yourself together, Mrs Cavanah,' said the woman. 'You've four children here who need their mother and you're frightening them with all this wailing.' She pushed a handkerchief into Kitty's hand and patted her shoulder. 'Let's care for these little ones first,' she said, not unkindly.

Kitty tried to stop her crying because she knew that what the woman was telling her was true. She owed it to her children to stay strong. She was all they had for now.

The woman brought some hot water and soap for them to wash themselves. Timothy was taken to another room and Kitty washed Peter as the girls stepped out of their wet clothing and washed themselves in front of the fire. The feeling gradually came back into her hands though her fingers were agony as she fumbled with the washcloth and towel.

'Here, see if these will fit him,' said the woman, handing Kitty some boys' clothing. Although the garments were patched and mended, they were clean. The cloth was good quality and better than the ragged clothes that she'd taken off her little son. She dressed Peter in the flannel undergarments, the shirt and trousers and the jacket. His cheeks were glowing and his hair was springing up around his head.

'He looks a treat,' said the woman. 'Get yourself washed now and I'll bring something for you to wear, then you can all go through to the soup kitchen and get a bite to eat.'

'What are you going to do with those?' asked Kitty as the woman gathered her discarded clothing into a pile.

'They'll have to go for rags,' she said. 'They're no use to you now. And they stink of the sea.'

When she'd towelled herself dry, Kitty picked up the clothes she'd been given. There was a petticoat, a gown and a plain shawl. She dressed herself, wondering who the clothes had belonged to. The ones she'd cast off had been shabby and worn but at least they'd been her own, woven and sewn by her own hand, and she began to cry again as she saw them taken away.

The woman came back with some thick stockings and a pair of boots for her to try on.

'Here,' she said. 'You can wear these.'

They were too big, but they seemed serviceable and the soles were solid.

'Pack them with some straw and they'll do you fine,' said the woman as Kitty fastened them up. She'd been barefoot for so long that they felt strange and heavy on her feet, but she was grateful for them, especially as the winter was coming.

Clothing and boots had been found for Maria and Agnes too, and Kitty barely recognized Timothy when she saw him freshly washed and dressed in his new clothes. She'd never seen her children so well turned out.

'Thank you,' she kept repeating to the woman. 'Thank you. I don't know what I would have done without your help.'

Some meal tickets were pushed into her hand and they were sent to join the queue for soup. It was doled out into bowls with a hunk of bread, and Kitty and her children found some upturned barrels to sit on whilst they ate. Although she was hungry, Kitty found it difficult to eat as she still felt sick from the seawater, but she made sure that the children had plenty.

'Where's Dada?' asked Agnes when her bowl was empty. 'Did he get off the ship?'

'He will have done, to be sure,' Kitty told her. 'Everyone who was in the water was pulled out. He must have come ashore on one of the other boats. He'll be looking for us. But this is a big city. Maybe we should go back down to the quayside to ask if anyone has seen him and the baby.'

'You were holding the baby when you fell into the sea,' Agnes told her. 'What happened to him?'

Kitty tried not to cry again in front of her older children, but the guilt of losing her youngest child threatened to overwhelm her. She ought to have held him more tightly. 'We'll find him soon,' she said, wishing that her words would come true.

'We didn't find him on the ship,' whispered Agnes, her lower lip trembling as she watched her mother. 'Did he drown?'

'No! No,' protested Kitty, refusing to believe it. 'We'll find him. Someone will be looking after him.'

She looked around at the crowd of people in the soup kitchen as if someone would suddenly produce her baby, but everyone was like her, huddled over their soup bowls in small groups. And, like her, there were several women alone with children.

She watched as some of the other families began to drift off, and now that she was feeling stronger, she picked up Peter and told the other children that they would go to enquire about their father.

27

As they walked, Kitty was able to take more notice of her surroundings than when she'd followed the crowd from the ship to seek relief. Everywhere was thronged with people and the roads were busy with carriages and carts filled with goods. She kept telling the children to stay back as they stared at the rushing wheels that passed them, tossing up mud and dung from the road. They were unused to the dangers and she was terrified that they might forget themselves and step into the path of some oncoming horse.

Some of the men seemed well-dressed, like the doctor who had come to her on the ship, but they never looked at her and her family and never stepped aside for them to pass. She was forced to weave in and out of their paths, trying to hold on to her children. Some turned their faces away as they walked by and on more than one occasion she heard the muttered words 'Irish filth'. It hurt her to think that she was so unwelcome here. It wasn't what she'd expected.

On almost every street corner, there were groups of beggars. Many, like her, were women with children crowded at their feet dressed in rags that barely covered them, holding out their filth-encrusted hands and repeating 'Please. Please. Spare a penny' to every passer-by. Kitty was surprised that they even hoped she would help them and she felt guilty that she couldn't as she hurried her own children past, not wanting them to witness such scenes when she'd promised them that they were going to a better life.

Unsure of her way, Kitty soon found herself in squalid streets with buildings grouped around courtyards that were swilled with filth. The stench was awful and the girls held their noses as they passed by the worst of it. There were no rich businessmen here. No beggars either. The people here had nothing to give. They stared at Kitty and her children as they went by and Kitty was aware that they were better dressed than most of the people who were sitting on the steps to their houses or pumping water into buckets in the yards.

Feeling uncomfortable, she began to walk back the way she'd come, but she soon realized that she had no idea which direction to take to get back to the quayside, and as the afternoon grew darker she simply sank down on a doorstep and clutched her children.

'Where are we going to sleep tonight?' asked Agnes.

'I don't know.' All Kitty wanted to do was cry. She had no idea where to go and what to do.

She heard something fall at her feet. Agnes reached out and picked it up. It was a penny. 'Thank you' she called after the man who had thrown it to her. It wouldn't buy much, but perhaps she could gather more money by simply sitting where she was and begging. The thought shamed her, but if she could make enough to pay for a room in a lodging house for tonight, they could sleep in safety and she might feel well enough to search harder for her husband tomorrow.

Behind her a door opened, casting a stream of light down the steps. 'Get off my doorstep!' roared a man.

'I'm sick to death of you filthy Irish beggars coming here with your diseases! If you want money, why don't you work like everyone else has to?'

'I . . .' Kitty hadn't the strength to try to explain her situation and it was clear the man had no interest in what she had to say. He had a broom in his hand and was brandishing it towards her. Maria was sobbing and she knew she must take her children to a safer place, although she had no idea where.

They set off walking again, the girls trailing their feet with weariness and Kitty's arms burning with the pain of carrying Peter. She wanted to cry, but she knew the children were looking to her to protect them.

'He's a bastard!' said a voice and Kitty was surprised to hear her native language being spoken. She looked down in the twilight to see a woman and two children whom she'd passed earlier. 'You must be newly come,' said the woman. 'Everyone knows not to beg outside his property.'

'I wasn't begging,' protested Kitty. 'We were just resting for a while.'

'How much have you made?' asked the woman as she got stiffly to her feet. Kitty showed her the penny. 'Is that all?' she asked her.

'I wasn't begging,' repeated Kitty.

'Have you got money then?' asked the woman eagerly, and Kitty felt a frisson of fear that she might be robbed.

'No!' she told her. 'This is all I have. My husband has all our money.'

'Where is he then?'

'I don't know,' she confessed, her tears welling up again. 'I've been looking for him. We got separated when we were rescued.'

'Rescued?'

'The ship we were on sank.'

The woman seemed to soften a little. 'I saw them wretches brought ashore,' she said. 'I didn't realize you were one of them. You look too well-dressed,' she accused as if she didn't really believe what Kitty was telling her.

'They sent us to the parish office. We got clothes and some soup.'

'You were lucky they didn't send you back,' said the woman.

'Back? What, back to Ireland?' Kitty asked.

'Yes. It costs them too much to keep feeding all the immigrants that are coming over, so they've started putting people on the boats and sending them back.'

'I can't go back!' Kitty told her. The thought of being out on that tossing sea again terrified her. Her heart raced with fear at the thought of it. Besides, there was nothing for her to go back to. Her home was destroyed. All she had was her family, and two of its members were missing. She began to feel a mounting panic at the situation she was in. It was worse than she'd thought. She had intended to return to the parish office the next day and try to get soup for the children again, but if what this woman was telling her was true, it might be too dangerous.

'I have to find my husband and my baby!' she told the woman. 'He's sure to be looking for us here in Liverpool. We were going to the docks to ask about him, but we lost our way.'

'I wouldn't go there now,' warned the woman. 'It'll be dark soon and it's not safe. Wait until morning,' she advised. 'Have you anywhere to sleep?' Kitty shook her head. 'You'd better come with me then,' she said. 'We haven't much room but I daresay we can fit you and the little ones in if you don't mind squeezing together.'

Kitty and the children followed the woman through the darkening streets. They turned corner after corner until Kitty began to feel uneasy about where they were going. The buildings grew shabbier with every turn and there were more and more people huddled together in the doorways who gazed at Kitty and her children dressed in mended clothes and with boots on their feet, and she could feel the ripples of envy and distrust. It made her pull the children closer to her.

At last they turned into one of the many narrow courts that stood back from the main streets. It was unpaved and a gulley ran down the centre, overflowing with household slops that formed fetid pools.

'Watch where you put your feet,' Kitty told the older children as she lifted Peter clear of the filth.

'Down here,' said the woman and Kitty caught a glimpse of her white face as she went down some steep steps to a wooden door.

'Don't fall,' Kitty warned Agnes as her daughter followed the woman down. 'Take your sister's hand,' she told Timothy.

They made their way down the steps and Kitty heard the woman push the door open. It groaned on its rusted hinges. Once inside, the woman struck a flint and lit a rush light. It barely illuminated the room, but Kitty was able to make out that they were in a stone-walled cellar with a low roof. There was no window, just a grille above the door that was on a level with the street. There was some straw and sacking piled into a corner, but as the woman set the rush light down on the brick floor Kitty could see that it was slick with moisture and that the bedding must be equally wet, but she was still immensely grateful for the offer of shelter.

'Sit down. You look exhausted,' said the woman. She kindled a fire in a small grate with a handful of damp sticks and added a few pieces of coal from a bucket. 'I follow the coal lorries and pick up what I can,' she explained. 'But it doesn't go far. Fetch some water from the pump,' she added to one of her own children, handing the girl a bucket. 'We'll make ourselves a hot drink.' She pulled a few coins from her pocket and handed them to her other child. 'Go and ask if there's any bread,' she instructed her. 'They sometimes let it go cheap at this time,' she explained to Kitty, 'and they're more likely to oblige when it's a child.'

'I must pay for something,' said Kitty as she retrieved

the penny from her pocket and held it out. The woman waved it away. 'Keep it,' she said. 'I made a fair amount today.'

'Is begging all you have to keep you?' she asked the woman.

'It's better than starving,' she told Kitty. 'It hurts my pride, but it gets easier, and we need to eat.'

'And pay the rent,' said Kitty, remembering their own struggles back in Ireland.

'I don't pay rent,' admitted the woman. 'These dwellings were closed up and condemned, but we had nowhere else to go. My husband, God rest him, knocked through the brickwork and found an old door to fit.'

'Don't you fear being turned out?' Kitty asked.

'They'll not turn us out,' she said. 'They'd rather see us here than roaming their fine streets. They hate us for begging. Some will toss a penny or two but many more will kick you or spit on you, on the children too.'

The first child came back with the water and the woman poured it into a pan and set it over the fire that was helping to illuminate the room. Kitty thought that if she stretched out her hands she would be able to touch all four walls. There would be barely room for them all to lie down, but it was much better than the ship, and at least they were out of the rain that had begun to pour down and trickle in through the grille where it was overflowing the gulley outside.

Footsteps clattered down the steps and the second child came in carrying a loaf.

'Well done,' said her mother. She broke the loaf into two hunks and handed one to Kitty.

'Thank you. You've been so kind,' she said as she shared it with her children. 'What shall I call you?' she asked.

'I'm Brigit.'

'Thank you, Brigit. I'm so grateful for the shelter,' she told her. 'We'll just rest here until daylight and then I must look for my husband again,' she said, hoping that she would be able to find her way back through the warren of streets to the quayside and that tomorrow she would have all her family with her.

4

After they'd eaten, Brigit shared out the straw and sacking and Kitty settled her children to sleep as best she could. Agnes had been silent the whole time. Timothy had asked for his dada. Maria had grumbled that the floor was hard but had been so tired that she'd soon fallen asleep, curled next to Kitty's legs. Peter had fallen asleep in her lap, sucking his thumb, and she'd held him there, keeping him from the wet floor as she leaned against the wall and dozed a little.

All night long there was noise from the courtyard above her. Men and women, the worse for drink, fornicating against the wall, vomiting and worse – and little by little it all trickled down through the grating.

She'd asked Brigit if there was a privy.

'Don't go there. It's filthy,' she'd said and passed Kitty a pot to put under her skirts to relieve herself and told her to throw the contents out into the gulley.

Kitty was so tired that she eventually slept a little, slumped over in the corner. When she woke she thought it must be nearly morning as there was a grey light around the grating and she could hear the clopping of horses' hooves and the clatter of wheels over the cobbles in the streets beyond the court. Brigit and the children were still asleep, so she waited, even though she was eager to get down to the docks to look for her husband and the baby. Her breasts ached for the child, and the last image she had of his little face as she'd tucked him into her shawl on the boat made her weep again.

'Mam?' Agnes's voice made her take a breath and try to calm herself. Her daughter was watching her. She looked worried. 'What are we going to do?' she asked.

Kitty shifted her son, who mumbled wearily in his sleep. Her legs felt numbed by his weight and the cold, but not enough to prevent her reaching down to scratch at a persistent itch which had bothered her all night long.

'We'll go to find your father as soon as it's daylight,' she told Agnes. She was aware that her elder daughter had been badly frightened the previous day and that now she must assure her children that they were safe and that she would care for them.

'Let's go now,' whispered Agnes. 'It stinks in here.'

Kitty agreed. The air was fetid with them all crowded in the cellar and she was afraid for their health. She woke Peter, Timothy and Maria and put a finger to her lips to bid them all to be quiet so as not to disturb Brigit and her children who were still sleeping soundly. She pulled on the door gently, but it wouldn't yield and she was forced to tug at it.

'Where are you going?' asked Brigit, woken by the noise.

'I'm going to find my husband,' Kitty told her with more confidence than she felt. 'I'm sorry we woke you and I'm really grateful to you for sheltering us for the night,' she added. 'But we can't impose on you.'

'I know it's not much,' replied Brigit, propping herself up on one elbow and rubbing her eyes, 'but the streets aren't safe,' she warned Kitty. 'It's not like home. You'll need to keep your wits about you.'

'I will,' Kitty promised. 'Thank you for helping us,' she said as she ushered her children up the steep steps into the courtyard.

Daylight revealed a scene that was even worse than Kitty remembered from the evening before. The rain had overflowed the gulley and the whole court was awash with filth. She raised her skirt and was thankful that they had been given boots and didn't have to paddle through the effluent barefoot. She told the children to follow in her steps as she trod from ash heap to ash heap until they reached the street. It was already busy with carts on their way to the docks, and with Peter in her arms and Timothy holding Maria by the hand, Kitty and Agnes followed them.

'How will we find Dada in this crowd?' asked Agnes when they reached the quayside.

'We'll ask if anyone has seen him,' replied Kitty, making her way towards some men who were loading bales of cotton to go to the warehouses. 'Have you heard of a man called Peter Cavanah asking for his family?' she enquired. 'Do you know if anyone has found a baby?' They all shook their heads and continued with their work.

Kitty made her way through the crowd, asking anyone she could, but they all dismissed her with a shrug or a curse. She asked some sailors who were coming ashore. 'I'm looking for my husband. He was on the *Sirius*.' She saw them exchange a glance.

'The *Sirius* went down yesterday,' said one.

'The passengers were rescued. I was rescued,' she insisted, 'but I got parted from my husband.'

One shook his head. He was Irish, like her. 'I'm sorry,' he said. 'I heard a lot were lost.'

'No!' she cried. 'That isn't true. I was there. The boats and ships rescued everyone from the water. I saw them.'

She could see the sailor was doubtful, but he hadn't seen what she'd seen and Kitty refused to believe his words. She continued through the dock, asking again and again for Peter Cavanah and the baby.

At last she felt Agnes pulling on her arm.

'It's no good, Mam,' said her daughter. 'We'll never find them here. We need to get some food.'

'I know. I know.' Kitty put a hand to her daughter's cold cheek. Agnes was always the practical one. She was so like her father, both in looks and temperament.

'Will they give us soup again?' Agnes asked.

Kitty knew that the children were all hungry and that they needed to be fed, but she was worried after what Brigit had told her that if she went back to the parish office they would send her back to Ireland. Still, not knowing what else she could do, she allowed Agnes to lead them away from the docks. 'Don't walk so fast,' Kitty warned her as a cart rushed past them. 'You must stay close.'

'Can you remember the way?' asked Agnes. Kitty paused on a street corner and gazed about at the tall brick buildings. They all looked the same to her.

'I think it was this way,' she said at last, and they set off walking down the street. As they walked, the red brick buildings gave way to stone built houses. Nothing looked familiar, and before long she had to admit to herself that they were lost again.

Agnes was looking around and eventually took her mother's hand. 'It wasn't this way,' she said. 'I think we should turn back.'

Kitty knew her daughter was right, but it wasn't so crowded here. The pavements weren't filled with drunks and barely clad beggars and men who threatened her. She felt safer.

'Let's just rest awhile,' she said, sitting down on a scrubbed doorstep. Her arms were aching from carrying Peter.

After a moment she heard the door behind her open. She turned to see a woman in a dark dress and white apron coming out. 'Get away!' shouted the woman. 'Get away, you filthy beggars!'

'I'm not a beggar,' protested Kitty, but then she was rendered speechless by the icy cold water that drenched her. She stood up gasping and wiping her eyes as she tried to recover her breath.

'That'll teach you!' shouted the woman. 'Get on your way!'

For a moment, Kitty was stunned. Then she felt her anger rising. How dared the woman call her a beggar and throw water over her like that? She was drenched and she wasn't too sure that the water had been clean. Agnes pulled on her sleeve, but Kitty turned back to the door, determined to bang on its shiny knocker until the woman came out and give her a piece of her mind.

'Let's go,' said Agnes, who had Peter on her hip. 'We'll get no welcome around here.'

Kitty saw that her daughter was right. She wrung out her shawl as best she could and settled it around her shoulders. The dampness had seeped through her gown to her petticoat and the wind was bitter. She needed to find somewhere to dry off and the soup kitchen, if they could find it, seemed to be the only solution.

They walked back the way they'd come, still asking everyone they passed if they'd heard of Peter Cavanah and if they knew if a baby had been found. The streets grew crowded and dirty as they got back into the centre of Liverpool, and she took Peter from Agnes to carry him herself.

'I'll ask the way,' said her daughter, approaching a woman who sat on a street corner. Kitty saw the woman draw her skirts away from Agnes and look up at her suspiciously, as if she thought she might be a thief. The idea made Kitty angry again, but she supposed she couldn't entirely blame the woman. She knew that if they were going to survive she would have to harden her own heart and trust no one.

'This way,' said Agnes when she came back, pointing out the direction they must take.

After a few minutes, Kitty recognized the building they had queued outside the day before. There was another line of ragged men, women and children standing there today. New arrivals, no doubt. Starving and impoverished families must be arriving every day asking to be fed and clothed. But they weren't to blame, she thought. Like her, most of them would have preferred to stay in their homes and farm their smallholdings if they'd been able to feed themselves. If they'd been given help in Ireland and provided with some corn to take the place of their ruined potato crops, then few would have made that perilous journey across the sea to meet with little but hatred.

She crossed the road and walked down the line of hungry people who were waiting for help, hoping to find her husband amongst them. There was still no sign of him and she waited her turn.

At last they were waved forward and the same men who had been sitting behind the desk the day before were there again. They glanced up and one gave her a hard stare.

'You were here yesterday,' he accused Kitty. 'You haven't just arrived.'

'No. But my children are hungry. I was hoping they could have the soup again,' she explained.

'Why did you not go to the workhouse?' he asked. 'You can't keep asking for food without working to earn it.'

'Yes, you must take your children to the workhouse,' the other man agreed. 'You can't simply wander the streets with them. They'll be fed there.'

'I won't be separated from them,' Kitty told him fiercely. 'I know they take children away from their mothers in those places!' The idea filled her with horror. It was bad enough being apart from her husband and baby; she must keep her other children close to her.

The man raised an eyebrow at her outburst and then sighed. 'I don't think there's much choice, Mrs Cavanah,' he told her. 'You don't want your children to starve, do you?'

'Of course not. That's why I came to ask for soup.'

The man drummed his fingers on the table for a moment before he relented. 'I'll give you tickets for today,' he agreed, 'but then you must go to the work-house and they will arrange for you to go home – where you belong,' he added as the tickets were held out to her.

Kitty thanked him, although she found the words hard to say. These Englishmen didn't seem to care if the Irish starved so long as they stayed in Ireland, out of sight.

The soup was good. It was hot and had a little meat in with the mix of vegetables. There were chunks of bread again as well, and Kitty ate her fill once the children had been fed. She lingered near the hot fire as long as she dared, waiting for her clothing and her hair to dry, but in the end they were told they must leave to make room for others.

She stood outside on the street, unsure what to do next. The workhouse was out of the question. As soon as she reached the gates, her sons and daughters would be taken away from her and housed in a dormitory with other children. She wouldn't be allowed to see them or care for them, and she couldn't allow that to happen. It was bad enough that their father was missing. She wouldn't allow them to lose their mother as well.

'Must we go to the workhouse?' asked Agnes.

'No,' said Kitty. 'We're not going there. We must stay together. It's what your father would want.'

Although she still refused to consider the prospect that her husband might not have survived, she'd begun to accept that he might not have reached Liverpool yet. She was sure he would have found them by now if he had. Perhaps the ship that had picked him up was still waiting to dock. She didn't know. But it was clear that she had to take responsibility for the rest of their children herself until they could all be reunited.

5

'Where will we go?' asked Agnes. 'I don't want to go back to that horrible cellar.'

Kitty didn't want to go back to the cellar either. She doubted they would be welcome anyway, but the only alternative she could see was sleeping on the street, and after the drenching she'd received that morning she would do anything to avoid that.

After they'd left the soup kitchen she'd begun to walk, with no clear intention. The streets all looked similar and now she realized that she didn't know how to find Brigit's place anyway.

Peter began to cry and she was forced to carry him even though she ached all over. Timothy looked weary and Maria was white-faced with exhaustion. Kitty realized that her children were going to become ill if she kept them walking around and around with no clear purpose.

In desperation, she sat them down in a quiet side street to rest with their backs up against a solid wall so no one could approach them unseen from behind. As they sat there a few people passed them by – men mostly, going about their business. Most kept their faces averted as if not looking at them would render them invisible, but one or two took pity on them and tossed her a farthing or two.

'I wish I knew where Brigit sent her child for that cheap bread,' said Kitty to Agnes as the skies began to darken. She knew that they needed to eat something before night fell and the shops closed up for the day. 'Perhaps we should go to look for food,' she suggested, pushing herself to her feet. Her legs were still itching incessantly and she felt compelled to scratch them. Agnes had complained too, and Kitty suspected that they'd all been badly bitten by fleas in the night.

They walked slowly back in the direction of the docks. The other beggars seemed to have abandoned their doorways now and disappeared back into the hidden underground cellars where they would sleep until the next day dawned.

The aroma from a fried fish stall drew her down a street she hadn't noticed before. She paused with the coins in her hand as she watched the vendor. After a moment he glanced up.

'What dost tha want?' he demanded.

'I want to buy food,' she told him, holding out the money. 'What can I get for this?' she asked, hoping that he was an honest man and wouldn't trick her.

The sight of her children seemed to soften him and he waved her forward. 'I've some scraps left that tha can have – for thy bairns,' he added as he piled bits of fish and batter on to a piece of newspaper and handed it to her.

Kitty thanked him and put the coins down on his counter, but he shook his head and pushed them back towards her. 'I hate to think of them little uns goin' famished,' he told her, and Kitty picked up the parcel with tears brimming at his small act of kindness.

They found a secluded corner and Kitty shared out the food amongst her children. It wasn't much and she knew that they would still be hungry when they'd finished, but she was grateful.

She lifted Peter on to her lap and pulled the shawl over him. 'Come near,' she told the others. 'We'll keep one another warm.'

The cold of the stone flags beneath her made Kitty ache with pain and her children fidgeted and moaned as they tried to find a way to sleep. The stars brightened in the sky and a full moon rose on the horizon, far out to sea. The night was bitterly cold and Kitty wished she had been able to find better shelter.

As the endless hours passed, marked by the chiming of bells from across the sleeping city, Kitty realized that she must make a plan. They would never survive the winter if they were forced to sleep in the open like this, and the few pennies she'd made from begging were nowhere near enough to keep them.

At dawn she was woken by footsteps and saw a sad procession making its way from an alleyway nearby. A woman was weeping copiously and a man had his arm around her shoulders. They were followed by a gaggle of thin children, coughing and shivering in the

49

half-light. They trudged after a man pushing a handcart and Kitty saw that a small body, probably a child, was lying there, wrapped in a threadbare blanket. It was obvious the child had died in the night and her heart grieved for the mother. She knew how the woman felt. Kitty felt the loss of her own baby acutely. Where was he? Who was caring for him? How long would it be before she found him?

Kitty roused herself. She knew that she mustn't allow herself sink into despair. She had her four other children to care for until she found him and her husband. She said a prayer and made the sign of the cross over her sons and daughters before waking them. They must move on from here before the men arrived to do their work.

Kitty took the money she'd been given from her pocket and counted it again. She had fourpence ha'penny. Somehow she must feed her children with it. She knew that she couldn't return to the soup kitchen. She would surely be turned away with nothing this time and told once more to go to the workhouse. Her only option was to do the same as Brigit had done – find a place where she could beg and hope that she could make enough to buy a proper meal.

She walked the stirring streets, wondering where would be a good place. Somewhere where the wealthy men were passing on their way to their businesses, she decided. She chose a spot near a street corner where passers-by would be forced to pause before they crossed the road. The footpath was fairly wide, but not so wide that she could easily be ignored. She settled herself down with the children around her.

'It may be better if you hold out your hands,' she told Agnes and Timothy. She'd seen the other women use their children to tug at the heartstrings of the wealthy men walking past.

Agnes pulled a face. 'I don't want to,' she complained. Kitty could hardly blame her. She didn't want to beg either. It was demeaning. She would rather work for her living, but she'd no idea how she could find a job, or if there were any jobs.

'Oy! You!' said a voice. Kitty looked up to see a fierce-faced woman with brown teeth glaring down at them. 'That's my spot!' she accused. 'Get on your way!'

'I was here first,' Kitty told her, trying to sound more sure of herself than she felt.

The woman shook her head. 'I can see you're fresh off the boat, but you need to learn. You have to work your way up to the best spots – and this spot is mine, so shift yourself.' Kitty sat firm. She couldn't see any reason to give way to the woman. The street didn't belong to her. 'Shift!' said the woman again, kicking out at her.

'Ouch!' Kitty winced and rubbed her thigh where the woman had struck her. 'Don't do that! I have children.'

'Aye, and I'll kick that little one in the head if you're not off my patch in under a minute,' she warned, glowering at Kitty. Kitty pulled Peter closer to her, but she could see that the woman meant what she said. In her naivety she'd thought that all the poor would look out for one another, the way people at home had done. Brigit had helped her, just as she would have helped others if she'd been able to. But it was clear that this woman was quite prepared to be violent to keep her favourite place on the street corner.

Reluctantly, Kitty got to her feet and picked up Peter. 'Come on,' she said to the other children. 'We'll find somewhere else.'

As they walked it became clear that all the best places were already taken, either by beggars or young lads who were busy with chalks, making pictures on the ground. She paused to watch one draw. He was talented and she gazed in awe as the image of a carriage drawn by four horses slowly took shape before her eyes. The boy looked up for a moment. 'You payin' to gawp?' he asked.

'I'm sorry. I haven't anything for you,' Kitty apologized. 'But your picture is beautiful. It's so lifelike.'

But the lad didn't seem impressed by her words of praise. 'Move away,' he told her. 'Leave space for the gents who'll throw me some money.'

It was only when Kitty turned down one of the side streets, where there were fewer people, that she was allowed to sit down without harassment. The children huddled close to her. She knew that they were thirsty and hungry, but she was reluctant to spend her money just yet. It would be better to wait until the end of the day and try to get some cheap bread or leftovers.

One or two passers-by tossed her a copper, but she knew that she could have made much more if she'd been allowed to beg on a busier road. By dinnertime Peter and Maria were pleading for food and she was forced to walk back towards the streets where the shops were. She bought a loaf of bread and they returned to their spot where Kitty shared it out. It wasn't much and she made sure that the children ate most of it. Whether she could get more money to buy them something for their supper she didn't know.

When darkness fell and the shops started to put up their shutters, Kitty approached a baker's shop where a woman was sweeping the floor and stacking baskets.

'Could you let me have anything cheap?' she asked. 'I have threepence.'

The woman paused and looked at the weary children clinging to Kitty's skirts. 'I'm sorry,' she said. 'I've nowt left.' Kitty turned away, disappointed, but the woman called her back. 'They'll give thee summat at t' night asylum if tha's desperate,' she told her.

'Night asylum?' repeated Kitty. 'I'll not go to the workhouse. They'll take the children away from me.'

'No. This isn't t' workhouse. It's a place on Free-mason's Row. Turn left, up there,' she said, indicating the way. 'But tha'll have to hurry. They shut the doors at six.'

Kitty thanked her and walked away. She was reluctant to go to any place where she might find herself separated from her children, but the night was cold and she didn't want the children to sleep on the street again. Peter was giving little whimpering cries and the others were staring at her, expecting her to make some provision for them. Kitty realized that she must find them food and a safe place to sleep.

She found the asylum easily enough by following the straggling line of starved and half-naked beggars through the gates and into the yard. Beyond the yard was a large house that looked like it might have belonged to gentry before the area became so run-down. They joined the queue at the door and waited patiently with the others in the cold. It was a relief when their turn came and they were able to step into the hallway, out of the biting wind.

'Name?' asked the man.

'Kitty Cavanah.' He wrote it down, along with the names and ages of her children.

'Have you any money?'

Kitty was about to say no, but her conscience forced her to be honest, hoping that it wouldn't mean she was turned away. 'I have threepence,' she admitted, 'but it isn't enough to buy food or lodging.'

'Put it here,' said the man, holding out a plate with a few other dull coppers on it. Reluctantly, Kitty parted with the money, worrying about how she would replace it and wondering if it had been the right thing to come here. The woman at the baker's shop had said they would help her but had made no mention of a charge.

The man opened the large chest that stood adjacent to his table and handed out portions of what he called *junk*. It was coarse bread, but the pieces were generous and they were sent through to the dormitory where they would sleep.

Kitty felt the warmth of the huge fire as soon as she stepped into the stone-floored room, even though the windows were left open to ventilate the space. It was welcome after the chill of the autumn day. There were two long forms on either side of the hearth and she saw that most of the women sitting there appeared much worse off than she was. Some were barely covered with clothing and what they had hung in rags about their thin bodies, their shoulders and elbows jutting through the flimsy fabric. As they stared back at her she was grateful for the clothing she and the children had been given. They were the only ones in the room who were not barefoot.

Kitty turned away to look at the bunks that were ranged down the sides of the room. They couldn't be described as beds. They were boxes, stacked three tiers high, made from wood. At one end of each bunk a plank served as a pillow, but there was no mattress or bedding – not even straw – and Kitty saw that it would be as hard as sleeping on the ground although it would be warmer and they were sheltered from the weather.

She lifted the children into a lower bunk and climbed

in beside them to share out the bread. They ate in silence. Then, wearily, Kitty folded her shawl as a pillow and they settled down as best they could to sleep.

Kitty was woken several times in the night as more women came in. Some lay on the bunks, but most preferred to spend the night sitting at the fireside, dozing and waking frequently as they slumped over or leaned on someone beside them. Some, like her, had children, and one had a baby whose piercing cries made Kitty's breasts ache unbearably and she felt the dampness where her milk tried to flow in response. She wept silently and covered her ears with her hands. She wanted her baby so much that she thought she would break with the grief of not knowing where he was.

They were woken by the ringing of a bell at daybreak. Kitty got the children down from the bunk and they all joined a line to get washed. In the bathroom Kitty was surprised to find that the water was warm and that in the yard there was a privy that was clean. They washed their hands and faces and then the superintendent told her that she and the children must do four hours' work in return for their accommodation.

'But I need to go and see if my husband has come,' she protested. 'Could I come back and do it later?'

'I'm sorry, it's the rule,' the woman in charge said. 'Four hours picking oakum. Then you get your breakfast. Then you can go.'

Kitty felt desperate. She hoped that keeping them here wasn't an excuse. She was suddenly terrified that what Brigit had warned her of would come true and that someone would come and force them back on to a boat to Ireland. But the huge gates at the end of the yard were securely locked and she could see that she had no choice.

She wasn't sure what the woman had meant by 'picking oakum'. She'd imagined that they would be gathering in some crop, but they were taken to a large room at the back at the building where the other women were already seated on benches that ran around the whitewashed walls. The superintendent handed her some lengths of fraying rope and explained that they were to pick the fibres apart.

With Peter at her feet, she and her other children began to prise apart the strands. It was a fiddly job even for an adult, and although the children worked quietly, Kitty could see that the task was hurting their fingers and she felt sorry that she'd had to bring them here.

'We'll finish soon,' she encouraged them. 'Then there'll be some breakfast.'

But the four hours seemed endless, even to Kitty. All the time she was working she kept imagining her husband, walking the streets of Liverpool searching for her. She hoped that he wouldn't give up and think that she and the children had been lost at sea. She was desperate to reunite her family – it would be too cruel if the chance was lost because she was stuck here at the same time her husband was looking for her at the docks.

At last the woman told them they could finish.

The last hour had been especially difficult for Kitty as Peter had continually pulled at her skirts and tried to climb into her lap. It had taken up so much time to keep setting him back on to the floor that some of the other women had grumbled at her, thinking she was shirking her task.

Kitty stood up and brushed the fibres from her skirt. Her fingers were red and sore and it made her upset when she saw her children's hands. This was no work for them, and she vowed that she would not bring them back here a second time if she could possibly help it.

They joined the queue for the door, where each person was being issued with another hunk of bread as they left. It was, at least, something to be grateful for.

'I've not seen you here before,' said the woman who was standing behind her. Kitty turned at the sound of the familiar lilting accent that reminded her of home and brought a lump to her throat. 'Are you alone with your children?' she asked.

'We sailed from Dublin a couple of days back,' Kitty told her. 'But our ship was wrecked coming across and I got separated from my husband.'

'I'm sorry to hear it,' said the woman. 'What will you do now?'

'I'll walk down to the docks again to see if he's come. We were meant to be going on to America. But he has the tickets and all our money.'

'I hope you find him,' said the woman. 'But . . .' She hesitated. 'What will you do if you can't?'

'He'll come,' Kitty told her, not wanting to address the question even though it was one that had already haunted her in the early hours of the morning as she'd struggled to sleep. It was something she tried to put out of her mind, although, deep down, she knew it must be answered, but how Kitty had no idea.

6

The quayside seemed busier than ever and Kitty was hopeful when she saw that some new ships had sailed in on the high tide. She pushed her way through the crowds, asking again if anyone had come across a Peter Cavanah, but they all shook their heads. She walked the children up and down the docks all day, dodging between the handcarts and the wagons and the stevedores with their hooks, asking about her husband and baby son, and by the end of the afternoon she was feeling despondent. It seemed that no more passengers had come ashore here from the *Sirius*.

The children were tired out and tearful from trailing after her. They had eaten nothing since the bread they'd been given that morning and she hadn't a single penny to buy more.

'We need to sit down for a bit, Mam,' said Agnes, pulling on her sleeve. 'No one has seen Dada.'

Kitty found a quiet corner and they rested for a while. Peter and Maria fell asleep, but Agnes and Timothy stayed awake beside her, staring out at the grey river that was teeming with boats. As they watched, one of the huge steamers began to move away from the quayside, the passengers thronging the rails as they left for new lives on the far side of the ocean. She and her family should have been on that ship, thought Kitty as she heard the paddles begin to slap against the water. It ought to have been taking them to a better place than this.

'We can't go on to America without him, can we?' said Agnes.

'No.' Kitty shook her head, thinking of the precious tickets and the money that might be lost for ever.

'Do you think Dada is drowned? And the baby?' asked Agnes.

'No. They can't be,' protested Kitty again, even though a heavy weight of doubt had formed in the pit of her stomach. She was starting to wonder if her certainty that her husband and youngest child were safe was misplaced – but she simply couldn't contemplate the awful alternative.

'Will we go back to that place again tonight?' asked Agnes, examining her bruised and bloodied fingers. 'Staying on the street makes me afraid,' she added as a scream pierced the night and there was the sound of shouting and running footsteps. 'At least we got fed, and it was warm.'

They sat on in desperate silence until the raindrops began to fall. First one or two, then they gathered in intensity, and it was clear there was going to be a downpour. So although it wasn't what Kitty wanted to do, she woke the younger ones and they made their way through the driving storm back to the night asylum.

*

As Kitty lay awake on the hard bunk, fretting, it gradually became clear to her that they couldn't remain in this city indefinitely. The asylum was no place to call home and they would surely perish if they had to spend winter on the streets.

Some of the women who'd been sitting near her earlier had been talking about going on to Stockport or Manchester to work in the mills there.

'You should come with us,' said one. 'You would find work and it would be better than staying here picking oakum.'

Kitty wondered if the time had come for her to move on. When she and her husband had discussed their future, back at home in Ireland, before they were offered the tickets to go to America, Peter had spoken of the possibility of getting work in the cotton mills in Lancashire. He had a cousin who'd left for a town called Blackburn some years ago and he had been sure that she would help them. He'd even talked about writing a letter to her. But the idea had been forgotten when the chance of going to America had come along. Now Kitty recalled it and wondered if seeking out this cousin might be the answer to her problems. And if her husband came, and he couldn't find her in Liverpool, surely he would guess that she had gone to Blackburn to seek help.

As they picked the oakum again the next morning, she whispered to her children that she had decided they should go to find their father's family. Agnes seemed doubtful. 'You've never said anything about this cousin before,' she said.

Kitty knew that Agnes was right to be dubious. She had no idea where Blackburn was, or how she would find this cousin Nan when she got there, but she knew she had to do something to keep her children safe and fed.

After they'd received their portion of breakfast bread, she saw the women she'd talked with the night before and went to speak to them.

'I've decided to go to Lancashire and try to track down my husband's relative,' she told them. 'You said you knew the way. Could we walk with you?' she asked.

'Sure, you'll be welcome,' they told her.

Kitty followed them out and her tears flowed unbidden as she watched them reunite with their husbands who had come out from the men's dormitory. How she wished that she could see her own husband waiting for her there in the yard.

Almost immediately, they set off at a brisk pace, and Kitty had to carry Peter and nag Maria to keep up so that they wouldn't be left behind. After a while of falling back and being forced to break into a jog to reach her travelling companions again, one of the women pulled on her husband's arm.

'Let me give the little girl a ride,' he said, hoisting Maria on to his shoulders. Kitty was grateful, even if her younger daughter cried at being carried by a stranger.

'Mine are almost grown now,' said the woman. 'I'd forgotten that little ones can't go so fast. Here, let me carry the boy for a while.' She took little Peter from Kitty's tired grasp and Kitty was thankful and grateful for the help.

The ragged party left the houses of Liverpool behind them and struck out down narrow, muddy lanes. Kitty was glad not to be alone and to have company to walk along with. She would never have known how to find her way out of the city otherwise, but both these families had relatives who were already in England who had sent instructions about how to reach them and where to find food and shelter along the way.

Whenever they passed a farm or a cluster of cottages near the roadside they asked for food. Sometimes they were lucky and were given a bit of stale bread or at least a drink of water, and Kitty wept with gratitude to the farmer's wife who gave her children a cup of warm milk each, straight from the milked cow. But many of the people whose homes they passed or whom they met on the road were not so kind, and although Kitty tried to shield the children from the worst of the abuse that was shouted at them, she knew that it hurt and bewildered them.

'Filthy Irish! Coming here with your fevers and expecting us to keep you! Get some work, you lazy good-for-nothings!' The anger and the insults wrenched at Kitty. She wished that they'd never had to leave their home and come here, because it was clear that they were despised for their poverty and desperation.

The first night they reached a town called Prescot. Kitty had expected that they would have to sleep in a barn or a hedgerow, but the families she walked with headed straight for a building that they called the vagrant shed to ask for relief. It was similar to the night asylum in Liverpool, and they were given bread and a bunk to sleep on. Kitty was grateful for the warmth and shelter.

'If they ask, say you have a job to go to,' one of the women had advised her. 'They'll give you a bed if they think you're travelling to work.'

'What job?' the man at the desk had asked, peering over the top of his thick spectacles. The woman had nudged her.

'Cotton weaver,' Kitty had replied. The man had looked doubtful, but he'd entered it in his book and waved her in. Kitty hated to lie, but she would rather do that than risk being sent back to Ireland.

There was work again the next morning. Kitty wondered why so many ropes had to be picked apart and what was done with the strands. It seemed a pointless task, and although she was willing to endure it, she was distraught every time she saw the damage to her children's hands.

'What's the use of it?' she whispered to one of the other women, even though they were not supposed to speak as they worked.

'I was told they mix it with tar to repair ships,' she whispered back. Kitty felt a shiver run through her at

66

the thought of so many holes in the wooden hulls of the sailing ships. No wonder the *Sirius* had gone down so quickly.

She kept back half the bread they were given to eat later, and they set off again on their long walk. Her body ached and she was constantly tired, but she knew it was much harder for her children, though they had stopped complaining and seemed resigned to what was to come. Kitty was grateful that some of her fellow travellers continued to help her carry Peter and Maria so that they could keep up their brisk pace, but Agnes and Timothy had to walk and Kitty worried about them.

They stopped to eat their bread in the early afternoon and soon after came across a farm near the roadside. One of the men went to ask for directions, and to see if any food could be spared. The farmer's wife came out with some milk and a few oatcakes. 'For t' children,' she said and Kitty thanked her gratefully. 'Where's tha headed?' she asked as she took back the cups.

'Blackburn. I have family there,' replied Kitty so that the woman wouldn't think she was a vagrant. 'I'm going to work in the mills,' she added.

'Tha needs to take the road to t' north at t' cross-roads then,' the woman told her. 'It'll take thee o'er t' moors to Bolton then down through Darwen.'

'To the north?' repeated Kitty to be sure she'd understood the directions. She often struggled to follow what the local people said. The accent was strange to her and they seemed to miss out half the words.

When they reached the crossroads, the man who was carrying Maria lifted her down from his shoulders and set her at the roadside.

'Come with us,' begged his wife. 'We'll find you somewhere to stay in Stockport. There's work there.'

Kitty was tempted. These people had been good to her and the prospect of setting off alone on the unknown road frightened her. But she was worried that if she went with them to Stockport she would never be reunited with her missing family.

'My husband will look for me in Blackburn,' she told them. 'I need to go there.'

'Well, the best of luck. God speed ye,' said the woman, clutching her close for a moment.

Kitty bit back her tears as she watched her friends go. She almost changed her mind and called after them to say that she would go with them after all, but she thought that finding cousin Nan was her best chance of being reunited with her husband and baby. Though how she would feed him she didn't know. Her milk had dried up. He would have to have cow's milk if they could get it, she thought. But maybe if she could get enough to eat her milk would flow again. She hoped so.

'Come on,' she said to the children. 'Let's see how far we can get before sundown.'

They trudged on. Agnes walked beside her in silence and Kitty suspected her daughter would have preferred to stay with the other families.

'It's not too late to catch up with the others and go to

Stockport,' said Agnes, glancing back to see if she could still see their travelling companions on the horizon.

'We need to find cousin Nan,' Kitty reminded her. Agnes didn't reply and Kitty fretted that her daughter was right and that she had made the wrong choice.

Kitty was unable to find a night shelter, and when it became too dark for them to go on safely they were forced to emulate the sheep and settle down in the shelter of a dry-stone wall to wait for morning.

It was freezing cold as an October frost settled on the short grass. Kitty wrapped her shawl around them as best she could and they huddled together for warmth. She watched the moon rise in the sky, changing from orange to yellow and white as it climbed. The stars twinkled above her and she recognized the patterns they made in the sky. Relieved that there was at least something familiar about this place, she dozed a little until dawn broke.

'Time to go on,' she said to the children as she woke them. 'At least there's no oakum to be picked.'

'No bread either,' grumbled Agnes.

'We'll find something,' replied Kitty with more conviction than she felt.

The road rose steeply as they walked, and Kitty could see hills rising in the distance. The green of the pastureland gradually turned to moorland where the wind whipped through the grasses, making them ripple across the landscape like waves on the sea.

They approached the outskirts of a town before

long and Kitty went to ask its name and beg a few pennies to buy something to eat. But it was clear that they were not welcome in Bolton.

'Come away from them. They might have the Irish Fever,' a woman had warned as she drew her children close. Another spat on the ground and cursed them. Kitty didn't linger. She wanted to tell them that she carried no disease, to plead with them to take pity on her children, but it was as if she wasn't a human being like them, but something to be feared. She hoped there would be a warmer welcome when she reached Blackburn.

7

Kitty paused and looked at the town in the valley below. They had smelt it even before they could see it – a mixture of clinging smog and overflowing sewers. At first, she thought that the whole place had been set alight, but then she saw that the dirty smoke was coming from chimneys – hundreds of them, each with its own wraith of dark grey rising from its tip and sinking down again to cover everything in filth and soot.

Beside her, Agnes's face was a picture of dismay. 'Is that Blackburn?' she asked.

'It must be,' said Kitty. 'Come on. Let's see if anyone can tell us where to find cousin Nan.'

Wearily, she led her children down the hill. They were forced to keep into the side of the road as the carts and carriages passed them, splashing up water from the muddy puddles that had formed in the ruts made by hundreds of wheels. The air grew smokier and fouler as they descended, and Kitty pulled her shawl over her mouth to prevent herself coughing. She bade the children do the same. She knew that they would not be welcome if people thought they were ill.

As they approached the outskirts of the town, Kitty's attention was drawn to a large building, set on an incline at the junction of two roads, with a high fence all around it. It was clear that this was the workhouse. She turned her face away and hurried the children past.

As they walked on Kitty became aware of a low, pounding noise that disturbed the air. At first she was unsure where it was coming from, but as she came nearer to the centre of the town she realized that it was from the brick buildings that stood on almost every street. They must be the mills. She hadn't imagined them to be so tall. She paused to watch as a cart halted near one and men began to unload bales of cotton like the ones that she'd seen on the quayside in Liverpool and carry them inside. She wondered if cousin Nan was in one of them, working at a spinning wheel or even at a loom. She couldn't imagine what it might be like.

Kitty saw a few men hanging about outside a public house. She approached them to make enquiries. 'I'm looking for Nan Cavanah,' she said. 'Do you know her?'

The men eyed her suspiciously. 'The Irish live down in Butcher's Court,' one told her.

'Where's that?' she asked.

'Down yon.' He nodded his head towards the far end of the road then turned away from her.

Kitty walked on, unsure of where she was going. She tried to ask some other passers-by but they crossed the street when they saw her coming and looked the other way. Not knowing what to do next, she followed some women with baskets over their arms towards the centre of the town. She saw that it was market day. The stalls, with canvas roofs, were arranged in lines on the market square and beside them stood a gabled building with a clock tower, its new stonework unsullied by the soot from the chimneys.

Kitty walked up and down between the stalls where fruit and vegetables were on offer, and passed one stacked with huge, round cheeses. Her mouth began to water as she stared at them. How she would have loved to taste a slice.

'Fourpence a half-pound,' the cheesemonger told her. She shook her head. She didn't have any money for bread, never mind a luxury like that.

'Do you know Nan Cavanah?' she asked him.

'Can't say as I do,' he replied and turned his attention to a paying customer.

Kitty walked on, asking everyone she could if they knew Peter's cousin, but nobody did. Then she noticed that many of the women were going into the new building through its wide-open doorway. Curiously, she followed them and found more stalls inside with an array of goods. Not just more fruit and vegetables, but stalls with lengths of material, needles, threads, buttons and hooks; stalls selling caps and aprons; butchers selling joints of meat; a tripe stall; a fish stall. Kitty stared at it all. She'd never seen so much food in one place and her belly growled at the smells all mingled together into an enticing aroma. She paused at a stall where a man was selling a dark liquid.

'Sarsaparilla?' he asked her. Kitty shook her head. She had no idea what it was and had no money to buy it anyway, but how she wished she could have just a little of all this produce to feed herself and her children.

She approached more stall holders and asked if they knew Nan. They all shook their heads and their smiles of welcome faded when they realized she wasn't bringing them her custom.

'Are you all right?' The sound of the Irish voice suddenly gave her hope.

'I'm looking for Nan Cavanah, my husband's cousin. Do you happen to know her?'

The woman shook her head. 'I can't say that I do. Do you not know where she lives?'

'I don't,' Kitty admitted. 'All I know is she came here to work some years ago.'

'Your husband's cousin, you say?' The woman glanced about. 'Where is your husband?'

'I lost him,' said Kitty and explained, tearfully, about the *Sirius*.

'I'm sorry,' the woman said. 'I can't imagine how hard that must have been for you. Let me try to help you to find your cousin. It shouldn't be hard. Most people from Ireland stick together,' she explained. 'Why don't you come home with me and we can ask about to see who knows her?'

Kitty went with the woman gratefully. 'I'm Aileen,' the woman told her as they walked.

'And I'm Kitty. Kitty Cavanah.'

'We haven't much,' Aileen warned her, 'but you're welcome to share what we have. I'll not see a mother and children from the old country go hungry or end up sleeping on the streets if we have a corner for them.'

'Thank you,' said Kitty as relief washed over her. The kindness was so unexpected after so many others had ignored or insulted her and she was grateful that some luck had come her way at last. They walked until they came to a collection of cramped houses clustered around a small courtyard. There was a stench of blood and offal and Kitty saw that there were two butcher's shops on the ground level. Some discarded bones had been thrown on to a pile in the corner where some mangy dogs were growling at one another with bared teeth. She lifted Peter in her arms and pulled Maria closer, afraid of the children being bitten if the dogs saw them as a threat to their food.

Aileen took them down some steps to a window-less cellar that was reminiscent of the one in Liverpool where Brigit had given her shelter. Even though it was the middle of the day, a lamp stood on the scarred wooden table to light the room. It was furnished with little else except an old mattress that was propped against the wall, a pile of boxes, which appeared to hold an assortment of discarded rubbish, and one chair where a man was warming himself at the fire and smoking a pipe that was adding to the fug of the atmosphere.

'Who's this?' he asked, not unkindly, as he gazed at the visitors who had crowded into his small home.

'It's Kitty Cavanah. She's come over from the old country. I found her on the street, searching for her cousin, Nan Cavanah. Do you know of her?'

'I can't say that I do,' he replied. 'But you're welcome. I'm Michael.' He held out a hand in greeting before turning to his wife. 'Did you bring the fish?' he asked. 'We always try to treat ourselves to a bit of fish at dinner time on a Friday,' he told Kitty.

'I wish I'd brought more,' said Aileen as she put the package down on the table and unwrapped it. Kitty saw that it was only a couple of fillets – a meagre portion.

'We've already eaten,' she said, not wanting to impose too much on the kindness of these strangers even though she could see her children eyeing the food hungrily.

'You'll drink some tea with us, though?' Aileen asked.

Kitty nodded eagerly. A hot drink would at least partly fill her aching, groaning stomach.

She repeated her story to Michael as Aileen fried the fish in a skillet over the fire. It smelt exquisite and Kitty wished that the children could have some of it. Maria watched so expectantly as it was put on to the plates that Aileen hesitated when she saw the child's face.

'Would they like a little bit?' she asked Kitty.

'Don't leave yourself short,' Kitty insisted, but Aileen cut the fish into even smaller portions and handed it out to the children, along with some oatcakes.

'It's like the feeding of the five thousand!' she laughed as she watched the eager children tuck in. 'Here.' She passed Kitty a morsel and a pile of oatcakes and Kitty thought she'd never tasted anything so good in her life.

8

Peggy Sharples walked back from the market with the parcel of haddock she'd just bought from the fishmonger. John always insisted that they had fish on a Friday.

'The world won't end if I make a bit of meat and tatie pie,' she'd once told him. But he'd frowned and she'd seen that it was important to him. It was his mother who'd taught him to be superstitious about it. And although John rarely saw her or his sisters and never went to church, he was somehow unable to shake off the fear that it was wrong to eat meat on a Friday and that if he did he would be punished for it in some way.

As she hurried towards the shop on Church Street that she ran with her husband, she found herself thinking about the woman with the four children again. She'd been wandering around the stalls, speaking to some of the stall holders as if she was making enquiries. Peggy had purposely avoided her, taking the aisle by the draper's stall so she wouldn't have to walk past her. She was probably Irish. There were more and more of them coming now, begging for food and bringing disease with them.

When she reached the shop, she glanced at her

display of hats and bonnets in the window. At first she'd struggled to make it look as appealing as it had when the shop belonged to Miss Cross, but she was learning all the time and was proud of her latest effort. At the centre of her display were several of the Jenny Lind hats that she'd ordered from London. Peggy had been unsure about them at first, as straw hats were regarded as something that the country women wore, and most of the society ladies still favoured bonnets. But when she'd lifted the first hat from its packaging and seen the turned-up brim, decorated with flowers at one side and a ribbon at the other, she'd been entranced and had immediately tried it on. She'd decided there and then that she would wear it whenever she was out to advertise it to the ladies of the town, and soon she had customers flocking to her shop asking for the latest fashion.

She pushed open the shop door and smiled at the tinkling of the little bell. 'Any customers?' she asked John. He was standing at the counter, sorting through the post.

'Not for hats,' he replied, and Peggy was glad, because although her husband was an excellent post-master, he had no clue about hats and gloves. 'I need to go out to deliver these,' he said. He'd begun to deliver letters by hand to the townsfolk a while ago, but now that the penny post was increasing in popularity so many more people were sending letters that it was becoming an onerous task. Peggy had been nagging him to take on a postboy to make the deliveries, but John was reluctant to trust the task to a lad.

'I'll just go and put this fish in the kitchen,' said Peggy. She opened the door to the stairs that led up to the rooms where they lived above the shop. 'Try not to be all afternoon delivering the letters,' she called as she went up. 'My mother will be bringing the children home later and I can't watch them and mind the shop at the same time. I'll have to close up.'

The stairs opened on to a small landing outside the kitchen. Peggy put her basket on the table and carried the parcel of fish to the stone slab in the larder. She would put the rest of her shopping away later, she decided, hurrying to hang up her jacket and put her hat away in the bedroom.

As she passed through the parlour, she glanced at John's aquarium. One of the sticklebacks was floating on the top of the water, obviously dead. Peggy sighed. He would fuss over it and the rest of the tank when he came back and saw it. He'd become obsessed with the thing and it was driving Peggy half mad. She decided to say nothing about it for now and hurried back down the stairs to mind the shop whilst he went out. Not for the first time, she thought that John didn't really understand how difficult it was to be a wife, a mother and a shopkeeper all at once.

Later that afternoon, Peggy tidied round the shop and swept the floor so it would be ready for the following day. No one would come in for hats and gloves so late in the afternoon, but there might be some parcels and letters for the post, especially from the local businesses before their offices closed for the evening. But the next time the bell tinkled it was her mother with Emily and Becky. Peggy scooped up her daughters, one in each arm, and kissed them.

'Have you been good?' she asked.

'Aye. They're always good.' Her mother smiled indulgently. 'Shall I take 'em upstairs?'

'Yes, please. Could you watch them until John gets back?' Peggy asked. 'I'm sure he won't be long, but I don't want to close when there might be people wanting to catch the last post.'

'Shall I give 'em their tea?' asked her mother.

'No. I'll see to them as soon as John comes,' Peggy said. She didn't want to impose further on her mother, and although she knew that she loved having her grandchildren, Peggy also knew that her two young daughters could be hard work – especially Emily, with her boundless energy and endless questions.

She continued to tidy the shop and received a handful of parcels whilst watching out for John. He seemed to be gone longer every day. At last he came. His pale cheeks were flushed with the brisk wind and when he took off his cap his fine ginger hair stood up on end. Peggy smoothed it down for him and kissed his cold cheek. 'My mother's brought the girls,' she said. 'I'll go and start the tea. Will you be long?' she asked, hoping he would say that he would close up the shop now.

He glanced at his pocket watch. 'I'll give it half an hour and then lock the door and take the bags to the station,' he said. Peggy nodded. She was grateful for the railway. Once the last bag of post had been put on the night train, the shop could be shut until the next morning.

Upstairs, little Becky had fallen asleep on her grandma's knee and Emily was playing with her doll on the hearthrug. Peggy wished that her mother had kept Becky awake. If she slept too long now she would cry later, and Peggy wanted a peaceful hour before she went to her own bed.

She threw another shovelful of coal on to the fire and lifted up her younger daughter.

'You'd best get off home now,' she told her mother. 'Dad'll be wondering where you've got to.'

'He'll be peering out of t' window lookin' for me and frettin' about his tea if he's got home from his meeting to find an empty house,' her mother laughed. 'He's as helpless as a babe when it comes to cookin' owt.'

Her mother fastened her bonnet and reached for the shawl she'd put over the back of the chair. Peggy had tried to persuade her to wear a jacket and a hat, but she'd said that she was too old for the new fashions and that what she'd always worn suited her well enough. She kissed the children and said she would see them the next day, then kissed Peggy on the cheek and went down the stairs. Peggy heard her call a farewell to John and then the shop bell tinkled. She looked out of the window to see her mother walk up Church Street. Peggy was glad that she wasn't going home to the old house on Water Street where she used to take in laundry. Her parents lived in a new house on Primrose Bank now. They had their own privy in the yard and a water tap in the kitchen. Her mother thought it was the height of luxury.

Peggy put the guard around the fire and began making the tea. By the time John came up, the girls had been fed and his piece of fish was ready to be fried and served with the potatoes she was keeping warm in the pan. She plated it up whilst he put his daughters to bed and kissed them goodnight.

'Have you had yours?' he asked as she set the plate in front of him.

'I ate with the girls,' she said. She poured out two cups of tea and took hers to a chair by the fire. 'I've been so busy in the shop I haven't even put a duster over any surfaces up here.' Peggy ran a finger across the edge of the fender and surveyed the grime in the candlelight. 'Maybe we should get a woman to help with the cleaning, as well as a postboy for the shop. I'm sure we could afford it. We're doing well, aren't we?' she asked.

She knew that John was reluctant to take on employees, partly because he was afraid of getting 'above himself', as he called it. She knew what he meant. They'd both been brought up in poor families and the idea of being an employer rather than an employee was a strange one.

'We're doing all right,' John replied. He blew on his forkful of fish to cool it before putting it in his mouth, then chewed on it thoughtfully. 'We'll see,' he promised at last. Peggy tried not to sigh out loud. His answer was always the same.

After he'd eaten, Peggy took the plates into the kitchen to wash them up. It was almost bedtime already and she was tired. She sighed as she heard him exclaiming over the stickleback.

'I don't know why they keep dying,' he said when she went back into the parlour. He was peering into the aquarium with a puzzled expression. 'The others seem lively enough. Perhaps it needs to be cleaned out again.'

'Not now,' Peggy said, hoping that he wouldn't start on the filthy task. 'It always makes such a mess and I'm too tired to clean up after you.'

John scooped the stickleback out of the water and threw it in with the rubbish. 'I'll do it on Sunday morning,' he said, 'and then I'll take the lasses down to the canal and see what else we can catch.'

9

As evening lengthened into night in Aileen and Michael's cellar, Kitty began to worry about where she and the children would spend the night.

'You must stay here,' Aileen insisted when Kitty told them she thought it was time to go. 'We'll make space. We'll not see you on the street with four small children. Michael will be quite comfortable in the chair, and you and I can sleep top to toe on the mattress with the children squeezed in between us.'

'Are you sure?' Kitty asked. 'I'm so grateful to you, but it seems such a lot to ask.'

'Nonsense,' Aileen told her. 'We'll manage.'

It was a tight fit, but Kitty was thankful that she'd found these new friends. Another night in the open would have been hard on the children, especially the younger ones.

It was impossible to tell when daylight came the next morning in the windowless cellar, but sounds of life in the yard above woke Kitty. Soon after, Aileen stirred and Kitty watched as she kindled the fire and picked up a bucket, taking it out to the pump in the yard to fill it. When she came back she was carrying a small sack and had an urchin, who looked about the same age as Maria, in her grasp. He wore a collarless shirt with a jacket over it. The sleeves were torn and frayed at the edges. His overlarge trousers were ripped into holes at the knees and fastened up around his waist with an old scarf. He was barefoot and pitifully thin.

'He wants to know what you'll give him,' Aileen told Michael, who was yawning and scratching as he poked the fire into a blaze.

'Empty it out then,' said Michael, and Kitty watched as Aileen shook the contents of the sack on to the table. She saw that it contained the remains of the bones that the dogs hadn't stolen, a few discarded nails, a short length of rope and a broken bottle. 'Here. A farthing,' Michael told the wretched child as he reached into his pocket before offering the coin. The child grabbed at it and, with the empty bag in his hand, scampered back up the steps to the street.

'It isn't even worth that much,' said Aileen, poking at the items still strewn across the table.

'I know. But how could I let a child go hungry?' asked Michael.

'You always were too soft.' Aileen put the bones into a sack, and added the rope and glass to an assortment of remnants in one of the wooden boxes. Then she counted the nails and put them in a leather bag.

Kitty was surprised. 'Is there some worth to those things?' she asked.

'There is,' replied Aileen. 'The rag and bone dealers

will pay money for what some folk throw away without a second thought.'

'Rags are sought after to make paper,' Michael explained to Kitty.

'But the bones? What use are they? Apart from boiling up to make a soup.'

'They go to make knife handles and the like,' said Michael. 'And the smaller pieces are ground up to fertilize the fields. Everything has its use. I'll be out there myself once it comes properly light,' he said, 'although it seems the child has beaten me to the bones. Have you seen him before?' he asked his wife.

'I haven't,' she said. 'And I don't think you should encourage him with your coins. You know that Mr Littler puts those bones out for us.'

'You're right,' agreed Michael, 'but I can't resist a young face.'

Aileen brought down the water to put some into the kettle and set it to boil. Kitty wasn't sure how long she would be welcome to stay, but she hoped that she and the children might at least be offered a hot drink before they went on their way.

'Nan Cavanah, did you say the name of your cousin was?' asked Michael when Aileen had handed him his cup of tea. 'I'll ask about to see if anyone knows her.'

'Might she have married?' queried Aileen.

'I suppose she might.' It hadn't occurred to Kitty that cousin Nan could have a different name now, making it even harder to track her down. 'It must have been a while since she came. I never knew her. She is my husband's cousin.'

'Well, Nan's not an uncommon name,' said Michael. 'But I'm sure someone will know of her if we ask around.'

Kitty took a cup of tea from Aileen, feeling more cheerful. 'I appreciate your help,' she said. 'I'm just not sure where to begin.'

'You might try the priest up at St Alban's,' suggested Aileen. 'He knows most folk – if your cousin is a church-going woman.'

When Michael had finished his drink, he stood up and pulled on a greasy coat and a grey cap, then picked up a bag and a stick that was honed to a point at the end. 'I'd best be off before any more of the urchins pick up the good stuff,' he said, making his way to the steps. He opened the door to the court, and Kitty could see that the sky was beginning to lighten above the roofs and in the distance she could hear the ringing of bells. At first she thought the sound was coming from the churches, but Aileen told her it was the mills, summoning the workers to their toil. 'If they aren't in by the time it stops, they lose a day's wages,' she told Kitty.

The children woke when Michael shut the door behind him. A cold draught blew across the cellar, making the fire smoke. Aileen gave them each a drink, but apologized that there was no food.

'You've been more than kind already,' Kitty told her. 'We can't impose on you any more. I'll feed my own children,' she reassured her new friend, although she had no idea how. 'I'm so grateful for the shelter,' she added.

'Go to see Father Kaye at the rectory,' urged Aileen. 'He might give you some food even if he doesn't know of your cousin.'

Kitty and the children climbed the steps into the court.

'Come back tonight if you don't find her,' said Aileen.

'Thank you,' Kitty replied with a grateful smile. She lifted Peter in her arms and bade the children follow her footsteps carefully through the filth. It was at least a relief to know they wouldn't have to sleep in the open if she didn't find Nan today, but she worried about how long Aileen and Michael would welcome her in their home when she had nothing to offer them in return.

She followed Aileen's directions towards St Alban's, on the far side of the town. As she made her way along the cobbled streets, she watched the shopkeepers opening up for the day ahead. She passed by a shop that sold hats and gloves and paused for a moment to look in the window. Kitty had never seen such hats before, with their upturned brims and fancy feathers, and she wished that she could try one on and look at herself in a mirror to see if it suited her. But although the items were not priced, she doubted that she would ever be able to afford one.

The woman who kept the shop saw her staring and glared at her from the other side of the window. Kitty moved on, not wanting to offend her. She didn't want another soaking.

The church was easy to find and Kitty knocked timidly on the door of the rectory that stood beside it. After a few moments, a woman in a coarse apron, her curly hair escaping from her cap in little coils, answered it.

'What dost tha want?' she asked, looking at Kitty and the children warily.

'I'm looking for Father Kaye. I was told he might be able to help me.'

The woman glanced at the children again and then back to Kitty. After a moment of hesitation in which Kitty thought she was to be sent away, she relented and invited them to step inside. 'And mind the childer all wipe their feet on t' mat,' she said.

Kitty stepped on to the coir matting behind the front door and vigorously wiped the soles of her boots, encouraging the children to do the same.

'Wait there,' said the woman, leaving her in the small tiled hallway with the crucifix on the wall. 'Don't touch nowt.'

Kitty could have retorted that there was nothing to touch, but she kept her silence and warned the children with a glance to keep quiet too. A moment later, the priest came out from a room at the back of the house. He was younger than Kitty had expected, with bright blue eyes and dark hair that fell over his forehead. He swept it back as he assessed her and the children, probably noting that they were shod and well-dressed by comparison with many.

'What can I do for you?' he asked.

'I'm seeking a woman by the name of Nan Cavanah,' she told him. 'She's my husband's cousin. I was told you might know her.'

'Nan Cavanah.' He ran the words around his tongue as he searched his memory. 'I can't say that I know that name,' he went on with a shake of his head.

Kitty felt the blow of disappointment. She supposed it would have been too easy to simply ask and be given an address.

'Have you come over from Ireland? asked the priest.

'I have. We've walked from the port at Liverpool.' She knew what his next question would be so she answered it. 'Our ship was wrecked and I was parted from my husband. I lost my baby too,' she managed to tell the priest before the sobbing overcame her.

'Come, come, now. Be brave,' said the priest. 'Come and sit down.' He put a gentle hand on her shoulder and ushered her into the front room. 'Sit here,' he said, bringing forward a bentwood chair from against the wall. 'Mrs Bowker!' he called. 'Bring a cup of tea for this lass – and some cups of milk for her children.'

He patted Kitty's shoulder and she wiped her face on a corner of her shawl, wishing that she had a handkerchief. 'Trust in God,' he advised. 'He will give you strength. Tell me what happened,' he encouraged as he sat down opposite her.

With the cup of hot tea in her hand, Kitty explained about the *Sirius* and their journey to Blackburn and everything in between.

Father Kaye listened whilst the children sat silently at her feet.

'I know all my parishioners,' he told her when she'd finished, 'but I know none by the name of Cavanah. Could this cousin have married?'

'It's probable,' Kitty admitted.

'Then all we know for sure is she's called Nan. It's a common name.'

Kitty's hopes sank even further. It seemed that finding her husband's cousin would be much harder than she had ever expected.

'I didn't know what else to do,' she said. 'I didn't want to stay in Liverpool and risk being sent back to Ireland. There's nothing for us there now.'

Father Kaye didn't reply and Kitty realized what he was thinking – that there was nothing for them here either if cousin Nan couldn't be found.

'I know my husband will come here to seek us out,' she told the priest. 'We must stay.'

'Mrs Cavanah . . . Kitty,' said Father Kaye. 'Have you considered the possibility that your husband may not come? He may have already been taken to the arms of the Lord. And the baby too. I know it isn't what you want to hear, but you must trust in God, and if it is His will you must accept that it is His plan for you. You must stand strong, for the sake of the children here. Pray for strength and it shall be given.'

Kitty shook her head. 'No,' she told him. 'I would know if they were . . . dead.' She whispered the last word. 'I must wait for them here,' she insisted. She would never give up hope.

'I'll see what I can do,' Father Kaye promised, and he gave her a shilling from the poor box to feed the children. Kitty thanked him profusely. It was much more than she'd expected.

She took the silent children back to the marketplace, grateful that they could at least have something to eat. It wasn't market day, but there were several street sellers touting their wares. Kitty hurried the children past the confectioner selling his sweets from a wide tray that hung from his neck on a thick leather strap, towards the man who was selling hot baked potatoes from a charcoal brazier. The smell of them made her long for home. She'd baked potatoes on her fire back in Ireland almost every day until the crop had failed.

'They don't have the rot, do they?' she asked suspiciously as she fingered the coins she'd been given, reluctant to part with them for something that might prove inedible.

'Not these,' said the man and he broke one open to show her the fluffy white flesh inside the crisp jacket. 'Nowt to beat 'em wi' a bit of butter and salt and pepper,' he encouraged her. Kitty didn't need much persuasion and she asked for three at tuppence apiece, feeling jealous that the crop here had provided such riches. These people had no idea how lucky they were, she thought. As the man sprinkled on the salt and pepper, she asked him if he knew anyone called Nan. He laughed and told her half the town called themselves by that name.

They ate as they walked. Kitty asked anyone who would stop about cousin Nan, but most people avoided them or hurried past. She wondered if she should start going down the streets knocking on the doors. She tried a few, but most of the houses were empty, their occupants hard at work in the mills, and the people who did answer either closed their door in her face or cursed at her to get off their doorstep.

Towards the end of the day, Kitty's thoughts turned to where she and the children would spend that night. She had hoped not to impose on Aileen and Michael again, but she couldn't go to the workhouse and risk being sent back to Ireland.

'What will we do if we can't find cousin Nan?' Agnes asked at last. Kitty sensed it was a question her daughter had been gathering the courage to ask for hours. She thought about replying that they would find her, but her daughter's serious face told her that she wouldn't accept any more platitudes. Agnes wanted an honest reply.

'I don't know,' she admitted.

As it grew dark and cold, Kitty realized that her only option was to ask Aileen and Michael if they could sleep in their cellar again. She knew that it was an imposition. There wasn't really room for them and she hated to have to rely on the kindness of strangers, but the only alternative was sleeping on the street, and she was afraid to do that. The streets here didn't seem any safer than the ones in Liverpool. There were too many people roaming them, often the worse for drink, and she was afraid that she might be robbed of the precious sixpence she had left, or worse.

Little Peter was exhausted and she lifted him into her arms as the other children followed wearily in her wake. She could see that Agnes was white-faced with anxiety, Timothy's face was resolute and Maria was trying not to cry. Kitty felt guilty that she was expecting too much from them. They had followed her around all day whilst she made her enquiries without complaint, but they were small and hungry and tired, and she knew that they needed something to eat and a safe place to sleep.

As she walked, she fought back her own tears. It would have been so different if her husband hadn't gone to help free that trapped boy on the ship. And although she knew that it was the right thing to do, she wished he'd put his own family first. In the past, he'd always been there to care for them. He'd protected them, and even though times had been hard in Ireland, she'd trusted him to make sure that they didn't starve. He'd always found a way, and even when they'd been turned out of their home he'd bargained hard for the tickets to America.

They should have been on their way by now. If only the *Sirius* hadn't foundered, they would have been sailing across that wide ocean to the better life she knew was waiting for them. Her husband would be by her side and her baby would be lying in her arms, suckling from the breasts that ached for him. Instead, she was alone with the older children in this strange town, trying to care for her incomplete family.

When they reached Aileen's door she reached down and knocked gently. It was opened almost immediately.

'It's me. Kitty,' she said as Aileen peered up into the darkness.

'Did you not find your cousin?' she asked.

'No. Father Kaye didn't know of her and I've asked everywhere, but no one has heard of her. I'm really sorry to be a nuisance,' she said, 'but there's nowhere else we can go – and you did say we could come back?' Kitty felt uncomfortable for asking and prayed that Aileen wouldn't turn her and the children away.

'You'd best come in,' said Aileen and with a wave of gratitude that made her gulp back tears, Kitty ushered the children down the steps and into the tiny room.

Aileen had a loaf of bread and some cheese. She cut some for the children and refused the sixpence that Kitty offered her. 'We had a good day,' she said. 'Michael's brought a jug of ale and some oysters.'

Kitty gratefully accepted the food. 'I'm beginning to wonder if cousin Nan isn't here any longer,' she said once the children were asleep and couldn't hear her doubts. 'She might have gone on somewhere else. Some of the people I walked with spoke of going to Stockport to find work.'

'So what will you do now?' asked Michael. He put a light to the tobacco in his small pipe and puffed, filling the cellar with thick acrid smoke. Kitty coughed.

'I don't know. I'm terrified of going to the workhouse,' she admitted.

'You can't go there!' protested Aileen. 'You can stay here for the time being, until you get settled. They can stay, can't they, Michael?' she asked her husband.

He didn't reply straight away and Kitty could see that he wasn't keen. She could hardly blame him. The cellar was overcrowded with them all in it and she couldn't reproach him for not wanting to sleep every night in the chair.

'I can't keep imposing on you,' she said.

'Stay for now,' said Michael. 'I'll not see a woman and children on the streets.' He drew on his pipe again and Kitty wondered if he was thinking she and her family were not his responsibility.

'I'll have to find work,' she said after a moment.

'And what about the children?' asked Aileen.

'Agnes is old enough to watch the younger ones. Timothy is old enough to work too. He's ten years old now. If we both work, maybe we can rent a room of our own.'

'What work can you do?' asked Michael. 'Can you weave?'

'I can spin,' said Kitty.

'Spinning is all done on machines here,' he told her. 'They may take you on at the factory, but it's more likely they'll turn you away. They don't like us,' he added. 'They only take on Irish if there's a strike and then they only pay us half of what they pay them.' He nodded his head in the general direction of the better streets. 'They tell us to go home and find work there. They've no idea what it's like and wouldn't care anyway if they knew.'

Kitty stared at her hands in the gloom of the flickering firelight. It worried her that she might not be able to find work here after all. She needed to work. She knew she couldn't rely on charity, because they would send her back to Ireland if she couldn't support herself and her children.

'What about gathering rags like you do?' she asked. 'Do you think I could do that? Could I earn enough to keep myself and my children?'

'It's not easy,' Michael warned her. 'And it can be dirty work. It's not always pleasant.'

'I'm not afraid of hard work,' she told him, determinedly.

10

It was the Irish woman again, thought Peggy later that morning as she saw her pause outside the window display and stare longingly at the Jenny Lind hats. She didn't look like she could afford to buy her next meal, never mind a hat, and Peggy wished that she would move on. She didn't want the likes of her lingering around the shop entrance putting off her regular customers.

'What's botherin' thee?' asked John as she turned away from the window.

'Nothing,' she said, remembering that she used to stare at the hats and gloves and ribbons in the window herself in the days when the shop had belonged to Miss Cross. She felt a little guilty as she moved behind the counter to unpack a parcel of silk handkerchiefs that had arrived that morning with the post from London. She supposed she couldn't blame the woman for looking. Goodness knows, she'd spent long enough arranging her display to make it enticing.

John had returned to sorting the letters into different piles for each street. Peggy frowned as she realized that he would be gone for a good while delivering them all. Sometimes she wondered if his reluctance to take on a postboy was because he enjoyed walking about, taking the letters to the houses, leaving her to run both the hat shop and the post office and to cook his dinner and care for the children.

'Something's botherin' thee,' he said as he heard her sigh.

'It was an Irish woman staring in,' said Peggy. 'I wish she wouldn't.'

'She's not doing any harm,' said John. He began to pack the sorted letters into his bag.

'She is if a customer comes whilst she's standing there,' Peggy told him. 'They don't like getting close to the Irish.'

'Well, she's gone now,' he said as he put on his cap, ready to go out. 'I won't be long,' he told her, opening the door. Peggy watched him walk up Church Street, whistling as he went, and she felt a moment of envy at his freedom. Although she loved her shop, and much preferred it to the class full of unruly children that she used to have to deal with when she was an assistant teacher, she sometimes yearned to be able to simply walk out and have some freedom for a while.

The doorbell tinkled again and Mrs Ibbotson came in with her daughter. Peggy put on her best smile and invited her customers to take a seat. 'What may I show you today?' she asked.

'These hats,' said Mrs Ibbotson. 'Are the ladies in London really wearing them?'

'They are, madam. They're immensely popular.'

Mrs Ibbotson seemed unconvinced, although it was obvious that her daughter was eager. 'Would you like to try one on, Miss Ibbotson?' encouraged Peggy. 'I think the one with the green trimmings would suit your colouring. In fact, I thought of you when I was ordering it.'

'Did you?' asked Miss Ibbotson, rising to the flattery. She turned to her mother. 'Please, Mama, may I try it?' she pleaded.

'Very well then,' said Mrs Ibbotson after a moment of hesitation. 'Please fetch the green one from the window,' she instructed Peggy.

Peggy removed it carefully from the display and brought it to the young lady who was eagerly removing her bonnet.

'I always thought that hats were a little ... you know ... common,' whispered Mrs Ibbotson as she watched Peggy fetch a mirror so that Miss Ibbotson could see her reflection. 'I always associate them with farm girls.'

'All the London ladies are wearing them,' Peggy assured her.

'Oh, please may I have it, Mama?' asked her daughter as she tilted her chin this way and that, watching the feather tremble with each movement. Mrs Ibbotson looked doubtful, but Peggy knew that she would be indulgent, and it wasn't long before Miss Ibbotson was walking out of the shop still wearing the hat, her bonnet in the hatbox, and Peggy was writing out the bill to be sent on to the house for settlement.

When the bill was done, Peggy chose another hat and was in the window adjusting her display when John returned looking flustered.

'What's the matter?' she asked.

'There's an Irish woman enquiring after a Nan Cavanah. I think she's the same one tha were talkin' about earlier. She stopped me in the street as I was deliverin',' he said.

Peggy could see that he was shaken by the encounter but couldn't fathom why it had disturbed him so much. 'But we don't know a Nan Cavanah, do we?' she asked, climbing backwards out of the window display.

'My mam's name was Nan Cavanah, before she was married,' he explained, taking off his cap and running his fingers through his hair. He looked worried.

'Do you think it's your mother she's looking for? What could she possibly want with her?' asked Peggy – although she suspected that it would be to do with money. Not that John's mother had any. She lived with her elder daughter, Susan, and her husband, Jimmy, and their children in a house on Moore Street. They got by but they had nothing to spare, and sometimes John had to help them out with a piece of meat or a sack of potatoes – even though Peggy resented it. She didn't like John's mother.

His family and hers had been neighbours once, a long time ago, on Paradise Lane. They'd rubbed along all right until the day John had his accident when his hand had been trapped in the spinning machine. When his mother had to take time off her work at the mill to seek help for him, the overlooker had promoted Peggy's mother to Nan's looms – and when Nan had come back she'd accused Peggy's mother of stealing her job. It had created a rift between the families that had grown and had barely healed when she married John. They were superficially polite to one another these days, but the insults and troubles of the past could never be completely forgotten or forgiven. The tentative truce didn't amount to a reconciliation, and Peggy tried to have as little to do with Nan as possible. More often than not, John went to visit her and his sister alone. Peggy didn't even like John taking the children to visit her, even though the woman was their grandmother. Her mother had always said that Nan Sharples was trouble, and Peggy hoped that she wasn't going to bring more trouble on them now with some poverty-stricken Irish relative turning up.

John hung up his cap and jacket and put away the bag. His hair was sticking up on end where he'd raked it with his fingers. 'Perhaps I should go to see my mam later,' he said. 'She'll be glad to see the children.'

'It'll be late by the time you're finished,' said Peggy, making an excuse. 'They'll be too tired.'

'I'll go alone then,' he said.

John kissed his little lasses goodnight and reassured Peggy that he wouldn't be late. He knew that she didn't want him to go to see his mother, but the encounter with the Irish lass had left him feeling unsettled. He was always aware of the difficult path he trod between his own family and Peggy's. Just when things were going well for them, he didn't want something to come along and upset all their good fortune, and he was fearful about why this Irish woman had come and what she wanted.

He walked briskly through the town to Moore Street, where he didn't knock but pushed open the door and called out a greeting.

'Well, tha's a sight for sore eyes!' said his sister. She kissed his cheek, but he knew it was a reprimand for not going to see them more often.

'Jimmy not in?' he asked, glancing around the small but spotlessly clean room.

'Gone to t' Spread Eagle for a pint. He'll not be gone long.'

'How is she?' asked John, nodding his head towards their mother.

'She's worsenin',' said his sister quietly. 'I wish tha'd come more often. It means t' world to 'er to see thee.'

John almost made the excuse again about being busy, but he kept quiet. They both knew that the real reason he stayed away was to please Peggy.

John went over to where his mother was sitting by the fire, a shawl wrapped tightly around her shoulders. 'Hello, Mam,' he said. She looked up at him and her tired face warmed into a smile.

'Tha's come!' she said, reaching out to touch his cheek. 'I thought as tha'd forgotten me.'

'I'd not forget thee, Mam,' said John, brushing her cheek with his lips and then sitting down opposite her, trying to reckon how long it had been since he'd last visited. Too long, he thought guiltily. He could see the change in her since last time he'd been. It was clear that she was unwell. 'Yon post office keeps me busy,' he said. He knew it was a poor excuse. 'How are you?' he asked.

'Middlin',' she replied as Susan put a cup of tea in his hand.

'I saw an Irish woman today, wi' a gaggle o' childer at her skirts,' said John. He took a sip of his tea. It was strong and sweet, the way he liked it. 'She were askin' after a Nan Cavanah.'

He saw that his sister recognized the name. 'That's what our mam was called before she was married. Why would she be looking for her?' she asked. 'What dost tha think she wants?'

'Money by the look of her,' replied John.

Susan pulled up a chair from the table and sat down beside him. 'Dost tha think she might be some relation?' she asked. 'Mam's never spoken much about any family in Ireland.'

'I suppose it's possible,' said John. 'How else would she know the name?'

'What dost tha think we should do?' asked Susan.

'Perhaps we should make some discreet enquiries,' John suggested. 'Try to find out what her name is and where she's come from.'

'What's tha whisperin' about?' demanded his mother. 'I bet tha's talkin' about me. I may be a bit deaf, but I'm not daft yet!' she told them.

'We're talkin about a young woman who's askin' after a Nan Cavanah!' said John, raising his voice. His mother's hearing had been damaged by the years working in the noisy mill.

'That were my name,' she replied.

'I know. I think she's come over from Ireland. Might she be a relative?' he asked.

'Could be,' agreed his mother. 'I had some cousins there. Used to write to 'em a bit when I first came. Told 'em they should come over – that there were work 'ere. But they never came.'

'This woman were only young, though,' said John. 'Much my age, I'd say, wi' a troop o' childer. Where did they live?' he went on. 'If we know the name of the place we can see if this woman says the same,' he added to Susan.

'We lived in County Wicklow,' their mother told them. 'Near a place called Rathdrum. It were a couple o' days' walk from Dublin. I went there to work in service before I decided to come to England. I were told there were work for those who could weave and spin, but it were very different from what I expected. There were regular work, though, and it were better than being at the beck and call of gentry in their fancy houses.'

John listened to his mother reminisce. He'd never

asked about her early life before. She was still talking when Jimmy came in from the pub and John realized how long he'd been sitting with his mother.

'I'd best go,' he said, standing up and reaching for his cap. 'Our Peggy'll be wondering where I've got to.'

'And what will she have to say about poor relations turning up on t' doorstep?' asked Susan.

John didn't reply. It was what was worrying him.

11

Kitty crept out of the cellar dwelling alongside Michael and Aileen. She took Timothy with her and left Agnes behind to care for Maria and Peter, telling them to stay inside and on no account to go wandering around the streets alone. Agnes nodded and asked if she would bring food back. Kitty had told her she would. She hoped that she'd be able to keep her promise.

It was half past five and just before dawn. At home there would have been a chorus of birds at this time, but here the streets were silent except for the noise of the scurrying rats that ran into the holes behind the brickwork of the dilapidated buildings as they approached.

Kitty and Timothy both carried a sack and Michael had found them each a stick, which he'd whittled to a sharp pointed end to pick up anything of value.

'Start with the houses up on Richmond Terrace,' Michael told them before he went off alone. 'I'll head up the hill.'

They walked through the centre of the town where the day was beginning. A man with a long pole was rapping on windows to wake the workers, and the stall holders were arriving in the marketplace with their fresh produce piled up on the backs of carts.

'Keep a look-out on the ground,' said Aileen as she bent to retrieve a lost nail from a horseshoe. 'You might find a copper or two that was dropped yesterday.'

The row of houses that Aileen led them to looked prosperous. They reminded Kitty of the one where she'd received a soaking in Liverpool.

'There's often some good stuff up here,' Aileen told her. 'But we need to be quick before it's all taken.'

'Do they mind?' Kitty asked as Aileen led them round to a back alley behind the houses. It was cobbled with a gulley running down the centre but was cleaner that the court they'd just come from.

'No,' Aileen reassured her. 'They probably don't even know that we come. They'll still be abed at this hour. But the servants know and sometimes they give us bones with quite a bit of meat left on them – enough to make a dinner from before they go to the dealer.

'Go down the steps and knock on the door,' Aileen instructed her as they reached the rear of the first house. 'One of the maids will probably answer. Ask if they have any rags. Take Timothy with you.'

Kitty went down the steep steps to the door of a room that was beneath ground level. She knocked tentatively, feeling anxious. She hated having to beg. No one came and Aileen called to her to knock more firmly. She did and a young girl came and opened the door a crack, her pale face peering out into the half-light.

'Have you any rags?' asked Kitty. 'Please,' she added.

The girl glanced at them and closed the door. Kitty was about to turn away but Aileen called to her to wait and after a few minutes it was opened again and the girl handed her some white cotton cloth.

'Thank you,' said Kitty.

'Let's have a look,' said Aileen as she took it from her and unrolled it. Kitty saw that it was a nightgown. It was of a good quality and had been embroidered around the neckline, but now it was frayed around the sleeves and badly soiled at the back. Kitty felt herself retch as she stared at it, but Aileen looked pleased. 'We'll soak it in some lye and that will come out,' she said. 'We'll get a good price for it. Put it in your sack and try the next house.'

As the sun rose higher in the sky and was obscured by the smoke from the mill chimneys, Aileen and Kitty worked their way to the end of the terrace. At most of the houses they were turned away empty-handed after Kitty's initial good fortune, but they managed to procure a few other rags and some bones, although there was very little meat left on them. Aileen seemed well satisfied with their haul and as it approached dinner time they made their way back to Butcher's Court.

The market was in full swing now and there were street traders crying their wares around the edges of the stalls on King William Street. Aileen bought some hot potatoes and muffins and said that they would share them.

'I'll pay you back as soon as I can,' promised Kitty. 'It

feels so wrong to keep accepting food from you when I know you don't have much yourself.'

'I'll not see you go hungry,' Aileen told her. 'Don't worry,' she added. 'I don't mind helping you out.'

They hurried back to the cellar to eat the food, Kitty eager to check on her younger children. She wasn't used to leaving them alone for long and she'd been worrying about them all morning, sometimes only just overcoming the desire to run back to the cellar to check on them. She could hear Peter crying as they approached the steps down to the door.

'Has he been crying long?' she asked Agnes as she dropped the stick and sack on to the floor and gathered her little boy up from the straw mattress, feeling his forehead with her hand and dreading it being hot to the touch. She couldn't bear to be parted from another child.

'I think he just missed you,' said Agnes. 'I did my best to keep him quiet.' Her elder daughter looked flustered and Kitty felt sorry for her. She knew it was a lot to ask of Agnes to take responsibility for the little ones.

'You've done all right,' she reassured her as Peter calmed now that he was in his mother's arms. 'We've brought some food.'

Aileen fetched water from the pump and set it to boil whilst they ate the potatoes before they went cold. The vendor had added a generous amount of butter and salt and they were tasty. Kitty could have eaten more but she was eager to see her children's stomachs filled before her own.

Aileen used some of the boiled water to make tea and after they'd drunk it she took the hot water and a tub up to the yard and put the rags they'd collected to soak. 'We need to wash all the white ones first,' she told Kitty. 'White fetches more money and the cleaner it is the better we'll be paid. Once they're pegged to dry we'll wash the coloureds. Then we'll boil up the bones for some broth before we sell them on.'

Whilst they were working, Michael came back. His bag was bulging with rags and some other small items that he'd found – a pan that had been boiled dry and had a hole in it and some rusty tongs. Aileen exclaimed over it all as if he'd found treasure.

'What do we do with them now?' asked Kitty as she watched the items being sorted into piles of white rags, coloured rags, bones, metal objects and other items.

'There's a dealer on Clifton Street,' Aileen told her. 'He'll weigh everything and give us the money. I'll give you a share,' she promised, 'but now that you know what to do, you'll have to go picking on your own tomorrow, and anything that you make will be yours so long as you chip in for food and coal.'

Aileen made it sound so easy, thought Kitty. She dreaded the prospect of having to go knocking on kitchen doors and searching along the back alleys on her own, but she was determined to earn some money so she could pay back Aileen and Michael for their kindness. She knew that she couldn't rely on the goodwill of her new friends for ever.

In the afternoon Kitty went with Aileen to see the rag dealer. His premises were on a street corner, and over the entrance hung a stuffed cloth object that might have been recognizable as an effigy or Aunt Sally if it hadn't been bleached and sodden by many summers and winters exposed to the weather. The shop window was crammed with an eclectic array of items: old linen garments, fragments of kerseymere and broadcloth, patches of chintz and damask, old jewellery with most of its stones missing, odd boots and shoes, and a pile of leather that appeared to be going mouldy.

Aileen pushed open the door and led the way inside. Used to living a frugal existence, Kitty had never seen so much stuff heaped up in one place, apparently in utter chaos. As she looked around, she saw pots and kettles, plates and dishes – mostly chipped and mismatched, piled up on barrels and shelves and vying for space with rolls of floor cloth, heaps of books, bottles of every shape and size imaginable, curtains, blankets, an old copper boiler, and a collection of fish kettles and stew pans that flanked the open doorway to a yard beyond.

Aileen nodded towards the bored-looking lad with a pock-marked face who was lounging behind the counter, his elbows on the only free surface in the whole of the shop.

'Mr Reynolds in the warehouse?'

'Aye.'

'This way,' said Aileen to Kitty, and they went across the cobbled yard to a long stone building. Kitty thought that the warehouse must have served as a barn for a farmer in the past, but it had been encroached upon by the industrial expansion and was now swallowed up amongst streets of close built sordid housing and the noise and smoke of the cotton mills. But it was the smell that took her breath away as Aileen pushed open the door for them to go inside. Kitty's stomach heaved and she covered her mouth with her shawl as she stared around in the gloom. The building was filled with tables. Women and girls were clustered around them sorting out the rags that the pickers had brought in. It was hot inside and the stench of the bones that were being sorted into the baskets on the floor was almost unbearable.

Aileen took her across to the dealer and introduced him as Mr Reynolds. He was a stocky man with a lush moustache and his cap pushed well back on his head over a mass of unruly red hair. He greeted them with an easy smile. 'What's tha got for me?' he asked. 'Empty it out here,' he said, indicating a table with weighing scales beside it.

'It's all sorted and washed,' Aileen told him as she piled the white rags on to the scale and watched as Mr Reynolds added his weights.

'Tha's a good lass,' he told her. 'Call it five pounds in weight. That's sevenpence ha'penny I'll pay thee for 'em. 'Ere, Molly, come and get these!' he called to a girl at the nearest table. 'Put 'em with t' cloth for t' paper mill. Now,' he went on, turning back to Aileen, 'hast tha got any coloureds?'

When all the cloth had been weighed, the bones assessed and the small metal items valued, Mr Reynolds pulled a stubby pencil from behind his ear and reckoned up the payment on a scrap of paper. 'One shillin' and thruppence,' he announced. To Kitty it seemed a fantastic amount of money to be paid for things that folks had thrown out as unwanted. 'Tha's done well today with thy new helper. What's thy name again?' he asked, and Kitty reminded him of it. 'Well, I daresay as I'll be seein' thee again. Hast tha come over from Ireland alone?' he asked curiously.

'No.' Kitty explained her story again, still unable to master her tears when she reached the part about her baby. She hated to keep having to tell it. The words rubbed raw at her grief every time.

'I'm right sorry to hear that,' said Mr Reynolds when she was finished. 'That must be right distressin'.'

'And you've never heard of a Nan Cavanah?' she asked him.

'No.' He shook his head. 'I know a few Nans, but none called Cavanah.' Kitty thanked him and she and Aileen turned to go, but he called after her. 'There's work 'ere for lasses sometimes,' he said. 'How old's thy daughters?'

'Agnes is twelve.'

'Old enough to be at work,' observed Mr Reynolds.

'I need her to look after the little ones,' Kitty told him.

'Well, if tha changes thy mind . . .'

Kitty thanked him again and they left the building. Even though the air outside was far from fresh, Kitty filled her lungs with it thankfully. 'How can they spend all day in there?' she asked Aileen.

'I suppose they're used to it,' she said. 'Work's work and folk are grateful for it. Agnes would do all right there,' she added. 'She's a bright girl, and quick. You could take Peter and Maria with you. Lots of other women take their children gathering.'

The next morning, Kitty wondered whether to take the younger children with her and send Agnes to look for work, but they seemed exhausted so she set out with just Timothy to see what they could find. She decided there would probably be nothing worth collecting on the streets they'd scoured the previous day, so she set off towards King Street where Aileen had said they might find something.

As she walked down the street, she stared up at the big houses that lined the road, all with freshly painted front doors, polished brass door knockers and leafy green plants placed in the front bay windows, partially hidden from the gaze of passers-by behind white net curtains. Kitty wondered who the people were who lived there.

A maid came out of one of the front doors and hung a carpet over the railing to beat it clean. She frowned at Kitty, who took Timothy's hand and hurried on, searching for a ginnel that would take them through to the rear.

The alleyway behind the houses looked suspiciously clean and Kitty wondered if someone had been there before her. She prodded her stick into some piles of waste but there was little of value to be found. After the easy pickings of the day before, it was a disappointment. Further along she found a few small bones that had come from a chicken that had been roasted, and she took them despite doubting that Mr Reynolds would give her much for them. There was cooking fat that had been discarded so she took that as well, knowing now that it would be sent off to the candlemakers to produce the stinking but cheap candles and rush lights that lit the homes of the poor. She added it to the sack that Tim was carrying before wiping her greasy hands on the apron Aileen had lent her. She wished that she had some other clothes to wear for the dirty work. The ones she had been given in Liverpool were becoming spoiled and it saddened her.

She and Timothy had worked their way down half of the street when she heard a door open. Her stomach lurched as she expected someone to shout at her, or throw something, but a plump woman came up the steps from a basement kitchen with a bundle of rags in her hand. She beckoned to Kitty.

'Mistress wants to know if these are any good to thee?' she said, holding them out. 'They're just scraps,' she added as Kitty reached for them eagerly. The material was mostly coloured but it was clean and wouldn't need to be washed.

'Thank you! That's so kind of you!' said Kitty, gratefully adding it to her clean sack. She hoped the money she would be paid for it would be enough to pay Aileen back for the food she'd bought for them.

The woman hesitated for a moment before she spoke again. 'Would t' lad like summat t' eat?' she asked. 'He looks fair clemmed.'

Kitty didn't understand the word but saw that the woman was looking at Timothy with genuine pity. In that moment she saw him with fresh eyes herself – a scrawny boy with barely enough flesh to cover the angular bones that jutted from his wrists. His eyes were overlarge in his thin, pale face and although he was clothed and shod it was clear that he was starving.

'That's very generous of you,' said Kitty, hardly able to believe their good fortune.

'Wait there,' instructed the woman and went inside, returning a few moments later with a thick slice of bread and butter and a cup of milk.

'Thank the lady, Timothy,' Kitty reminded her son as he pushed the food eagerly into his mouth.

'Thank you,' said Timothy with his mouth full.

'I'm sorry he hasn't better manners,' apologised Kitty. 'He's very hungry,' she added, although she knew it was no excuse.

'Tha's Irish,' observed the woman.

'Yes,' said Kitty, relieved that this woman at least was not judging her harshly for it. 'We came to find my husband's cousin, Nan Cavanah,' she explained. 'Do you happen to know her?' she asked hopefully.

'Can't say as I do,' replied the woman. 'Is tha husband out lookin' for her?'

And Kitty found herself telling her painful tale all over again.

The woman shook her head in sympathy as she listened. 'I'm right sorry for thee,' she said. 'I'd not wish it on anyone to go through what you have. I hope tha finds thy family soon.'

She went back to her work and Kitty moved on. The encounter had left her tearful. It was the first kindness she'd received in the town from anyone who wasn't Irish and she was immensely grateful for it.

When the sacks were full, she and Timothy walked back to Butcher's Court. Kitty's stomach was aching with hunger and she hurried past the hot potato man and the other street vendors, not wanting to spend any money until she knew how much her morning's haul would bring.

'There's some lovely stuff here,' said Aileen, examining the offcuts of material that Kitty had been given. 'These are much too good to go for rags. They could go for quilting. Make sure you get a fair price,' she warned her. 'Accept nothing less than fourpence a pound even though it is coloured stuff.'

Down on Clifton Street, Mr Reynolds greeted her with a welcoming smile when she pushed open the door of his shop.

'Tha's been busy,' he observed when he saw the filled sacks. 'What's tha brought me?'

'Fats mostly,' she said. 'But I've a few other things.'

'Bring 'em through to the back,' he said and called to

the lad to mind the shop for him whilst he was out. He led the way across the yard and into the warehouse where Kitty tried to overcome the stench that nauseated her.

She watched closely as Mr Reynolds looked critically at the finds she emptied on to the table. She knew that he would try to pay her as little as he could. He picked a few things up, turned them over and nodded before weighing in the metal and counting up the bones. 'No rags?' he asked. 'Are they in the wash?'

'There's these,' said Kitty as she took the bundle of fabrics from her clean sack and looked for somewhere to put them down where they wouldn't get spoiled. She watched the man's face and saw the gleam that lit his eyes for a moment before he rearranged his expression into a sterner look. She knew that she'd kept the best until last but that he would bargain hard with her.

'Aileen says these are too good for rags. That they can go for quilting,' she said, eager to make it clear to him that she couldn't be tricked.

'Aye,' he said as he looked at them. 'Put them on the scales,' he told her. 'I'll give thee thruppence a pound.'

'Aileen said to take no less than fourpence a pound.'

'Did she now? And why she would want to be putting such nonsensical ideas in thy head, I don't know.' He looked at the rags again. 'Thruppence ha'penny. Take it or leave it,' he said. 'It's my best offer.'

Kitty hesitated a moment longer, to be sure that he wouldn't increase his price if she waited.

'All right. Fourpence,' he agreed at last.

'I'll take it,' she said and Mr Reynold's face warmed to a smile.

'Tha's a quick learner,' he said as he counted out her money. 'Tha'll do well at this trade.'

That night Kitty lay awake on the crowded cellar floor. Whichever way she turned she was touching someone, and every time unfamiliar skin touched hers, Kitty recoiled with a jolt. She could hear Michael coughing and trying to find a comfortable position in the chair. They couldn't go on like this. It wasn't fair to either Michael or Aileen. She needed to find a place of her own.

'There's the dosshouse,' Michael suggested when Kitty raised the topic the next morning.

Aileen shook her head. 'A woman alone with children wouldn't be safe there,' she told him. 'You can't go sleeping in a room with strange men,' she said to Kitty. 'You can stay here as long as you like.'

'I'm grateful to you. I really am,' said Kitty. 'But it's not fair on you to have to keep putting us up like this. You don't have the room.'

'The one on Nab Lane is women and children only,' Michael said and, although Kitty was grateful that Aileen was so welcoming, she knew that sooner or later Michael would insist on having his bed back and she didn't want it to lead to a falling-out. No, it was up to her to find somewhere else, and if the only alternative was the dosshouse then that was where she would go.

She gathered enough rags to receive another decent payment from Mr Reynolds later in the day. So, after she'd bought some food for the children, she left the younger ones with Agnes, who was helping Aileen to wash rags, and she went to look for the dosshouse that Michael had told her about.

Kitty found the place on Nab Lane. It was three storeys of blackened brickwork and grimy windows. The door stood open and she saw a woman mopping out the entrance hall, although on closer inspection she saw that the mop was tangled and threadbare, and the water in the bucket so dirty it seemed to be adding more filth to the floor than it was taking up.

'Do you have any beds?' Kitty asked her.

'Aye. Fourpence a night,' replied the woman. 'Just thee?' she asked.

'No. I've children as well.'

The woman leaned on the mop and looked her up and down. She took in Kitty's clothes and seemed to decide that she was good for the money. 'How many childer?' she asked.

'Four,' said Kitty, her heart breaking that she couldn't say five. 'It's just until my husband gets here,' she added, not wanting the woman to judge her.

The woman sniffed and wiped her runny nose on the back of her hand. She didn't seem interested in Kitty's circumstances. 'How old's thy childer?' the woman asked her. 'I don't have boys over ten. They have to go in the men's house.'

'He's only nine,' Kitty lied. She had no intention of sending Timothy in anywhere alone, and he was so small and skinny that he could easily pass for younger than his years.

'Two beds or three?' she asked.

'Two,' said Kitty firmly. It would be a huge improvement on their present arrangements.

'We open at six,' said the woman. 'First to come gets the beds. I don't reserve 'em,' she explained. 'And t' same goes for every night. Tha's rentin' 'em for twelve hours,' she told Kitty. 'Tha's to be out by six in t' mornin' because someone else'll be sleepin' in 'em durin' t' daytime.'

Kitty went back to collect her other children and to tell Aileen and Michael that they could have their bed back that night.

'I'm so thankful I met you,' she told them. 'I don't know what would have happened to us otherwise. We would have to sleep on the street.'

'We were glad to help,' Aileen reassured her, 'and we're here for you if you need anything – anything at all.'

Her friend's words made Kitty cry. She seemed to do nothing but cry these days. Sometimes from grief, but sometimes, like now, because she was overwhelmed by the kindness of others.

She hugged Aileen and thanked her and Michael again. She knew she owed them a lot.

*

By a quarter to six, Kitty and the children were in a queue for the dosshouse beds. Kitty recognized some of the other women. She exchanged a brief smile with one of the young girls who worked at the rag and bone shop. Most of the others were single women, but some, like her, had children with them. There were Irish accents amongst the broad Lancashire voices and Kitty wondered if any of these women knew Nan Cavanah, but the ones she asked shook their heads and said, no, they'd never heard of her.

The door opened promptly at six as a church clock chimed in the distance. The woman she'd spoken to earlier positioned herself at the entrance and took the money as they went in.

'Two beds,' Kitty reminded her when it was her turn and handed over eightpence.

'Up the stairs,' said the woman. 'Take any that tha fancies.'

Kitty picked up Peter and, ushering the children ahead of her, climbed the steep steps. All the beds on the first floor were already taken so they continued up into the attic. As she walked down the narrow aisle between the close packed rows of wooden beds, Kitty began to think that her money had been taken for nothing. On each side of her every one of them had someone either lying on them or sitting on the edge, pulling off muddy boots and damp shawls.

'Get a move on!' someone shouted and Kitty felt a sharp finger poked into her back. She urged the children on even though she could see that they were reaching the end of the attic with no sign of any spaces. She wondered what would happen when they reached the far wall. People were following her closely and the stairs they'd just climbed were thronged with women. There was no way back.

But when she reached the last bed she saw that there was a low opening. She hesitated but the woman behind her told her to get on through and stop messing about.

'Go on,' said Kitty, sending Agnes first, followed by Peter. When Maria had crawled under the low beam, Kitty dropped to a crouch and in the gloom of the few flickering candles that lit the space, she saw that there was another attic on the far side. Most of the beds here were occupied as well, but she managed to find two together at the far end, near to the stairs that led down to the floor below.

She told Agnes to sit on one and she claimed the other as she watched the stream of women pass her and clump down the steps, still searching. The doss-house must run the length of the street, she realized, even though there was only one entrance.

Relieved to have found somewhere, she turned her attention to the beds. They were raised up from the floor and the attic wasn't as damp as Aileen and Michael's cellar. Each bed was made from wood, simi-lar to the ones they'd slept in at the asylum in Liverpool, but here there was bedding – a mattress of rough tick sacking filled with straw. Kitty poked at it, hoping that it was clean. There were no blankets. They would have to put their shawls over themselves to keep warm — although she didn't think that warmth would be a problem with so many bodies packed in so close to one another.

Kitty had brought some bread and dripping. She shared it out with the children as they sat and watched the other women settle down. No one spoke much but the silence was punctuated by the regular coughing from almost all the beds. The smoke and dampness in this town was healthy for no one, thought Kitty, pining for the fresh clean air of her homeland.

The younger children were soon asleep and the candles were either blown out or had guttered and failed in the draught blowing in under the eaves. Kitty closed her eyes and tried to get comfortable on the prickly sacking. She felt exhausted. She hadn't slept properly for weeks now and the constant worry over her situation was wearing her down, but still she lay awake in the pitch blackness. Tomorrow they must be up early and out to see what rags and bones they could gather from the back streets. She needed to make enough money each day to buy food and pay for their beds. Beyond that, she shivered to contemplate.

13

Before dawn the next morning, Kitty and her children were back on the street with their sacks and the sticks, hunting along the back alleys. Kitty had tasked Maria with keeping her eyes to the ground, looking for any discarded nails or other small items of metal that she could weigh in at Mr Reynold's warehouse. She tried to make it seem like a game even though her daughter was unenthusiastic and complained of hunger.

As daylight strengthened, it was easier to see, and Kitty led her family down the back of King Street again, poking her stick into any pile of dirt she could find to see if it contained anything of worth. But there was little there that she hadn't seen the other day and she realized that she must widen her search and try some of the other streets.

As she passed the back of the house where the woman had come out to her before, she paused. She could see a light in the kitchen and imagined the woman preparing a breakfast. She hesitated, wondering if she dared to knock on the door and ask for food for her children, but the shame of having to beg made her reluctant. She had a few pennies left in her purse and as soon as the market began and the street sellers came out she would see what she could afford to buy for them. In the meantime, they must continue their search for anything they could sell, or goodness only knew where they would be sleeping that night.

Bessie Anderton yawned as she opened the curtains of the nursery. Her husband, Joshua, had been up very early to catch the coach to Manchester where he had a business meeting with some railway men, and she'd got up with him and sleepily eaten the breakfast of scrambled eggs that Dorothy had cooked.

Her baby daughter was still sleeping. Julia was a good child, thought Bessie. She usually slept through the night now that she was three months old, and even though Bessie knew it was foolish to disturb her just yet, the love she felt overwhelmed her and she couldn't resist the urge to pick the baby up and hold her solid weight in her arms and kiss the dark curls that were escaping the little cap.

As she rocked the sleepy infant in her arms, murmuring nonsense words of affection and pressing her lips to the child's warm head, a movement in the back alley below caught her eye and Bessie saw that it was the woman again, poking about in the piles of rubbish. She had more children with her today – as well as the boy there were two girls and a younger child of about two years old. The elder girl was carrying the little one on her hip whilst her mother and the others added a few items to a sack that the boy held open.

Bessie saw the woman glance at the house. When she'd seen her the day before she'd felt so sorry for her that she'd sent Dorothy out with a few offcuts of material and told her to give the child something to eat. It seemed that the woman had come back to see what else was on offer.

Bessie was wondering whether to go down and ask Dorothy to feed them again, but as she hesitated she saw them move on and disappear from view – probably to root through the waste behind another street. Bessie found it saddening. No one should have to search through rubbish to feed their children.

She guessed that they had come over from Ireland. More and more were arriving. Not that they were made welcome. Most people resented them and argued that they should be sent back where they'd come from and that it wasn't up to English people to provide them with poor relief. Bessie had some sympathy for their views. It wasn't always easy for people to get work and she understood their fear that the newcomers would take their jobs. But she hated it when she heard abuse shouted at the Irish on the streets. She sometimes wanted to intervene, but she wasn't brave enough. Besides, it was easier for her to be charitable when she had enough money to live comfortably. She knew she was lucky – although she hadn't always been well off. When she was a child, her mother had worked hard to feed her and her sister, Peggy. She'd taken in other folks' dirty clothing to launder and their home had always seemed full of wet, steaming washing hanging to dry and the slightly scorched smell of fresh linen being pressed with the heavy irons her mother kept on the grate. They hadn't been well off, but they'd never been so poor as the woman and her family who were gathering rags.

Julia began to whimper and Bessie sat down on the nursing chair and began to suckle her, enjoying the closeness of the child and the intimacy of her soft little mouth at her breast. She caressed Julia's soft hair with her thumb as the baby's eyes locked on to hers. They were darkening now to the same brown hue as her father's. Bessie smiled down at her. The overpowering love she had for this little girl still surprised her. She'd never expected the feelings of motherhood to be so fierce, and she gave thanks that Julia would grow up wanting for nothing.

Footsteps on the stairs brought Dorothy to the door with a cup of chocolate in her hand.

'I guessed you must be nursing her. It were so quiet,' she observed as she put the cup down on a side table.

'I think she's had enough,' replied Bessie as she lifted the child to her shoulder and gently rubbed her back.

'Do you want me to take her? You have Mrs Thwaites coming for an early fitting,' Dorothy reminded her.

Reluctantly, Bessie handed the baby to her maid and went to the bedroom to rearrange her clothing and make herself decent. As she did, Bessie wondered if she could find the opportunity to raise the matter of the Irish beggars with Mrs Thwaites. Mr Thwaites was on the relief committee and Bessie knew that her client had the ear of her husband.

'Irish,' replied Mrs Thwaites when Bessie mentioned the family in the back alley. She looked like she'd tasted sour milk. 'They should be sent back. Mr Thwaites says there's barely funds to support the locals who're deserving without us having to feed those we have no responsibility for.'

Bessie thought it was for the best that she had a couple of pins pressed between her lips as she adjusted the seam under her client's left arm. It gave her a moment to frame her reply.

'I don't think they would come except for the failure of their potato crop,' she said. 'It's the children I feel sorry for. The ones I saw were obviously starving. I sent my maid out with food for one of them yesterday.'

Bessie glanced up to see Mrs Thwaites shaking her head. 'I wouldn't do that,' she advised. 'You don't know what diseases they're bringing with them, and you have your little girl to consider. You wouldn't want to lose her to the typhus fever.'

The prospect sent a shiver of alarm through Bessie. She knew how fragile babies could be and the thought of anything happening to Julia made her want to weep with the horror of it.

'I'm surprised that your husband would allow it,' went on Mrs Thwaites as she lowered her arm and moved about to get a feel for the fit of her gown.

Bessie didn't reply. She knew that Joshua would never forbid her to help another suffering soul, but she was also painfully aware that it was only his money and status that made him acceptable, if grudgingly, to the local worthies.

She watched Mrs Thwaites turn this way and that before the long mirror in the fitting room.

'That's much better,' she announced at last. 'When will it be ready?'

'By Friday,' promised Bessie, understanding that any conversation about the needy family was finished.

'Good. I'm planning to wear it to the ball at the assembly rooms.'

Bessie helped her client out of the gown and back into her day clothes. She knew that she trod a slippery path between the gentry and the working classes, not being either one or the other. But it also gave her a perspective on both, which was sometimes helpful but more often frustrating, as neither would even try to see from the point of view of the other.

Perhaps it was up to her to find out more about the Irish immigrants, she thought. Maybe there was more she could do to help them than offer sympathy and the odd slice of bread.

When her sack was full, Kitty decided it was time to find something for the children to eat. They walked back to the square where Kitty saw that bread would be cheaper than hot potatoes, and she left Agnes in charge of the younger ones whilst she went to buy a loaf. There was nothing to put on it and it was dry to eat. Kitty would have loved some butter or cheese, but she didn't know how much she would get from Mr Reynolds today and she didn't want to be short for the dosshouse that night.

Some of the rags she'd found were quite dirty, but they would have to stay that way. She had nowhere to wash them and she hated to keep asking for favours from Aileen. The rag and bone man weighed them in and gave her sixpence for the lot, but Kitty knew it would have been more if they'd been clean. She sighed. It wasn't enough for two beds, and even if they could all manage to get into one, which was probably impossible as they were so narrow, she would only be left with tuppence for food until she could go scavenging again the next day. What she'd received the day before had been exceptional, she realized, and she couldn't expect such valuable handouts every morning.

Mr Reynolds noticed her disappointment. 'I can set yon lass on at the sortin' tables,' he reminded her.

Kitty looked at Agnes and then at the girls who were sorting bones. They looked covered in grease right up to the elbows.

'I'll find 'er summat to wear as an apron,' offered Mr Reynolds. 'One and six a week. Regular income. Sundays off.'

'What do you think?' Kitty asked her daughter. 'Could you do it?'

'Don't be mollycoddlin' t' lass,' advised Mr Reynolds. 'It's a good job for 'er!'

'I can do it,' said Agnes and Kitty was proud of her determination. 'So long as you can manage without me helping to watch the little ones.'

'They're not so little!' observed Mr Reynolds. 'They're old enough to pick. Even t' babby can be taught to pick up owt shiny. Over there,' he directed Agnes, handing her a torn length of cloth to wrap around herself. 'Sally'll show thee what to do.'

14

The rag and bone shop was closed on Sundays so Agnes had the day off, but Aileen had told Kitty that they should still go picking and store whatever they found in the cellar until the following day.

'There's no day of rest for the hungry,' she'd remarked. So, as soon as they were turned out of the dosshouse at six o'clock, they took to the back streets and narrow alleys to search for rags.

It was quiet and it took Kitty a while to realize it was because the mills didn't work on a Sunday and there was hardly anyone else about. There was a peacefulness that she relished as they worked their way steadily through the backs, examining everything they found and filling the sacks with whatever might bring a ha'pence or a penny.

At the end of one street they came out by a canal. A few empty barges were tied up by a warehouse but there was no work going on. The excited voices of some children attracted her attention and she walked towards them, curious to see if they were pickers who had found something valuable.

On the towpath by the canal she saw a man with two little girls. The man had a net and was dipping it into the water. The little girls sat with their legs dangling down to the water, watching him – a pot filled with water was on the ground between them. They were obviously not gatherers. They were well-dressed and looked prosperous and Kitty was bemused by the sight. Surely they weren't fishing for their dinner, she thought, although she could see no other reason for their actions.

The elder of the two children noticed Kitty and her family and looked at them curiously. 'What are they doing?' she asked the man.

He glanced up. 'Rag gatherers,' he said. 'Look! I've got a stickleback!'

The child's attention was diverted to the catch and Kitty ushered her own children away. The man looked familiar, and she thought that she'd probably already asked him about Nan Cavanah and she didn't want to intrude.

The sight had made her sad, though, as she remembered how her husband had played with their own children back in Ireland, teaching them songs and rhymes and games. Even though he had worked hard he'd always had time for the little ones.

'What were they doing?' asked Maria.

Kitty knew she'd wanted to go and watch.

'Fishing,' Timothy told his little sister. 'Dada used to take us fishing,' he said and Kitty, hearing the sadness in his voice, put her arm around his shoulders and squeezed him to her. She knew that the children were missing their father. Whenever they asked about him, Kitty always said that he would soon come, but she was beginning to wonder how long the answer would satisfy them, especially Agnes.

As they walked, the church bells began to ring, and Kitty decided to take the children to the morning mass at St Alban's. They could sit at the back, she thought, hoping that they would be made welcome despite their dishevelled appearance.

When they reached the doors she saw that other people going in were dressed no better than her family and it gave her the courage she needed. She didn't dare leave her sack outside in case it was stolen, so even though it smelt bad she took it in with them and pushed it underneath the pew. As soon as the mass began she found comfort in the familiar words that the priest spoke. At least there was something here that was the same as home.

'Mrs Cavanah,' Father Kaye greeted her when the service was finished. She was surprised and touched that he had remembered her name. 'Did you find your cousin?' he asked.

Kitty shook her head. 'No. I'm still searching,' she replied.

'Have you found a place to live?'

Kitty explained about the dosshouse and her work as a rag gatherer. Father Kaye listened with sympathy but could offer no solution other than to promise he would tell her if he heard anything about Nan Cavanah.

'Bless you all,' he said before moving on to speak to someone else, and Kitty picked up the sack to take it back to Aileen and Michael's cellar and to see what she could find for the children to eat when there was no market or costermongers to buy food from.

'Are we going to stay here for ever?' asked Agnes later that afternoon. They'd left their pickings with Aileen and Michael and shared some bread and a cup of tea, but the cellar was too cramped for them to linger, and Kitty had decided to take the children for a walk until it was time to go and pay for their beds.

They'd climbed the hill above the town and Kitty was glad of the fresh air even though it was a bitterly cold day and her face felt numbed with the wind that blew up here. She could see for miles, but it was all strange to her. Unlike her home, where she could name every village and farm and smallholding that she could see, she had no idea what these places were called and who lived in them.

They were sitting on a rock that jutted out from the grassy slope and Kitty had Peter on her lap, shielding him from the weather with her arms.

'I don't know,' Kitty admitted to her daughter. 'But I don't want to leave just yet. Besides, where would we go?'

'We could go to find those people in Stockport – the ones we travelled with,' said Agnes. 'They were nice. They said there was work.'

'You've got work,' Kitty reminded her daughter.

'But we might find better work,' she insisted.

Kitty reached out an arm and hugged her daughter

close. 'I'm sorry,' she said, 'but the money you earned this week has really helped us. We needed it,' she said, hating to have to think of her daughter being miserable all day long just so that she could help to feed her younger sister and brothers. 'I know it's hard,' she went on, 'but it won't be for ever. Things will get better,' she promised, even though she had no idea how their situation could improve. It was becoming clear to her that no one had heard of anyone by the name of Nan Cavanah – and as for her husband coming, tears filled her eyes at the thought of him. The last image she had of him was heaving at the ship's mast to try to free the trapped boy. After that he'd been gone. He couldn't have drowned. He just couldn't. She refused to even consider it.

Kitty sighed and wiped her face on the back of her hand. 'We'd better get going,' she said. 'We need to get in the queue at the dosshouse so we don't miss the beds.'

Next day, when Kitty took her findings down to Mr Reynold's warehouse to be weighed in, he had news for her.

'Someone mentioned a Nan Sharples last night,' he told her as he counted out sixpence ha'penny into her outstretched hand. 'Said as he thought she might have come over from Ireland a while ago.'

'Was she originally called Cavanah?' asked Kitty, feeling a rush of excitement that her search might be over. But Mr Reynolds shook his head.

'He didn't know. He said she lives with her daughter on Moore Street. Didn't know the number.'

'I'll find it. Thank you so much,' Kitty added, hoping that this could be the breakthrough she had hoped and prayed for.

She glanced across to where Agnes was standing at one of the tables, sorting out bones and putting them into baskets according to size. Her daughter looked up and smiled briefly before wiping her forehead on the back of her grimy hand and reaching across the table for more. Kitty gave her a quick wave and hurried out from the stench to where Timothy and the younger children were waiting for her. 'Let's get some dinner,' she told them, eager to get them fed so that she could go to look for this Nan Sharples.

They went to the market square and bought some mutton pies. Kitty carried one back to the rag and bone shop for Agnes where she asked a woman if she could give her directions to Moore Street.

When she found it, Kitty decided to begin at the nearest end and work her way down. At the first two houses the women told her they didn't know anyone by that name. At the third she was spat at and called a filthy Irish, but at the fourth the woman was more amenable.

'They live at number twenty-eight,' she told Kitty. 'Jimmy and Susan Slater and her mother. I'm fairly sure she's called Nan Sharples.'

Kitty thanked her and walked down to number

twenty-eight. The door was dirty with the mud that had been thrown up from the wheels of passing carts, but the knocker looked like it had been polished and the curtains at the window seemed clean. With Peter in her arms, and Maria and Timothy on either side of her, she knocked tentatively on the door. At first there was no reply and, disappointed, she realized she would have to come back later when the occupants were home from work. Then she heard a shuffling and a latch clicked and the door was drawn open a crack. A face, creased with age, peeped out at her.

'What dost tha want?' asked the woman suspiciously.

Kitty stared at her, searching for any resemblance to her husband and his family. Certainly the woman's hair appeared to have been red before it had greyed, and Kitty thought there was something familiar about her sharp eyes and jutting chin.

'I'm looking for Nan Cavanah,' she said.

'What?' asked the woman. 'Tha needs to speak up.'

'Nan Cavanah!' repeated Kitty, aware that the whole street could probably hear her and imagining the twitching of curtains behind her back. 'She's my husband's cousin.'

'Oh aye,' replied the woman, still holding the door almost shut. 'And what cousin would that be, then?'

'His name's Peter Cavanah, son of Timothy and Marie Cavanah. They lived in Rathdrum,' she added, and her heart leapt and began to beat a little faster as she saw the names were familiar to the woman.

'Tha'd best come in,' she said and opened the door wider for them to go inside.

The parlour that Kitty stepped into was neat and clean. 'Wipe your boots on the mat,' she told the children.

'Sit down,' the woman invited and pointed to a wooden chair by the hearth. Kitty perched on the edge of it and watched as the woman lowered herself into the one opposite with a sigh.

'Are you Nan?' asked Kitty nervously.

'Aye, I'm Nan,' she agreed as she looked Kitty up and down. 'Nan Sharples now, but I was Nan Cavanah a long time ago.'

Kitty wasn't sure if she felt relief or disappointment. It was a mixture of both. It was a huge relief to eventually find cousin Nan, but Kitty doubted that the frail woman who sat opposite her could be of any help at all. When her husband had spoken of his cousin, Kitty had envisaged a woman about his age, or maybe slightly older – someone still in the prime of life, energetic and capable, who would welcome them with open arms and help them find work and a place to live. But the reality was very different.

Nan looked at the children. 'These yours?' she asked, leaning forward to study them.

Kitty nodded. 'Yes. I've another daughter too. Agnes. She's working at the rag and bone shop.'

Nan raised an eyebrow. 'Dirty place,' she observed.

'It's the only work she can get,' Kitty told her.

'And where's Peter, thy husband?'

Kitty told her about the boat. It was painful having to shout about it, but every time her voice dropped Nan bawled at her to speak up. 'He thought that you would help us,' she ended.

Nan was shaking her head. 'I don't know what tha expects me to do,' she told Kitty. 'I have nowt.' She spread her hands to emphasize the words. 'I live here with my daughter and son-in-law. There's no room for thee,' she added, glancing at the wide-eyed children who were sitting in silence on the rag rug. 'Where's tha stayin' now?' she asked Kitty.

'I'm paying for beds at the dosshouse.'

'Filthy place. Tha'll get vermin,' she warned, drawing her shawl more closely around her shoulders. She was silent for a moment as she stared into the fire and Kitty was unsure what to do next. She'd pinned all her hopes on finding this cousin and it had never occurred to her that it might end like this. She'd expected cousin Nan to be more welcoming when she eventually found her, but this woman didn't seem much interested in them, and Kitty wondered if she'd really understood what she'd told her. It seemed rude to simply get up and leave, but the silence dragged on for so long that she felt uncomfortable.

Then Nan began to speak again. 'I were sixteen when I first come 'ere,' she told Kitty. 'I came with a friend. Bridie were her name. I wonder whatever happened to her,' she mused. 'I've not seen her in years.

We were workin' in service in Dublin,' she went on, 'but we didn't like the woman we worked for and we thought we'd be better off as us own bosses. So we saved our wages and got on a boat to Liverpool. We thought we were comin' to paradise.' Kitty nodded. She understood that only too well. 'I went to Stockport first. Then came here. Got work in a mill and met my Joe.'

'My husband said you used to write home.'

'Aye. I did for a while. If I could find someone to put it down for me. But they wanted payin', them as could write. Thought they were above us workin' folk.' She sniffed. 'I never held wi' readin' and writin',' she explained. 'Never did anyone any good. They get above themselves. Look at our John,' she added.

'Who's John?' Kitty asked curiously.

'My youngest. He can read and write. That's why he never comes to see me. Thinks he's too important.' She sniffed again.

'Does he live in Blackburn?' asked Kitty, wondering if perhaps this John could help her. If he could read and write then perhaps he could spare a bit of money as well.

'Aye.' Nan looked at her fiercely. 'But it's no use tha thinkin' he'll do owt for thee,' she warned Kitty. 'Stay away from him and his wife, that's my advice.' She settled the shawl more firmly around her shoulders. 'What will tha do now?' she asked.

'I don't know,' replied Kitty. 'I suppose I'll have to manage somehow.'

'Don't rely on a man to help thee,' Nan advised. 'Waste o' time, most of 'em. Take my Joe. Drunk himself into a state and got himself shot down without a moment's thought for how I'd manage without him.'

Kitty was shocked and unsure what to say. She couldn't believe that it was true and wondered if the woman was making it up. Perhaps her mind was as damaged as her hearing by working in the mills.

'I suppose I'd better go,' she said, feeling ill at ease now in the woman's company.

'Aye. Tha'd best,' agreed Nan. 'Take care o' them young uns,' she said, waving a hand towards the children.

'I will,' said Kitty, although she had no idea how.

A few moments later, they were back on the street with the door closed behind them.

'What now?' said Timothy. Kitty could see the fear on his face. He was old enough to understand the implications of what had just happened, and she knew that she would be unable to deceive him by trying to make something positive from it.

'It looks like we'll have to find a way of managing without her help,' she told him. 'Aileen and Michael make a living from rag gathering, and so must we. I have you to help me, and Agnes has a job now. We'll be all right,' she said, struggling to believe her own words of reassurance.

15

When Peggy heard the shop doorbell she turned from the gloves she was arranging on her counter, expecting to see a customer, but it was John's sister Susan who stood on the threshold, looking uncomfortable.

'Is John not here?' she asked. She seemed anxious and Peggy wondered if something was wrong. Perhaps John's mother was poorly. She hoped not. John had enough to do without being summoned down to Moore Street and expected to pay out for the doctor.

'He's out delivering the post,' said Peggy. She wondered whether to invite Susan to sit down on the chair she kept for her customers, but decided against it. She didn't want her getting too comfortable or staying too long. 'Is something wrong?' she asked.

'Well . . .' Susan hesitated and Peggy saw it was something she didn't really want to discuss with her. 'I just wanted a word with John. How long will he be?'

'He can be gone a while,' said Peggy.

Susan looked undecided about what to do. It was obvious she was reluctant to go home without speaking to her brother.

'Which street is he delivering to?' she asked. 'I could go to look for him.'

'I don't know. He sorts the letters himself. Would you like to wait?' she said at last.

'No! No,' Susan waved a hand in refusal. 'I'll have a walk around and see if I can see him.'

She retreated from the shop, the bell jingling behind her, and Peggy watched as she hurried off up Church Street. Something was wrong. That much was clear and she hoped it wasn't going to make trouble for them.

Peggy found that she couldn't settle to anything as she waited, and she walked to the window again and again to look for her husband coming home, afraid of the news he might bring with him. At last she saw him coming down the street with his empty bag slung over his shoulder. She couldn't fathom the expression on his face.

'Your Susan was in here looking for you!' she burst out as soon as he came through the door.

'Susan? Here?' A sudden shadow of worry clouded his face. 'What did she want?'

'She wouldn't say. She just said she needed a word with you.'

'I wonder what's wrong,' he said, putting the bag away. 'I'd better go round to see. You can manage, can't you?'

'She said she'd go and look for you. She might not be back home,' Peggy told him. 'Besides, my mother will be bringing the children in a minute. I'll have to close the shop if you go out again,' she told him, knowing that he wouldn't want people to miss the last post.

'It'll be something and nothing,' she added, hoping she was right.

John stood behind the counter looking undecided. Peggy felt guilty. She knew she ought to tell him to go and reassure himself that nothing serious was amiss – it was just that she was always afraid of him getting mixed up with his family's troubles. Nothing good ever came of it.

Peggy turned as she heard the door open, thinking that it would be her mother. But it was Susan again. 'John!' she burst out. 'I've been lookin' everywhere for thee!'

'Aye. Peggy said. What's to do?' he asked, guiding his sister towards the chair.

'It's that Irish woman,' Susan said. 'She's been to see our mam whilst we were out at work.'

'Did Mam let her in the house?' asked John, looking concerned.

'Aye. And her childer as well.' John frowned.

'It's not like Mam to be lettin' folk in,' said John.

'I know. She knows not to let strangers in,' said Susan. 'I don't know what made her do it this time. The woman must have spun a pretty tale. Mam seems to think she's genuinely a cousin, but how can we know? She could be anybody.' Susan shrugged. 'What are we goin' to do? It worries me,' she went on. 'It seems suspicious that she came in the daytime when Jimmy and me were out. Jimmy wants to find her and warn her off, but what if she really is a relative fallen on hard times?'

Peggy felt irritated. John's sisters were always turning

to him and expecting him to sort out their problems. It made Peggy cross. John owed them nothing. His loyalty should be to her and their children.

'She probably just thought your mother was a soft touch, being in the house on her own,' Peggy said. 'You'll have to tell her to keep the door locked.'

John pushed a hand through his hair as he thought about what Susan had told him. 'I think I'll have to talk to our mam first,' he said. 'Find out what was said.'

Susan shook her head. 'She doesn't always remember things these days.'

'But what if this woman is genuine?' John asked her. 'What if she really is a relative?'

'If she is then she must be a distant one,' Peggy interrupted. 'She's not your responsibility. If she can't manage, she can always go to the workhouse.'

Both Susan and John stared at her and Peggy knew they thought she was callous. She was just wondering whether to say something in her own defence when the door opened again and this time it was her mother with the children.

Peggy ushered them upstairs to the parlour.

'What's going on?' asked her mother as she helped the girls out of their coats and hats. 'It's not like John's sister to come to the shop.'

'It's about some Irish woman who's been hanging around,' Peggy told her. 'She's been to see John's mother claiming that she's a relative. Probably wanting money. Susan wants John to warn her off.'

'Nan Sharples did come from Ireland. I remember her telling me once, when we used to speak to one another,' her mother added.

'It doesn't mean she's related to everyone who lives there!' Peggy pointed out. She watched her daughters go straight to the aquarium to check that the stickle-backs were all still alive.

'No. But something's brought that lass to Blackburn,' said her mother. 'I think I've seen her. Does she have four childer with her?'

Peggy nodded. 'Yes. That's her. I caught her staring into my shop window the other day.'

'What's wrong with that?' asked her mother. Peggy saw that she was trying not to laugh and it irritated her.

'I don't want her sort hanging about. She'll put off my paying customers.'

'When did tha get so self-important, our Peggy?' asked her mother. 'We were poor when thee and Bessie were childer. Don't ever forget that.'

'We never went begging on the streets, though!'

'I don't think this lass is a beggar,' said her mother. 'I saw her with a sack. I think she's gatherin' rags.'

'Well, that's not a proper job, is it?' asked Peggy.

'It's probably the only work she can get. Don't look down on folk who're worse off than thee,' her mother told her. 'Tha wouldn't be as well as off as this if it hadn't been for George Anderton.'

Peggy didn't reply. She hated to be reminded that she owed anything to her sister Bessie's real father.

She still found it hard to believe that her mother had had an affair with another man and that her younger sister was not really her sister at all, but only a half-sister – although it explained why she looked so different and why she'd never really seemed to fit into their family. It was true that as well as helping Bessie, George Anderton had helped her and John to take on this shop. Not that it was a gift. They paid rent to him for it and made their own money by working hard. It wasn't the same as taking charity, but Peggy would have much preferred any help to have come from her own father.

'I'll be off then,' said her mother. She kissed the girls and began to go back downstairs. 'Think about it, Peggy,' she called from halfway down. 'It does no harm to give other folk a helping hand.'

Peggy went into the kitchen to start making the tea. She could do with a helping hand herself, she thought, never mind some Irish woman. If John was going to help anyone he could start by finding someone to do some chores about the house.

16

Kitty sat on the edge of the dosshouse bed. It was too dark to see anything and she guessed it must be about three o'clock in the morning. She'd been lying awake for what seemed like hours, listening to the distant clocks chime and the symphony of snoring from the crowded beds in the attic as other women turned and muttered in their sleep. In the end she'd got up and wrapped her shawl around her shoulders. Her mind wouldn't settle and she relived her meeting with Nan Sharples over and over again in her imagination.

'What will we do now?' Agnes had asked once again when Kitty had told her about cousin Nan.

'She said she had a son, John. He might help us,' Kitty had replied, trying to find something positive to tell Agnes, even if it had been clear from the encounter that this son was unlikely to do anything for them.

But perhaps she should look for him. She knew his name. John Sharples. Maybe she should ask if anyone knew him and where he lived. She hated the thought of having to ask for help, but if he was a cousin then surely he might do something for them? It was obvious that Nan had nothing, but a man who could read and write must have a good job. It seemed the only possible thing to try.

Kitty lay down again to try to snatch what sleep she could before she had to get up again to go scouring the streets.

Next morning, Bessie opened the curtains of the nursery. The Irish woman was there again. 'Come and look,' she called to Joshua. 'There's the woman I was telling you about.'

Joshua came over to the window and stood shoulder to shoulder with her. Bessie leaned in towards him. She loved the solid feel of his dark body and imagined his muscular arms under the sleeves of his freshly washed and ironed shirt. He was still fastening the buttons as he watched the woman. It was barely light and they'd only just got up.

'She sure looks thin,' he observed. 'She has decent clothes, though, the children too.' They watched as she turned over some piles of rubbish, bending to pick up something that looked filthy and adding it to her sack.

'She wouldn't be doing that if she had any money,' said Bessie, wrinkling her nose at the thought of grubbing through the filth for a living. 'She must have fallen on hard times.' They both watched for a while longer and suddenly the woman looked up, aware of being observed. Bessie drew back feeling guilty. 'Do you think we should do something to help her?' she asked.

Joshua stopped knotting the cravat at his neck and

allowed it to hang loose as he continued to watch. 'I think we should,' he said after a moment.

He turned away from the window and went down the two flights of stairs to the kitchen. Bessie hurried after him and was in time to see the surprise on Dorothy's face as he strode in.

'Miss Dorothy!' he said. 'There's a woman and children out back and they look mighty hungry. Will you offer them a bite to eat?'

Dorothy's eyebrows were raised and she glanced at Bessie who'd followed her husband in.

'It's the same woman as the other day,' said Bessie. 'She has more children with her this morning. Offer them some bread and milk.'

Dorothy put down the fork she'd been using to whisk eggs for breakfast and, wiping her hands on her apron, she went to open the back door and call to the woman.

Kitty picked up Peter and grasped Maria's hand when she heard the door being opened behind her. 'Quickly. Pick up the sack,' she told Timothy. 'Let's go.'

She'd seen the people at the upstairs window, watching, and she guessed that they'd told their maid to send her away. Even though it was the house where Timothy had been fed, Kitty knew that it was usually the maids who offered help and that the gentry who lived there didn't want people like her looking through their rubbish. Even though they'd discarded it in their back alleys because they didn't want it themselves, they still resented her helping herself to it.

'Don't go!' called the woman.

Kitty hesitated and glanced over her shoulder. The woman was beckoning to her.

Kitty walked towards her warily. She almost braced herself for a shower of cold water.

'Would the childer like a bite t'eat?' asked the woman.

'That's kind of you. Thank you,' she said, trying to sound as appreciative as she could whilst still keeping her dignity. 'But we weren't here to beg,' she added.

'Come down the steps,' said the woman. Kitty took the children down the flight of scrubbed stone steps that led to the kitchen door. She suspected that the woman preferred her to be out of sight of the other houses. 'Wait there a minute,' she instructed them.

Timothy and Maria sat down on the steps but Kitty waited with Peter in her arms for the woman to reappear. She'd closed the door behind her so it was clear they weren't going to be welcomed inside. Not that Kitty could blame the woman. She was aware that they stank. But it was a fine morning, if cold, and in the hours before the mill chimneys began to belch their smoke there was a refreshing, crisp feeling in the autumnal air.

A few minutes later the door was opened again and the woman held a plate with four thick slices of fresh bread spread with a generous covering of butter. Kitty saw her children's faces glow with anticipation as they looked to her for permission to take the food. Kitty wished that their hands were cleaner, but there was nowhere to wash them and she didn't want to appear difficult by asking, so she nodded to them and the older two reached out and took a slice each.

'Say thank you!' she reminded them. 'I'm very grateful,' she told the woman as she took a slice for Peter. She hesitated as she saw that the older two had sat down again on the steps to eat. 'Do you mind?' she asked.

'No. Better there than in the alley,' said the woman, convincing Kitty that she would prefer they weren't overlooked. 'Take a slice for yourself,' she added after Kitty had put Peter down and folded the bread over to stop his hands being smeared by the butter.

Kitty reached for the final slice. 'Thank you,' she said. 'Are you sure your master and mistress won't mind?'

'It was them as told me to offer thee summat t' eat,' said the woman. 'They're kind folks.'

'Will you thank them for me, please?' said Kitty. 'Tell them I'm grateful. We're not beggars,' she added again. 'We're trying to earn an honest living, but it's not easy.'

'Did tha find thy cousin?' asked the woman and Kitty felt tears well in her eyes at the question, partly because she was touched that the woman had remembered her story and partly because the discovery of Nan had been so disappointing.

'I did, but she's an old woman now. She has nothing, so she can't help us,' Kitty explained.

'I'm sorry to hear it,' said the maid. Then she went back inside and closed the door and Kitty sat down with the children to eat. She was grateful but she knew that she couldn't rely on the kindness of strangers to feed her family for her. They were her responsibility and it was up to her to provide for them, so as soon as the bread was finished she chivvied them to their feet and they resumed their work.

'I feel like we should do more,' said Bessie to Joshua as they ate their scrambled eggs and toast in the breakfast room which caught the best of the early-morning sunshine. 'I've told Dorothy to feed them if they come again. You don't mind, do you?' she asked him.

'Why would I mind?' he asked. 'Don't forget that I know what it's like to go hungry, and if your father hadn't taken me in and fed me I wouldn't be sitting here today.'

Bessie looked at her husband. He looked well-fed and prosperous in his smart clothes, ready to go out and do business. She couldn't imagine what he'd looked like as a starving runaway slave, stealing apples from her father's orchard.

'I was lucky,' he added, meeting her gaze. 'And I feel as if it's my responsibility to pass on the kindness. It's what your father would want,' he added.

Bessie nodded. She knew that he was right. Her father would help anyone if he thought they were genuinely in need, although he was quick to spot imposters and tricksters.

Joshua placed his knife and fork neatly side by side on his plate and drained his teacup. 'I'd better go,' he said. 'I've a meeting with the railway men at nine.'

He kissed her and told her he'd see her later. Bessie sat a while longer, enjoying the indulgence of not having to rush to do anything. It was very different from the days when she'd been roused by the knocker-up to begin work at her looms in the mill at six o'clock. She'd hated having to get up so early and the heat and the noise of the mill had never been pleasant, even though she'd prided herself on her work and had enjoyed the sight of the neatly woven fabric growing row by row as the shuttles had flown from side to side, threading the weft through the warp threads. She could afford to be a lady of leisure now that she was married to Joshua, but sitting idle never normally appealed to her and she enjoyed the seamstress's business that she ran, stitching for the ladies of the town. She enjoyed their company and hearing about their lives, even if they never would accept her as one of their own.

Bessie roused herself and began to load the breakfast pots on to the tray to be taken down to the kitchen. She would have taken it down herself, but she knew Dorothy would tell her off, so she left them neatly stacked and went up to the nursery.

17

'Did tha find Nan Sharples?' Mr Reynolds asked Kitty after he'd weighed in her morning's finds and paid her for them.

'I did. Thanks,' she told him. 'Though she's in no position to help us. But she said she had a son, John Sharples. Do you know him?'

'There's a John Sharples who's the postmaster,' replied Mr Reynolds, wiping his hands on a greasy towel. 'On Church Street,' he added. 'Same place as th' hat shop.'

'Oh, there!' said Kitty, remembering how the woman in that particular shop had glared at her for daring to look at the window display. She wondered if this was the wife that Nan had spoken of. 'Is he married?' she asked Mr Reynolds.

The rag dealer raised a quizzical eyebrow as if he thought Kitty might be set on marrying the postmaster herself if he was still a single man.

'Aye, he's wed,' he told Kitty. 'Sorry to disappoint thee.'

Kitty blushed. 'It wasn't why I was asking,' she told him.

He laughed and winked at her. 'I'm only teasin' thee,'

he said. 'Seems tha might have dropped lucky after all if he's the son of thy cousin,' he added.

Kitty hoped that he was right, but she suspected that it might not be that simple. It was clear from what Nan had said that there had been some sort of split in the family and she didn't think that this John would welcome her visit, but it was the only option left to her and she resolved to try.

She decided it would be easier to go alone. She didn't want to annoy Mrs Sharples by having a crowd of them in her shop. So she went in search of Aileen to ask if she would keep an eye on the children for a while.

'I don't need a minder,' grumbled Timothy as they walked. 'I'm old enough to look after myself.'

'Maybe so,' Kitty told him. 'But I don't think you're old enough to look after Maria and Peter.'

'So just leave them with Aileen. I want to go to watch the blacksmith shoeing the horses.'

'We'll see,' said Kitty, hoping that he would change his mind when they reached Butcher's Court. She needed to know where her children were if she was to have peace of mind.

Luckily, Aileen was at home. Or at least she was out in the courtyard, pegging up some rags that she'd just washed. Kitty hoped that she would soon have a place with her own with space for a tub so that Mr Reynolds would pay her the rate for clean rags. She didn't want charity. She was eager to work, but she needed a little bit of help and that was what family were for, she told herself as she felt her stomach flutter with anxiety at the prospect of what she was planning to do.

Kitty explained where she was going and asked Aileen if she could watch the children for a while, and if she had any jobs that Timothy could do in return. Her friend agreed readily and set him to pumping some extra water for the wash tub. He didn't complain but Kitty knew he resented not being allowed to go and look at the horses.

'I'm glad you've found your family,' Aileen said. 'I'm sure they'll be able to help you.'

As Kitty walked up Church Street she wished she could be as sure as Aileen that help would be forthcoming. Her friend was such a kind soul that it had never occurred to her that Kitty's cousins would be anything less than welcoming.

Kitty's pace slowed as the shop came into sight. She was reluctant to go in, but she knew that she must try to speak to these people. They were her family – well, her husband's family. How could they turn her away when she so desperately needed their help?

She approached the door cautiously and tried to look in to see if there were any customers inside. She didn't want things to get off to a bad start by interrupting something important. But the shop looked empty, so she took a breath to steady her nerves and pushed open the door. A bell jingled, startling her. She almost turned and ran out, but she told herself not to be so silly. She had as much right to go into the shop as anyone else and what she was going to say wasn't unreasonable. There was no reason not to introduce herself to her relatives.

The woman, who had been on her knees behind the counter, emptying a box, rose slowly into sight with a pile of handkerchiefs in her hands. She stared at Kitty in disbelief.

'What do you want?' she demanded. 'I've no rags for you here. You'd better go.' Still clutching the handkerchieves, she glanced behind her, towards a door that was partly open to reveal a flight of stairs. Kitty sought to reassure her.

'I don't want rags,' she said. 'I'm here to speak to John Sharples.'

The woman put her hankies down on the counter and crossed her arms. She raised her chin and Kitty saw that she was frightened – although what it was she was afraid of Kitty couldn't imagine.

'He isn't here. Please go!'

Kitty felt disappointment flood through her. 'When will he be back?' she asked.

The woman shook her head. 'I don't know. You'll have to leave now,' she repeated, glancing towards the street as if she was wondering if help might be forthcoming.

'I'm family!' burst out Kitty. 'Nan Sharples is my husband's cousin, so John is his cousin too.' She felt on the verge of tears but she was determined to say her piece. 'My husband always said that if we came here our family would help us.'

The woman continued to stare at her. 'I don't know about any Irish cousins,' she said at last. 'Why would I believe you?'

'Because it's true! I spoke to Nan and she believed who I was.'

'My husband's mother isn't well and her memory is failing. She's confused,' the woman told her. 'You could be anybody. You must go now,' she added, glancing towards the window again as if she was hoping that somebody would come in and rescue her.

'Will you tell your husband I called?' Kitty pleaded. She was desperate to speak to John Sharples and hoped that he would be more willing to listen to her than his wife. 'Tell him Kitty Cavanah called. Peter Cavanah's wife.'

The woman nodded briefly. She seemed willing to agree just to be rid of her. Kitty wanted to ask if she could call again, but it was obvious the woman couldn't be rid of her quickly enough, and so she turned and retreated to the door where the bell jangled as she opened and closed it and she found herself once more on the street, no nearer to getting the help she desperately needed.

Kitty hurried away from the shop, feeling that she had been demeaned by the woman – Mrs Sharples. It was clear that she wasn't wanted there, not by her at least, and she walked as fast as she could to put distance between her and the excruciating encounter. No wonder there had been a falling-out between Nan

Sharples and her son. With a wife like that it was no wonder she didn't want anything to do with him.

Despondently, Kitty walked back to collect her children from Aileen.

'Did you find him?' asked her friend when she'd invited Kitty into the cellar room and brewed a pot of tea for them to drink. 'What did he say?'

'He wasn't there,' she admitted. 'I only spoke to his wife.' Kitty took a sip of the weak tea. 'She wasn't very welcoming,' she admitted. 'I don't think she believed me.'

As the shop door had closed behind the Irish woman, Peggy had let out her breath even though she'd been unaware that she was holding it. She felt herself deflate slightly and her legs were suddenly weak. She stumbled out from behind her counter and sat down on the chair, hoping that no customers would come in before she'd had time to recover herself.

She wasn't sure what it was about the encounter that had made her so afraid. She wasn't usually nervous about being alone in the shop. She knew most of her regular customers and had nothing to fear from them. But the Irish woman was different, and it wasn't just the fear that she carried disease, although that did worry Peggy and she was glad that her daughters were with their grandmother. It was hard enough keeping children safe from disease without exposing them to the Irish Fever. No, it was fear of what the woman wanted and how they could be rid of her.

The trouble was that John was a soft touch. He hated to see anyone go without anything and, far too often, he would give credit to his customers when Peggy knew that there was no hope of ever getting the money. She would scold him about it, but he always shook his head and said that the person in question would pay eventually, even though they rarely did. But Peggy suspected that this would be even worse. This woman wasn't looking for the price of a penny stamp; she would want to take as much as she could get for herself and her brood of unruly children. At least she hadn't brought them with her today, thought Peggy, imagining in horror the mess they could have left in her spotlessly clean and tidy shop.

She wondered if the woman was in the habit of visiting towns and seeking out people she could claim kinship with. Although she professed to be poor and was posing as a rag gatherer, it was clear that her clothes and boots were not those of someone who was destitute. Her children were all well-clothed and shod too. It wasn't often you saw pauper children with shoes or boots on their feet, thought Peggy. It was all very suspicious.

She looked up as the door was opened again and was relieved to see that it was her husband. His face took on a worried frown at the sight of her.

'What's to do?' he asked her, hurrying across to where she was sitting. 'Hast tha been taken poorly?'

'I'm all right,' she reassured him. 'I've just had a bit

of a fright. That Irish woman has been in. Right into the shop, bold as brass, asking for you.'

John frowned. 'What did she want?' he asked.

'Well, it's obvious, isn't it?' replied Peggy. 'She wants money. I sent her on her way, but it was a bit frightening being here alone when she came in. I wish you'd get a boy to do the deliveries.'

'Did she threaten thee or summat?' he asked, looking concerned.

'No,' Peggy admitted. 'Not directly anyway. But I'm sure it's money she's after. And goodness knows what disease she's carrying. I don't want her coming in here. We have the children to consider.'

John went to put away the post bag and take off his cap. 'Shall I make thee a cup o' tea?' he asked.

'No.' Peggy stood up. 'I'll do it. I'm all right now that you've come back.'

18

As soon as Kitty saw Agnes come out of the rag warehouse that evening she knew that her daughter was poorly. She was almost white. There was a sheen of sweat on her face and she was coughing. It was little wonder she was ill, working so hard in this stinking place, thought Kitty, taking her daughter in her arms and hugging her.

'I don't feel well,' Agnes told her mother.

'You're just tired,' Kitty tried to reassure her, even though she suspected it was something far worse. 'We'll go and pay for some beds and you'll be better come morning when you've had a good sleep.'

But Agnes was clearly feverish and Kitty was unsure what to do. She had no idea where she might find a doctor, or if she could afford to pay for one. She glanced in her purse and saw that she would have a little to spare after the beds were paid for. It would probably be best if she got Agnes laid down and then went to look for a chemist to see if she could afford to buy a powder that might help her feel better.

Agnes walked with her in silence as they traversed the streets towards the dosshouse. Kitty would have liked to help her along, but Peter was fractious and crying and she was forced to carry him – and to tell the truth she felt weary herself. The exchange with Mrs Sharples in the hat shop had left her feeling worried and upset.

'Three beds,' said Kitty to the woman, counting out the money into her palm.

'Three, is it?' she asked with a raised eyebrow. 'Tha must be makin' a good livin'.'

Kitty didn't reply. She didn't want to draw attention to Agnes being unwell in case the woman refused to let them in, but she thought that it would be safer for Agnes to sleep alone tonight.

They climbed the rickety stairs towards the beds in the attic. Kitty was keen to get three together, and despite her earlier choice of beds at the end of the room, she'd discovered that they were left until last because they were close to the piss pots, which stank worse and worse as the night progressed and they were filled to overflowing.

She had to go up to the highest floor where the roof was so low she was forced to crouch as she made her way along. Here, she managed to find two adjacent beds and one opposite to them. Agnes sank down on to the nearest looking utterly exhausted.

'Let's take off your gown,' Kitty said. As she helped Agnes, she realized that her daughter's teeth were chattering uncontrollably as she shivered with the chills. It was clear that she had a fever and the skin on her chest and back was hot to the touch. Agnes continued to shiver, even after she'd been covered with both her own and Kitty's shawls. Kitty had no cloth to wring out in cold water to put on her forehead. She'd weighed in everything that she'd found and she was afraid to ask for help in case the other boarders objected to them being there and they were turned out into the night.

'Stay here,' she told the other children, 'and keep an eye on your sister. I'm going to see if I can get a powder from the chemist's shop.'

Kitty hurried back down the wooden steps, provoking the wrath of the women who were trying to come up, and eventually got back out on to the street again. She'd seen the chemist shop a few streets away and she hurried towards it, breaking into a run now and again, afraid that it might shut before she could reach it.

The lamps were still burning in the interior as she reached the door and pushed it open to be met by an almost overwhelming aroma. Kitty recognized lavender and camphor mixed with the smells of other oils and herbs, ranged in glass jars of all colours on the shelves behind the high mahogany counter.

A man in a waistcoat and spectacles, his hair slicked down with a pomade that added to the other scents, turned to look at her.

'Please,' begged Kitty. 'Please. I need something for my daughter. She has a fever.'

The man frowned and Kitty knew that he had recognized her accent as Irish. She prayed that he wouldn't turn her away empty-handed.

'I can pay,' she assured him, counting out pennies on to the counter. 'How much do you want?'

The man turned and reached up on to the shelves behind him and took down two large bottles. 'Wait there,' he instructed her as he carried them into his dispensary. The door was left ajar and Kitty watched anxiously as he took a smaller bottle from a drawer and placed a funnel into its opening. He measured out various liquids into it, then pushed in a cork, gave it a thorough shake and came back to the counter.

'Give her a teaspoonful three times a day,' he instructed. 'That'll be sixpence, please.'

'Thank you!' Kitty paid and left the shop, clutching the bottle against her chest, terrified of dropping it. She retraced her footsteps to Nab Lane and was hot and breathless herself by the time she'd climbed back up the stairs to reach Agnes. It was only then she realized that she had no spoon. Too tired to search for one and eager to get the medicine into her daughter, she bade Agnes sit up a little and take a sip. Then she pushed the cork firmly back into the bottle and stood it on the floor, where she hoped it would be safe from being knocked over.

All around her women were chatting about their day, but an overwhelming tiredness struck Kitty and once she'd seen her children settled she climbed into the bed beside Maria and lay down. Her heart was still beating frantically from the climb to the attic, and although she tried to sleep she found it difficult to rest. When sleep eventually came it was filled with visions of men beating pans and pounding staves and she too began to shiver.

Kitty woke in the night and found she too was drenched in sweat. She pushed herself up and fumbled for her tinderbox to strike a light for a candle to check on Agnes. In the flickering glow, she saw that Agnes was sleeping, but her hair was slick with sweat and she'd pushed the shawls aside. Kitty eased herself out of bed to cover her daughter again, but her own head began to spin and her heart pounded. It was clear that whatever was making Agnes sick was making her ill as well. She lay down again, feeling weak and wondering what she would do if she felt no better by the time morning came.

She was woken again when the women around her began to stir. She could hear Peter crying because he was wet and Timothy was calling for her to come and get him.

'In a minute,' she called, aware that her voice sounded croaky. As soon as she tried to sit up, she began to cough and every muscle in her body ached.

She turned her head and it throbbed. 'Agnes,' she whispered. 'How are you?'

Her daughter coughed and when Kitty caught sight of her, she could see that her face was flushed and her eyes bright. 'I hurt,' complained her daughter. 'Everything hurts.'

'Mam?' She turned her head painfully to see Timothy looking down at her with a concerned expression. 'Are you not getting up?' he asked. 'Peter's soaked the bed.'

Kitty groaned and flopped back against the hard

pillow. 'Just give me a minute,' she said. 'Help Maria get dressed. I'll be there in a minute.'

Timothy looked doubtful. 'Are you ill as well?' he asked.

'I'll be all right,' she reassured him, trying to swing her legs over the side of the bed. The gloomy attic swayed and she clutched at the wooden edge of the bed to try to steady herself. She was close to tears and she had no idea what she was going to do. 'Pass me that medicine bottle,' she said.

Timothy bent to retrieve it and handed it to her. Kitty struggled to get the cork out so Timothy took it from her and pulled on it himself. He handed the foul-smelling mixture back to her and Kitty raised it to her lips and forced a sip down her raw, aching throat. It burned like fire. She wiped the rim on her petticoat. 'Give Agnes a dose,' she told him. 'Not too much,' she warned. She put her hands to her throbbing head and realized how hot she felt.

One by one, the women and children from the other beds clattered down the wooden stairs and eventually the attic was silent and empty except for Kitty and her family.

'You're going to have to get up, Mam!' Timothy told her urgently. She could hear the fear in his voice.

'I'll be all right in a minute,' she repeated, although she doubted that she would be. How on earth was she going to manage?. It was clear that she wasn't well enough to go rag gathering – and no rags meant no money, which meant she wouldn't be able to afford to pay for beds that night. Where would she go? She couldn't ask Aileen to take them in when they were ill, but she had no idea what else to do.

'What's tha doin' still 'ere?' demanded a voice. 'It's gone six.'

'My mam's poorly. And my sister,' Timothy told the dosshouse woman before Kitty could prevent him.

'Poorly?' Kitty saw the woman take a step back and cover her mouth and nose with the edge of her grimy shawl. She peered at Kitty and at Agnes who was still prostrate in the bed. 'Tha shouldn't have come in if tha were poorly,' she told them. 'I'll not have illness 'ere. They'll close me down. Tha needs to be gone.'

'Can we not stay for a while?' Kitty asked. 'My daughter's not fit to be out of bed.'

The woman shook her head. 'They'll close me down,' she repeated.

'I'll pay,' whispered Kitty, although she knew that there wasn't enough money in her purse. 'Timothy,' she said to her son, 'will you run to Aileen's place and ask if she can possibly lend us a few pennies? Tell her Agnes is poorly and needs a bed. Tell her I'll pay her back as soon as I can.'

'No!' The woman tried to grasp Timothy, but he wriggled past her and his footsteps faded down the stairs. 'Tha's done it now!' complained the woman, sounding angry. 'As soon as word gets out they'll send the inspector and I'll be put out of business. Filthy

Irish!' She spat on the floor. 'I should never 'ave let thee in!'

To Kitty's relief she clumped off down the stairs and they were left in peace. She sank back on to the bed, aware that Maria was staring at her in alarm and Peter was crying. She needed to get up and take the wet cloths off him, but no matter how determined she was, the room began to spin every time she tried to get up. And when she did manage to stand, her legs felt so wobbly she doubted they would hold her long enough to get down the stairs, never mind find somewhere for them to spend the day. She tried not to cry, but the sobs rose in her throat as she grasped Agnes's hand and told her not to worry – she would look after her and everything would be all right.

Kitty lost track of time as she waited and it wasn't until she heard Aileen's voice that she roused.

'They can't stop 'ere!' the dosshouse woman was telling her friend. 'I needs 'em gone afore th' inspector comes. If he sees 'em he'll shut me down!'

'Kitty?' She heard Aileen call her name and she tried to sit up.

'I'm all right,' she told her.

'You're not all right,' replied Aileen. 'It's the fever. You probably caught it in this place.'

'My place is clean!' Kitty heard the dosshouse woman protest. 'It's the filthy Irish that have brought disease here. They should all go back where they've come from. We don't want 'em here!'

'Can you get up? Can you walk?' asked Aileen, ignoring the woman's insults. 'I'll take you home. I should never have let you come here. We should have made room for you.'

Kitty was about to protest that there wasn't room for them and she couldn't keep taking advantage of Aileen's hospitality, but her words were silenced when they all heard a heavy tread coming up the stairs.

'Oh, this is all I need,' the dosshouse woman grumbled as a man ducked into the attic under the low rafters. 'Bloody inspector.'

'What's wrong with them?' Kitty heard the man ask.

'How should I know?' asked the woman. 'Whatever it is, they didn't catch it here.'

'Maybe so, but you'll have to wash all this bedding and fumigate the mattresses. Has a doctor seen them?' he asked.

'I got medicine from the chemist. I'll be better soon,' said Kitty.

'I take it you've nowhere else to go?' said the man.

'I'll look after them,' Aileen told him.

'Where do you live?' asked the inspector. 'Butcher's Court? If this is typhus I can't allow it to take a hold there. They'll have to go to the workhouse infirmary.'

The word sent a rush of fear through Kitty. 'No,' she managed to protest. 'I'll not go there.'

'You don't have any choice,' replied the inspector. 'I'll write a note for your admission and send a cart.

You and the girl will go into the infirmary. The other children will be cared for on the wards unless they become ill as well. What's your name?' he asked.

'Kitty Cavanah.

'And four children?'

'Five,' she protested as she heard Aileen explaining her circumstances to the inspector.

When the man had gone away, Kitty clutched at Aileen's arm. 'I don't want to go to the workhouse,' she said urgently. 'I've worked so hard to keep us out of there. They'll take the children away from me,' she sobbed, reaching to try to pull Maria and Peter closer to her. 'And then they'll send us back to Ireland.'

'I'll take the little ones,' offered Aileen. 'They won't take up much room.' Kitty watched as she picked Peter up in her arms and grasped Maria by the hand. 'I'll take them now, before the cart comes,' she told Kitty. 'I'll look after them until you're better,' she promised, although Kitty could see the doubt that shaded her friend's face and she knew that Aileen was wondering if she would ever come out of the workhouse alive.

'Take Timothy as well,' pleaded Kitty as Aileen dragged a distraught Maria away from her.

'Where is he?'

Kitty looked around the attic, but her elder son was nowhere to be seen. 'He must have gone down,' she said. 'Will you find him? Please?'

'I will,' she promised.

Kitty heard Maria's cries fade into the distance as Aileen took her away. It felt like all her worst fears were coming true. The workhouse was the place she dreaded most and now there was nothing she could do until the cart came to take her there. All her strength had left her and she was unable to protect her children.

'Mam,' whispered Agnes, 'are we going to die?'

'No, of course not,' she reassured her daughter. 'It's just a bit of fever. We'll be better in a day or two and then we can get back to our work again.'

'I wish we could go home,' said Agnes.

The dosshouse woman had come upstairs with a broom and her dirty mop in a bucket of water and almost chased Kitty and Agnes down the stairs. Kitty hardly remembered negotiating the narrow steps on trembling legs as she tried to support her daughter. Outside the bright light had hurt her eyes and they were pushed on to the back of a cart where some handfuls of straw had been thrown down. Then they were jolted away until they reached the high wall and the gatehouse of the workhouse that had made her shudder when she'd passed it on her way into Blackburn.

They paused at the gatehouse and Kitty could hear men talking, but she couldn't make out their words. Then they were jolted across the cobbled yard to an ominous-looking doorway where Kitty saw a woman in an apron and cap waiting for them.

'Get 'em down,' she told the men. 'Bring 'em this way. They're goin' to t' fever ward.'

The building was dark inside and dank. Kitty felt as if they were on their way to hell. Surely there would be no return from this place. She tried to put an arm around Agnes to reassure her, even though she was struggling to keep herself upright as she walked.

When they reached the crowded ward, filled with other coughing and wretched beings, it was a relief to lie down on a bed, even though the straw mattress smelt musty and the sheets felt damp. Kitty hoped that at least they were clean. Agnes was put in the bed beside her and she clutched her daughter's hand. It was icy cold and Agnes was still shivering.

'Is there another blanket?' she asked the nurse.

'No. We're short,' she replied. 'Tha's lucky to get one at all.'

Kitty pulled her daughter closer to try to quell her trembling. She stroked her soft hair and tried to reassure her. 'They'll take care of us here,' she said. 'We'll soon be better and then we'll find a place of our own to sleep so we don't have to go back to that dosshouse.' It was where they had caught this fever, Kitty was sure. She knew that she hadn't brought it with her from Ireland, no matter what they told her.

'I want to go home,' moaned Agnes again.

'I know. Soon,' promised Kitty, kissing her daughter's head, although she knew that home was now a distant dream and they could never go back there. 'Perhaps your dada will come soon,' she said. 'He has the tickets. We can go to America. It'll be all right,' she promised, trying to soothe her sick daughter as tiredness overwhelmed her and she fell into a doze filled with men shouting at her and her home burning before her eyes, making her feel hotter and hotter.

19

Bessie tipped the handle of the baby carriage towards her to manoeuvre it down the three steps at the front door on to the street. She was getting the hang of it now and no longer needed to call for Dorothy to help her lift it down. When all the wheels were safely on the footpath, she looked around to see their neighbour, Mrs Briggs, the wife of the mill owner. She seemed to be lingering and Bessie wasn't surprised when the woman called her over.

'May I have a word with you, Mrs Anderton?' she said. 'There have been some Irish in the back alley. A woman and children. Have you seen them?'

'I have,' replied Bessie warily, wondering what the woman was leading up to. When they'd first married and moved into this house, she and Joshua had been pleased that they would have such eminent neighbours – a mill owner on one side and a doctor on the other. But it had soon transpired that their new neighbours were not quite as enamoured with them. There had never been any unpleasantness, but here on King Street it had soon become apparent to Bessie and Joshua that they would not be regarded as the equals of their neighbours. They were never invited to visit and rarely spoken to unless there was some complaint to be made.

'It isn't something to be encouraged,' said Mrs Briggs. She made no accusations, but Bessie wondered if she'd seen Dorothy giving the family food. 'We don't want them spreading the typhus fever,' she added.

'I don't think they were doing any harm,' said Bessie, hoping that the woman wasn't going to make trouble. Mrs Briggs visibly bristled and drew herself up so that she could look down at Bessie. The mill owner's wife was more than twice Bessie's age and Bessie knew that she thought of her as a child – too young to be a married woman and a mother.

'I don't want people like that near my house,' she said. 'I don't want them to be encouraged.' She put an emphasis on the last word to make sure Bessie understood that she had indeed seen Dorothy handing out the food.

Bessie wasn't sure how to respond. She knew that she'd done nothing wrong by helping the Irish woman. 'They were only gathering rags, trying to make a living. There's no harm in it,' she told Mrs Briggs quietly, determined to be reasonable and not be bullied, though she really didn't want to have a falling-out with her neighbour.

'They're bringing the Irish Fever,' said Mrs Briggs. 'That's why my husband won't have them working in his mill. He doesn't want disease to spread amongst his other hands.' Bessie didn't reply. She didn't know what to say that would stop the woman from haranguing her. 'If I see them again I'll report them. I'll make sure they're told to go and not return,' Mrs Briggs told Bessie before turning and stalking off up the street.

Bessie watched her go. The exchange had left her feeling helpless and angry.

'I had a bit of trouble with Mrs Briggs earlier,' Bessie told Joshua that evening after Julia was asleep and they'd settled down in front of the fire for an hour or so.

'What trouble?' he asked.

She could see that he was wary. Bessie knew that he disliked the woman as much as she did.

'Nothing much,' she quickly reassured him. She knew that any hint of her being treated less than well made him angry. He was very protective of her. 'She called me over to complain about the rag gatherers being in the back. I think she knew we'd given them something to eat the other day. She trotted out all the usual stuff about them bringing disease. She said she'd report them if she saw them again.'

Joshua moved to the edge of his chair and reached out his hands to the flames. Bessie could see that the news had disturbed him. 'I don't want trouble,' he said after a moment, 'but that woman sure makes me cross.'

'Me too,' replied Bessie. 'And I don't want trouble either. But if the Irish family come back again, what do you think we should do? Should we turn them away?'

she asked him. 'I hate to think of those children being hungry.' She put her sewing aside and reached out for Joshua's hand. 'Why is it wrong to do a good thing?' she asked.

'It isn't,' he said firmly.

'So should we feed them again?' she asked him. 'Despite Mrs Briggs?'

He frowned. Bessie could see that he was as conflicted as she was. They were both aware that they trod a precarious path in this town. They had both risen in the world – in his case a huge rise from being a plantation slave in the deep south of America. He'd run away from his owner and made it as far as her father's farm in Wisconsin. Her father had taken him in, fed him and clothed him and cared for him. But Joshua had still not been safe from the slave hunters who might capture him and take him back to the cotton fields. So when her father had come back to Blackburn on a visit he had brought Joshua with him, so that he could be truly free. He was employed now as her father's land agent, overseeing his affairs and investments on this side of the great ocean.

Bessie herself had been a mill lass, toiling fourteen hours a day at weaving looms until the man she discovered was her birth father had forbidden it. She'd wanted to go back to America with him, but she'd fallen in love with Joshua and when she'd discovered that he must stay, she'd stayed too, although it had broken her heart to part from the father she'd only just met.

They were both aware that there were people who looked down on them and thought that they were beneath them. And then there were the ones who judged Joshua on the colour of his skin. He always shrugged it off and said that it had been worse in America, but Bessie knew that it hurt him when men he was doing business with were reluctant to shake his hand or when their wives crossed the street if they saw him coming. They judged her too for marrying him. She'd heard the whispers and she tried not to care because there was no man on earth kinder than her husband, but it was still hard at times when she heard derogatory words muttered as she passed people by in the street.

'Your father took me in and fed me when I was a runaway,' Joshua said quietly. 'I see no reason not to pass that kindness on. We'll not be bullied by the likes of the Briggs. They go to their church every Sunday and talk about their Christianity, but I see little of what they preach in their dealings with folk.'

Bessie nodded. She knew that he was right. She would tell Dorothy to give the family food if they came again, but she hoped that it would go unnoticed by Mrs Briggs.

The next morning, when Bessie opened the nursery curtains, she looked out for any sign of the Irish family. Despite her resolve, she was plagued with a feeling of guilt, as if she was doing something wrong. She hoped that if the family came, they would come early before

Mrs Briggs had risen from her bed so that there was no chance of her seeing them.

It was a dull morning with a light drizzle in the air and the backs looked empty. Bessie lingered, watching the magpies in the trees beyond the street and enjoying her brief moment of peace before the day began. Then a movement caught her eye. It wasn't the woman she'd seen before, but a smaller figure, moving stealthily in the shadow of the stone wall that separated the houses from the alley beyond.

As the figure moved into the open to prod at a pile of rubbish with a stick, Bessie recognized him as the son of the Irish woman. Wondering where the rest of his family were this morning, she lifted her skirts in her hands to run down the stairs to the kitchen where Dorothy looked up in alarm at her sudden, breathless appearance.

'Whatever's the matter, Mrs Anderton?' she asked. 'Is Julia poorly?'

'No.' Bessie shook her head. 'There's a boy in the back alley. I think he's one of the family who came before. Will you call to him? But quietly,' she added. 'Don't let Mrs Briggs hear you.'

She watched as Dorothy opened the door and gave a low call. 'He's coming,' she said.

'Bring him in,' said Bessie. 'I want to talk to him.'

Dorothy beckoned to the boy again and he came slowly down the steps. 'Step inside,' she told him, but the boy hesitated, unsure. 'Step inside,' Dorothy told him again. 'Leave that bag and stick outside and wipe your feet on the mat.'

Bessie watched as the boy appeared in the doorway and stared at her. He was clearly frightened.

'It's all right,' she told him. 'We'll not harm you. Would you like something to eat?'

The offer of food and the aroma of the bacon that Dorothy had been frying for breakfast was enough to encourage him to cross the threshold. He wiped his feet as he was bidden and then stared suspiciously at the two women. 'What do you want?' he asked.

'Are you alone today?' asked Bessie. He nodded nervously and glanced back towards the door that Dorothy had closed behind him, as if he was checking that he knew the way out. 'Where's your mother?' asked Bessie.

The boy shook his head and looked close to tears, but then he balled his hands into fists and took on a determined look. 'I'll not go!' he protested. 'I'll not go to that place! You'll have to catch me first!'

He turned and dashed towards the door to make his escape, but the latch got the better of him and Bessie had crossed the kitchen in a moment and put a hand on his arm to restrain him.

'Let me go!' he shouted, as he wrestled with the door handle again. 'Let me out!'

'It's all right. It's all right.' Bessie tried to soothe him. She was worried that he would manage to get the door open and run before she could find out what it was that was making him so afraid.

'What's happening?' They all turned to see Joshua in the kitchen doorway. 'What's all the fuss?' he asked as he took in the scene.

Whilst Bessie's attention was distracted the boy saw his opportunity and wrenched open the door.

'Go after him,' she begged Joshua, as the boy shot up the steps, but her husband was shaking his head.

'It won't do any good to go chasing him through the streets, Bessie,' he told her. 'Let him go for now.'

'But he was so frightened,' she protested. 'I'm worried about him. I think someone else is looking for him. He kept saying *I'll not go to that place*. Do you think he's in trouble?'

Joshua was shaking his head. He pulled forward a chair and sat Bessie down. 'Ain't nothing you can do right now,' he told her.

'He's left his bag and stick behind,' observed Dorothy as she closed the door. 'He might come back for them in a while. I'll listen out for him.'

'At least leave some food for him,' said Bessie. 'Put some of that bacon between slices of bread and wrap it up. If he comes back at least he can have something to eat.' She turned to Joshua. 'I only wanted to talk to him,' she said. 'I'm worried that something's happened to his mother and the rest of his family.'

'They're probably just scavenging a different street,' said Joshua.

Dorothy put a cup of tea down on the table beside Bessie. 'Drink that,' she told her. 'There's no need to get so upset . . .' Bessie suspected she'd been going to add *about an Irish child*, but had thought better of it.

'I'll make some enquiries,' promised Joshua as he got ready to leave the house. 'Someone may have seen them. Don't worry,' he added as he kissed her.

But Bessie was worried even though she couldn't quite explain it to herself. It was as if by offering food to the family they had suddenly become her responsibility.

'Has the boy come back?' she asked Dorothy when she brought Bessie her morning chocolate as she fed Julia.

'No.' She shook her head. 'The bag and stick are still there. He probably won't come back until after dark now,' she predicted.

'Will you watch Julia for a while?' asked Bessie. 'I have an errand to run.'

Dorothy didn't ask what her errand was and Bessie felt guilty as she put on a plain bonnet and her oldest jacket. She knew that both her maid and her husband would disapprove of what she intended to do, but she was determined to discover what the boy was so afraid of and what had happened to his mother.

Bessie knew that most of the Irish lived in the cellars around Butcher's Court. It was a place that most people avoided, but she wanted to see for herself if it was really as bad as people said. Growing up, she'd known poverty herself and she knew that there was no shame in it. Her mother had worked hard to care for her and

Peggy and provide for them, even during the hard times when there was no work at the mill. Her father . . . she struggled to think of Titus as anything other than her father, even though she now knew that her real father was George Anderton . . . Titus had always worked hard too and had hated the times when he couldn't bring in a wage to support his family. He'd campaigned endlessly for fair pay and rights for the working man. It was his passion and had got him into trouble on more than one occasion. Bessie wondered what he thought about the Irish immigrants. She rarely saw him these days and had never had the sort of relationship with him that would have allowed her to discuss such things. He'd always been much closer to Peggy, but he would have a view on it. She was sure of that.

As she approached Butcher's Court her courage almost failed her. The scene was very different from the terraced streets where she'd grown up, and it was clear that the poverty here was much worse than anything she'd ever experienced. There was a low, narrow entry, very dark and damp. Two more turns brought her to a small, filth-strewn courtyard where a woman was pegging out some washing on a rope that was tied to makeshift fastenings on the buildings at either side. The items she was hanging with care weren't even recognizable as clothing and Bessie was horrified that this was all the family had to wear.

As Bessie stood watching, the woman removed the last of the wooden pegs from her mouth and met her gaze.

'Can I help you?' she asked, clearly puzzled by Bessie's presence. Her accent was unmistakably Irish.

'I'm looking for someone. Perhaps you can help me,' said Bessie. 'There's a woman and some children who've come to my house a few times. My maid gave them some remnants of material from a dress I'd been sewing . . .' She fell silent as the other woman began to shake her head.

'It's no good coming here wanting your stuff back,' she told her. 'It'll all have gone to the rag shop to be weighed in.' She sized Bessie up for a moment. 'Best take it up with your maid if it was a mistake,' she advised her. 'I'm sorry. There's nothing I can do about it.'

'But the other woman who gathers rags,' persisted Bessie. 'Where can I find her? Do you know her?'

'Like I said. There's no way you can get anything back,' repeated the woman as she grasped a wooden prop and hooked the end on to the washing line to lift it further from the ground. The tattered remains of the clothing that had been washed turned and flapped in the breeze that was coming down the ginnel – a breeze that carried with it the stench of the offal that had been left on the stone slabs in the slaughterhouse whilst the better cuts were being taken to be displayed in the shop. Bessie noticed the mangy dogs that were hanging around the open doorway looking for an opportune moment to snatch some food. The butcher saw them too and shouted at them to get away before banging shut the door.

'I don't want anything back,' Bessie told the woman as she turned her attention back to her. 'It was willingly given. I wanted to help. But the lad who was with her came to the back alley alone today and he seemed afraid. I was going to feed him, but he ran off.'

'Young lad?' said the woman as she picked up her wicker basket. It was clear to Bessie that this news meant something to her. She must know the family in question, but it was obvious that she didn't trust Bessie and wasn't going to give anything away.

'He was about nine or ten years old,' Bessie went on. 'Not badly dressed,' she added, glancing again at the washing.

The woman followed her gaze. 'Those aren't what we wear,' she said and a smile tugged at her lips as she tried not to laugh. 'Those are for rags. But I'll get more for them if they're clean.'

'Oh. I see. I did think . . .' Bessie felt embarrassed as the woman began to laugh.

'We're not well off,' she told Bessie, 'but we do keep ourselves decent.'

Behind the woman, Bessie saw a small head appear as a little girl climbed up the steep steps from a cellar. She was dragging an even smaller boy behind her and Bessie immediately recognized them as the children of the woman she was looking for.

'He's wet himself,' announced the girl, still grasping the hand of the infant who had a dark stain at the front of his trousers.

Bessie heard the woman sigh. 'Take him inside. I'll be there in a minute,' she said, ushering the children away with a backward glance in Bessie's direction.

'I only want to help,' called Bessie. 'I'm not here to make trouble for you.'

She saw the woman hesitate. 'If you see the lad again, tell him that he's to come to Aileen's,' she said.

'I will. But is there anything else I can do? Where is the children's mother? Is she unwell?' asked Bessie, wondering if the woman she was seeking was ill in the cellar below. 'I could ask the doctor to call.'

The woman laughed again, but this time it was with derision and held no amusement. 'Doctors won't come here,' she said. 'They're too afraid.'

'I'm sure they're not.'

'They are. Afraid of the fever and afraid they won't get paid. We're expected to live in hovels like these, with all this filth,' she said, waving a hand towards the blood from the butcher's that was trickling out from under his door and running down the gulley towards the pump where the residents drew their drinking water. 'And then they blame us for the illness it causes.'

'I do want to help,' insisted Bessie. She opened her purse and took out the coins she had brought with her – two florins. 'Here,' she said, offering them on her outstretched palm. 'Please take these.'

The woman hesitated, but then shook her head again. 'I don't need your charity,' she told her. 'Go back to your fancy house and don't bother about us.'

Bessie watched as the woman followed the children down the steps. For a moment she considered following her, but what good would it do? She desperately wanted to help these people, but she could see that they were proud and there was nothing to be gained by forcing her favours on them.

She turned away, feeling frustrated, and walked back towards the town centre. Rather than going straight home, she walked up Church Street to her sister Peggy's shop. She pushed open the door and the bell brought Peggy hurrying to her counter, but Bessie saw the flash of disappointment on her face that it wasn't a customer before she set it into a smile of greeting.

'What brings you here?' she asked.

'I was just passing,' said Bessie. 'And I haven't seen you for a while.'

'I've been busy,' replied Peggy, managing to make it sound like an accusation rather than a reason.

'I know. That's why I thought I should make the effort,' Bessie told her. 'Can I sit down?' she asked.

'Aye. But you'll have to go if I get a customer,' Peggy warned.

Bessie lowered herself on to the bentwood chair. She suddenly felt weary and wished she'd gone straight home. She'd wanted to confide in her sister, but Peggy had distanced herself from her since they'd both married. Bessie suspected it was because Peggy resented that all her good fortune had come from Bessie's father rather than her own. The discovery that George Anderton was Bessie's real father had changed their relationship. Peggy had always been the favourite child whom Titus had thought would rise in the world, whilst he never had any ambitions for Bessie other than the mill. So, when Bessie had suddenly risen far above her sister and gone to live in the house on King Street that her birth father had bought for her and Joshua, Peggy had been left feeling disappointed, even though George Anderton had agreed to rent her and John Sharples the shop that Peggy had always craved.

'I've been down to Butcher's Court,' Bessie told her sister.

'Why on earth would you want to go there? Are you mad?' demanded Peggy, wrinkling her nose at the very thought of it. 'I hope you didn't catch owt,' she added, making Bessie wonder if she was going to be asked to leave.

'No. I wasn't there long. I was looking for a family that I've seen in our backs a few times. The woman's come over from Ireland, but she lost her husband and baby on the boat and she's been left with nothing apart from a brood of children to feed.'

'Oh her!' said Peggy.

'Do you know her?' asked Bessie.

'Aye. She's latched on to our John and his family,' replied Peggy. 'She's claiming to be a cousin. It's nonsense, of course. She came right into the shop one day looking for him. If she comes again I'll fetch the constable!'

'What makes you think it's nonsense that she's a cousin?' asked Bessie curiously as she watched Peggy begin to rearrange her display of gloves. It reminded her of the first time she'd come into this shop and sat on this chair. It had been run by Miss Cross then and it was the day her father, her real father, had told her she was his daughter. He'd wanted to give her a gift and he'd brought her in here and bought her the most exquisite pair of lavender-coloured gloves. She still had them at home, wrapped in tissue paper in her chest of drawers in the bedroom. They were amongst her most treasured possessions.

'Couldn't she be related?' she asked her sister. 'Isn't his mother Irish?'

'They can't all be cousins! Or maybe they can. They stick close together,' sniffed Peggy. 'But she's only after money. I've told John to send her on her way if she comes near him again.'

'I felt sorry for her,' admitted Bessie. 'I thought I ought to see if there was anything I could do to help. That's why I went to Butcher's Court. But it's a horrible place.'

'So I've heard.'

'I spoke to another woman called Aileen. The younger children were with her, but she seemed worried about the older lad. I think he's run away.'

'Don't get involved,' advised Peggy. 'It isn't anything to do with you. And you don't want to be taking the fever home to Julia.'

Bessie felt a moment of anxiety as she considered the possibility. Peggy was right in a way. Her own child must come first, but still she felt that she couldn't ignore the plight of the woman and her family.

She jumped up from the chair as the door opened, but it was only John.

'Hello, Bessie!' He seemed genuinely pleased to see her and kissed her cheek in greeting before putting away his post bag.

'Bessie's been talking about that Irish woman. I've told her not to get involved,' Peggy told him.

Bessie explained to John about giving the woman rags and food and her concerns for the family.

'I'd stay away from Butcher's Court,' he said. 'Does Joshua know tha's been down there?'

'I just went on the spur of the moment,' she replied. She hoped that her husband would be more understanding than her sister.

'It's full of disease – typhus, cholera. It's not safe,' John warned her grimly. 'Don't go again.'

'I think the woman might be ill,' said Bessie. 'I offered to send a doctor, but the woman, Aileen, refused.'

She watched as John frowned. He seemed about to say something but hesitated and Bessie wondered if he would have spoken more freely if Peggy hadn't been there. She wanted to ask him about the woman's claims that she was his cousin, because if they were true then something would have to be done to help her. They couldn't simply turn her away.

'I'd best go,' she said.

'I'll see thee to the door,' said John and when Bessie was outside he closed it behind him so that Peggy couldn't hear. 'The woman's name is Kitty Cavanah,' he told her. 'She says she's a cousin of my mother. She went to see her and she mentioned Rathdrum and my mother says that's where our family came from.' He glanced back inside the shop, but Peggy seemed engrossed. 'It seems a bit of a coincidence if it isn't true. But I don't know what to believe. Peggy says she's just a trickster looking for money, but she seemed desperate to me.'

'When did you last speak to her?' asked Bessie.

He shook his head. 'A few days ago. I haven't seen her since. I thought Peggy was probably right when she said that she'd moved on.'

'She wouldn't go without her children.'

'But this Aileen wouldn't tell you anything?'

'No. She seemed afraid.'

'Leave it with me,' said John. 'I'll see what I can find out. And best not mention to Joshua where tha's been,' he added before going back inside the shop.

20

Aileen hurried Maria and Peter down the steps and shut the cellar door firmly. The last thing she wanted was some busybody coming around asking questions.

'Sit down,' she told Maria. 'I told you to stay inside!' She knew that she was being harsh and that the little girl didn't understand how important it was that she and her brother stayed hidden. She saw the child's lip tremble and felt guilty. 'Sit down,' she repeated more gently, 'and I'll get your brother cleaned up.'

She stripped the wet clothing off Peter and wiped him with a wet rag, then wondered what she could dress him in until his trousers were washed and dried. She had a few spare clothes but none that would fit a baby, and it seemed that Kitty and her children owned nothing except what they had arrived in. Eventually she wrapped a towel around the child's waist and pinned it. It would have to do for now, and it wasn't as if anyone was going to see him.

'When's Mam coming back?' asked Maria when Aileen was finished.

'Soon,' she told her. 'Just be a good girl until then.'

The problem was, thought Aileen, that she wasn't sure whether Kitty or Agnes would come out of that place alive. Few did. Most came out in a cheap wooden box and were taken to a pauper's grave outside the parish church without even a priest to say a mass for their souls. As she carried the soiled clothing up into the yard and put it into the half-barrel where she soaked her rags, Aileen wondered if she'd been too quick to take on the children. She just hoped that they wouldn't become ill as well and pass the typhus fever on to her and Michael. But what else could she have done? She couldn't have seen them taken to the workhouse. Irish children were not treated well in that place. It was bad enough Kitty and Agnes being taken to the hospital there.

She was worried about Timothy too. He'd run off before the cart came to take his mother and sister away. She'd had no idea where he'd gone, but if it was him that the woman had seen then at least he'd stayed in Blackburn – or he had until that morning. The woman had said he'd seemed afraid, and Aileen knew that he would be. Unlike the two little ones, he was old enough to realize that with his mother in the workhouse hospital he was vulnerable to being taken into care himself. She hoped she could find him soon and reassure him that he would be safe with her and Michael, for the time being at least. Aileen knew that if Kitty did die then a big decision would have to be made. Michael hadn't complained about her looking after the little ones for a few days, but taking on a whole new family at their age was a different proposition. They'd both thought that parenthood was long behind them – and Aileen thought longingly of the two sons she'd brought up to manhood. They were married now and had both gone off to America to work in the mills there, in a place called New Bedford. They sent letters home sometimes and Michael read them to her in the firelight. They spoke of hard work but good wages, and the houses they described seemed like palaces to Aileen. Her sons had made the right choice, even if she did miss them and longed to see the little grandchildren she would never know. But it was a country for young people, she thought. It was such a shame that Kitty and her husband hadn't been able to complete their journey.

If Timothy was still trying to gather rags then she must ask Mr Reynolds if he'd seen him when she went down later, she decided. Aileen just hoped that the incident with the woman who'd called hadn't frightened him so badly that he'd decided to leave town.

'Young lad?' asked Mr Reynolds when she'd weighed in her rags and bones later that afternoon.

'Aye. He's brother to Agnes who was working at the sorting tables.'

'The one who took sick?' Aileen nodded. 'No,' said Mr Reynolds. 'I've not seen him today.'

'If he does come in, will you send him to me? I promised Kitty I'd look after her children until she's better.'

'How is she? And her daughter?'

'I don't know,' said Aileen. 'They don't allow visitors and they tell you nothing. They say they can only speak to her family – but she's got no family.'

'I hope they pull through,' said Mr Reynolds. 'She were a nice woman and her daughter were a hard worker. I could do with more like that,' he commented, glaring at the lasses who were chatting as they worked. 'Give over gassin' and get on!' he shouted across to them.

Aileen thanked him and hurried home to where Michael was watching the children. She would take them out with her tomorrow, she decided. It wouldn't be easy, but it would give her the chance to ask about amongst the other gatherers if they'd seen Timothy. If she could find him, he could at least make himself useful by looking after the little ones whilst she worked.

Kitty lay in the hospital bed with Agnes beside her. She could see a spider weaving its web in a corner of the lime washed wall near to the bed. If she reached out a hand she could probably touch it, she thought, but the effort was too much for her and she knew she must concentrate all her strength on staying alive. She must not die. She'd survived the shipwreck and she must survive this too, because who would care for her children if she didn't get better? She crept her fingers across the dampened bedclothes and touched her daughter, as she had several times already, to reassure herself that Agnes still lived. She felt hot, but she was still breathing.

Kitty heard a door slam at the end of the ward. The noise hurt her head more than she thought possible and when she turned it gently to look, she saw a man in a suit, standing beside the nurse. He was looking at each patient in turn as he made his way down the rows of beds which had been crammed together in this building that seemed little more than a shed. Above her Kitty could see a wooden roof and she could hear rain dripping on to the stone floor where it was leaking. Eventually, the man and the nurse reached the bed where she and Agnes were lying.

'These are Irish immigrants. They have the fever as well,' she heard the nurse say.

Kitty tried to meet the doctor's eye. She wanted to ask him what cures he recommended. They had been given nothing yet except a drink of tepid water, and she had no idea what had happened to the medicine she'd bought from the chemist.

She tried to lift her head, but it felt too heavy and thudded back on to the hard pillow. Every part of her body ached and one moment she was roasting hot, the next she was shivering as if she'd been caught outside without her shawl in the depths of winter.

She tried to speak, but the doctor was already moving on, crossing to the long row of beds that faced hers. Each one was filled with a prone figure. Some were shivering under their blanket. Others had cast their blanket aside. Some tossed and turned. Some were very still, and Kitty feared that they had died. She'd seen two bodies carried out already and she was terrified that the same fate awaited herself and Agnes.

She hoped that Aileen had kept her promise to look after her other children and that they were safe and hadn't fallen ill as well. Why had she come to this place? Maybe she should have listened to Agnes and gone to Stockport after all. But her husband would never have looked for them there, she reminded herself, as she clung on to the hope that he would come soon. At least he could care for the children if she didn't get better.

Bessie reached her home and let herself in at the front door. She was standing in the hallway, tugging off her bonnet, when she heard Dorothy coming up the steps from the kitchen.

'There you are!' exclaimed her maid. 'I was beginning to worry.' She glanced at Bessie's clothing. 'Where have you been?' she asked.

Bessie frowned. Although she loved Dorothy dearly and could never have managed without her, there were times when she thought that the woman forgot herself. It was true that Dorothy was old enough to be her mother, but she wasn't her mother, and if it hadn't been for the anxious look on the maid's face she thought she might have been tempted to set her straight about her position in this household. When she'd left home to be married, Bessie had never envisaged having to explain herself to anyone other than her husband.

'Is everything all right?' she asked. She couldn't hear Julia crying and hoped that she was still asleep. She was sure she hadn't been gone long.

'Julia was fractious. She was hungry. I've given her a little bit of pap and she's sleeping now.'

'I'll go up,' said Bessie, feeling guilty that she had neglected her own child in favour of the Irish waifs.

'She's in the kitchen,' said Dorothy. 'I've set her in a basket near the range.'

Bessie handed her bonnet to the maid and hurried down the back steps without a word. She knew she should have been grateful, but she felt irritated. She was sure that Julia couldn't have been hungry so soon after her last feed and she felt cross that Dorothy might be judging her to be an inadequate mother.

'I only did what I thought was right,' complained Dorothy after she'd put the bonnet away and followed Bessie down to the kitchen. 'Are you going to feed her in here?' she asked as she watched Bessie sit down on the faded kitchen chair with the baby in her arms.

Bessie didn't reply. She didn't tell Dorothy that she needed her company after her visit to Butcher's Court and her exchange with her sister. She would have liked to confide in her maid, but she didn't think Dorothy would approve of what she'd done. It was why she'd slipped out without telling her where she was going.

'Have you seen the Irish boy again?' she asked as Julia settled down to suckle.

Dorothy picked up her smoothing iron from the range and spat on it to see if it was hot. The iron sizzled and she returned to ironing the bedsheets and table-cloths she'd folded into a neat pile after fetching them down from the washing line.

'No,' she said as she worked. 'His stick and sack are still there. The bacon sandwich has gone. Could have been rats, though.'

'If you do see him, tell him that Aileen is looking for him and that he's to go to her,' said Bessie. She saw the maid raise an eyebrow slightly, but Dorothy didn't ask how she'd elicited this information. She kept her thoughts to herself, but Bessie knew she suspected where her mistress had spent the afternoon and she didn't approve.

John had said nothing more to Peggy about the Irish woman after Bessie had gone, but he'd decided that he must speak to his mother and sisters about her. If there was any chance that she was family, then surely he had an obligation to do something to help her, especially as it seemed that her husband was drowned at sea.

So, after the shop had been locked up for the day and his daughters had been put to bed, he made an excuse about needing something for his aquarium and hurried down to Moore Street.

His mother was dozing in the chair by the fire and Susan was baking bread.

'Jimmy's gone to the White Horse for half a pint,' she told him.

'It's thee I've come to see – and my mam.'

'Well, sit thee down then. I'd pour thee some tea but as tha can see I'm up to the elbows in flour and dough.'

'I'll do it misself,' he said, hanging up his cap and setting some cups on the table before reaching for the brown pot that was keeping warm. He handed one filled cup to his mother and sat down opposite her. He could see the sharpness of her shoulder blades through her shawl where she was hunched over with the hardship of her life's work.

'I've come to talk about the Irish family,' he said to Susan. 'I'm sorry our Peggy were rude when tha called about it. She doesn't mean any harm.'

'It pays to be careful,' Susan told him.

'Aye, but if Kitty Cavanah really is a cousin, we can't let her and her children starve. If we are kin, then we have a responsibility.'

'Aye. But how can we be certain she's a cousin?' asked Susan.

'I don't know. But what she said about Rathdrum seems too much of a coincidence.'

'Rathdrum?' interrupted their mother. 'Our family came from Rathdrum. That lass that came. She said she was a cousin – or married to a cousin.'

'Did tha believe her, Mam?' asked John.

'Why wouldn't I?' she asked.

'Perhaps it's best to let it lie,' suggested Susan. 'It's not like we have a lot to give anyway.'

'Happen so,' said John and took a long drink from his steaming tea. He could see the sense in turning a blind eye, but the sight of the Irish widow and her children had moved him to want to help them whether they were family or not.

21

The next morning, Aileen was up early. Maria and Peter were reluctant to be roused, but she didn't want to risk leaving them alone whilst she went out to work. She gave them both a bowl of pobbies, laced with as much sugar as she dared to spare. For herself, she made do with a cup of sweetened tea. She would eat later, she told herself.

Michael had already gone out and she followed him up the steps, which were slick with an icy covering of early frost. She carried Peter, his slightly damp pants restored to him, on her hip and carried a sack and stick in the other hand. With a shorter stick and a sack of her own Maria trailed after her. She was still asking when her mam was coming back and Aileen was still telling her soon, although she wondered how long she could keep up her reassurance before she was forced to tell the little girl what she feared would be the truth.

They began in the alleyway at the back of Richmond Terrace. There were some other gatherers there already and it was a street Aileen would usually have dismissed so late after daylight, but she was keen to ask if anyone had seen Timothy.

'Son of the new woman, do you say?' asked a man

sorting through a pile of refuse as he listened to Aileen's story. 'I saw him with her a few days ago. They were on Fish Lane. I almost told them they were wasting their time. There's nothing to be found down there where folks are wearing their rags.'

'But have you seen him since?' persisted Aileen.

The man shook his head. 'I can't say that I have. Why do you want to know?'

'We think he's had a fright and run off. His mother's worried about him,' she added, not saying that Kitty had the fever. She didn't want to create a panic. 'If you do see him, will you tell him to go to Aileen's?'

'I will for sure,' agreed the man and continued with his work.

'Not much today,' remarked Mr Reynolds when Aileen went to weigh in her finds later that morning.

Aileen knew that it was true. Between looking after Maria and Peter and making enquiries about Timothy, she'd only collected a fraction of what she usually did. It was reflected in the price too, she reflected as she put away the coins she'd been paid in her purse and straightened her skirts. Less money and more mouths to feed wasn't a good combination and she considered once again the wisdom of taking on Kitty's children. If it was true that Nan Sharples and her son John, who ran the post office, were family, it was clear to Aileen that there were others who had more obligations and who were also in a better position to offer help to these little ones. Perhaps she should go to find these cousins her-self and point out that they had a responsibility to their family members.

As she was taking the children back to Butcher's Court, Aileen caught sight of John Sharples himself coming down Mincing Lane. He had the strap of the leather bag that he used to deliver letters slung across his upper body and he was whistling as he walked, as if he hadn't a care in the world.

It seemed too good an opportunity to miss and, grasping the children, one in either hand, she waited for a couple of carts to pass before hurrying across the street to confront him.

He glanced up as he saw her coming towards him but seemed to dismiss the possibility of any interaction with her. Most folk were the same. The Irish were invis-ible to them.

'Mr Sharples?'

He stopped as she confronted him, standing directly in his path so that he couldn't easily get past her. He looked quizzical and concerned.

'I've no letters for Butcher's Court,' he told her.

'I need to speak to you, about Kitty Cavanah.'

Aileen saw that he recognized the name and rather than hurrying off he shifted the weight of his bag on his shoulder.

'What about her?' he asked carefully.

'These are her children,' Aileen told him. 'Two of them anyway. I'm looking after them.'

'Where is she?' asked John Sharples.

'She . . .' Aileen hesitated, wishing that she'd thought out what she was going to say rather than acting on impulse. 'She's not well,' she told him.

'I'm sorry to hear that,' he replied. 'What ails her?'

Aileen decided to be honest. 'They say it's the typhus fever. She and her daughter Agnes are in the workhouse hospital.'

She saw a look of concern flicker across his face.

'I'm not sure what I can do to help,' he told her.

'She says your mother is her cousin,' persisted Aileen. 'And I'm not in any position to help, although I'm doing my best, but I've little enough as it is and now that I've got extra mouths to feed, it's going to be a struggle.'

John Sharples looked uncomfortable. He dug a hand into his pocket and took out a shilling, which he offered her. This time Aileen swallowed her pride and took the money.

'Buy the children some food,' he said. 'But if you are struggling you could always go to the parish and see what they can do for you.'

'But family should help family,' Aileen told him. 'She's your cousin. You should take some responsibility.'

She saw that he had the grace to look a little shamefaced.

'It's not that straightforward,' he said.

'Do you not believe what she says?' challenged Aileen, feeling increasingly cross that this well-dressed man who had money to spare wouldn't acknowledge his relations who were worse off than him. 'I'm looking after these two little ones even though they're not my family,' she told him. 'But I know when to do the right thing and I'll not see babes like these starve on the street.'

John Sharples met her angry stare for a moment, then pulled his cap down further over his face and stepped into the street to get past her.

'I have to get on,' he told her. 'I've got post to deliver. But I'll see what I can do,' he said, although Aileen didn't think it was much of a promise.

John felt guilty as he hurried away. He'd been taken by surprise when the woman stopped him on the street and her accusatory attitude had made him defensive. But he'd been shocked to hear that Kitty and her other daughter were in the hospital. They must be very sick to have been taken there. A wave of anxiety overcame him as he remembered that the woman had been in the shop and had spoken to Peggy. What if she'd brought the fever in with her? He thought of his own little girls and his throat tightened as he considered the possibility of them falling ill.

The other person who seemed concerned about the Irish family was Bessie. His sister-in-law had always had a softer nature than his wife, although it was Peggy's strong-minded tenacity that made him love her. He wondered whether he should call on Bessie when the letters were delivered and tell her about Kitty being in the hospital. It was always uncertain whether people would come out of there alive, he knew, and the towns-folk only ever whispered its name, some making the sign of the cross as they did, hoping that they would never be so unlucky as to find themselves within its dark stone walls.

If Kitty Cavanah died, what would become of her children? Would the woman Aileen keep them? Or would she take them to the workhouse? They weren't her responsibility, as she'd rightly pointed out. And John's conscience pricked him as he finished his round, with a little voice telling him again and again that he couldn't do nothing and allow that to happen.

Bessie was finishing a dress fitting when she heard the bell ring at the front door. It was very unusual for anyone to call except for her clients, and she knew that she didn't have any more appointments that afternoon.

'The dress will be ready next Wednesday,' she told Mrs Fisher. 'I would call my maid to show you out, but I think she's gone to answer the doorbell. I'll walk downstairs with you myself,' she said as she helped her customer on with her outside coat and held up a look-ing glass for her to adjust her bonnet.

Halfway down the stairs she saw it was John standing in the hallway, trying to flatten his unruly hair after handing his hat to Dorothy. She thanked Mrs Fisher and allowed Dorothy to take her to the front door whilst she ushered John into the parlour.

'Is everything all right?' she asked, hoping that there

was nothing amiss with her sister or her nieces. 'Has Peggy sent thee?'

'No. She doesn't know I've come,' he confessed. 'I've come about Kitty Cavanah. She's in the fever hospital.'

'Is she?' Bessie looked alarmed. 'I thought the woman Aileen was caring for her.'

'She's caring for the younger children. She stopped me in the street earlier to harangue me.' He told Bessie what had been said between them.

'What are we going to do?' she asked when he'd finished the tale. It had obviously upset him, but Bessie thought she wasn't the one he should be confiding in. 'You need to talk to our Peggy about it,' she said.

'She's certain the woman's a trickster – and maybe she is,' replied John, 'but the sight of them little childer made me feel so guilty. We've done all right, haven't we?' he asked. 'And we've known poverty. Remember what it was like on Paradise Lane?'

'I remember,' she assured him, 'and I'm grateful that the fates have been generous to us.'

'The fates and thy father.'

'Aye, him as well,' she agreed. 'We must do something for them,' she told John. 'It's only right to help those who are less fortunate.'

'I know,' he said. 'I've not the money to fully pay for their keep, but I feel I should do summat. I wondered if tha's any suggestions.'

Bessie thought about it as she rang for Dorothy to

bring them some tea. She knew that John always enjoyed a fresh brew.

'I suppose the best way we can help is to find them somewhere to live and a way to earn their own living,' she said. 'But the mill owners don't like taking on Irish unless they have to, and I doubt the woman has the skills to be a powerloom weaver. And then there are the children.' She paused. 'Has anyone seen the lad again, do you know? He's not been back here.'

'I've not seen him,' said John. 'Dost tha think they could earn enough gathering the rags to afford rent on a house?'

'I doubt it,' said Bessie. 'Or the Irish wouldn't be living in those filthy cellars. It isn't a proper job. Maybe she could take in washing like my mam did. Or be a baby minder? That would mean she could watch her own childer as well.'

'Would folk leave their bairns with an Irish woman?' asked John.

'Probably not,' Bessie agreed. She watched Dorothy set the tea tray down on the table and pour two cups for them. 'And I doubt it would bring in much of a wage anyway. The older children could work, I suppose, but it's not easy for a woman when she doesn't have a husband's wage to support her. And if she goes to the parish they'll send her back to Ireland.'

'Perhaps that would be for the best,' John suggested.

'No,' Bessie told him. 'Their harvest has failed again. That's why they're all coming over. I doubt they would have come in the first place if they hadn't been desperate.'

'Dost tha think she's genuine when she claims she's a cousin?' John asked.

'I couldn't say.' Bessie offered John the sugar. 'But I think her need is genuine. I feel sorry for her. I pray she pulls through the fever. She doesn't deserve to die alone, so far from her home. Maybe when she's better we can try to find her some work. She might suit a scullery maid. But then she'd have to live in, and what about the children?'

It wasn't until John was walking home that a thought struck him. It had been Bessie's comment about scullery maids that had made him recall that Peggy had been pestering him to find someone to help her about the house for a while now. He wondered how she would respond to the idea that they employ the Irish woman. Not well, he feared, and yet he wondered if it was worth making the suggestion. Or maybe they could employ the daughter? He wasn't sure how old she was, but old enough for some basic domestic tasks, he was sure. Of course, the Irish woman had to recover from the fever first – and he wouldn't say anything about that to Peggy. Whatever she said, he'd made up his mind that he must help this family. He had to give Kitty Cavanah the benefit of the doubt and believe that she was a cousin. He would never be able to live with his conscience otherwise.

22

Kitty had no idea how many days and nights she'd been lying in the hospital bed. But her head didn't seem to hurt so much this morning and even though her legs wobbled like jelly when she eased herself to her feet, she managed to walk to the privy to relieve herself and felt proud of her achievement. Agnes seemed better too. She'd managed to get up a few days ago and the doctor had said that she could go home today. Not that she had a home to go to. Kitty could only hope that Agnes could find her way to Butcher's Court and that Aileen would take her in. She had no way of sending a message and they couldn't go together because the doctor wouldn't release her until he was sure that she was fever free. She'd pleaded to go with Agnes, but he'd been stubborn, and the truth was that even though she had managed the short walk to the privy, she knew she was incapable of walking from the workhouse hospital all the way back into Blackburn.

When she got back to the bed, Agnes was dressed and sitting on the edge of it.

'I don't want to go without you,' she told her mother. 'What if Aileen won't help me?'

'She will,' Kitty reassured the whey-faced child.

She knew that the only other option was for Agnes to be admitted to the workhouse, and she feared that would mean her daughter being put on a boat back to Ireland, alone.

'I'm not sure I can remember the way.'

'If you leave here and take the main road back towards Blackburn, you'll remember where it is.'

'Shall I go back to my job at the warehouse?' asked Agnes.

'In a day or two, when you feel strong enough. It'll help Aileen if you can pay her to keep you and your brothers and sister until I can come to get you.'

'How long will they make you stay here?'

'Not long,' Kitty promised. 'As soon as they're sure the fever has gone, I'll come to find you.'

She hugged her daughter, feeling the angles of her bones beneath her clothing. There was no spare flesh on the girl at all, and Kitty was thankful that she'd pulled through the illness as quickly as she had. There had been many others who'd been roughly stitched into sacking and carried out to be dumped in a communal grave. She and Agnes were both lucky to be alive, even though the nursing had been minimal and the doctor had seemed more concerned with his reputation than healing the sick.

Kitty cried when Agnes was taken away to be shown out through the high iron gates. She felt a failure as a mother, fretting and worrying about all her children out there without her to care for them. Even though she was certain Aileen would have kept her promise to care for them, she still felt guilty. And as for the baby – she pushed away an image of him being tossed on the fierce waves. She couldn't bear it.

Aileen was getting the little ones something to eat, food bought with John Sharples's shilling. She spread a good coating of fresh butter on some slices of bread and handed them to Maria and Peter. She'd eat later, when Michael came back, she told herself, trying to ignore her own nagging hunger. It seemed wrong to take the food that was meant for the children.

She gasped and crossed herself in alarm when a noise outside made her turn to see who was coming down the cellar steps. For a moment she thought that Agnes must have passed over and here was her ghost come to find her brother and sister. The white-faced apparition that had manifested itself in her doorway was almost translucent, and it was only when Agnes spoke that she was convinced the child was real.

'Sit down.' Aileen grasped the girl by the arm and steered her towards Michael's chair. 'Your mother?' she asked, fearing that Kitty had died.

'They won't let her out yet,' Agnes told her. She was so exhausted she could barely speak.

Aileen poured the girl a cup of the tea she'd just brewed and wished she had something more fortifying to add to it than a spoonful of sugar, but the drink seemed to revive Agnes a little. She ate a slice of the bread as she explained that her mother would come to collect them as soon as her fever had gone.

'Where's Timothy?' Agnes asked. 'Is he working?'

'I've not seen him today,' said Aileen, not wanting to alarm her. 'But I'm sure he'll come before long.' She prayed that someone had passed on her message to him. Even though she knew it wasn't her fault that Timothy had run away, she still felt as if she was responsible.

'I'll go back to work for Mr Reynolds, as soon as I feel well,' Agnes promised.

'We'll see,' said Aileen. It was obvious that the child wouldn't be fit to stand for hours at the sorting tables for a while yet, and meanwhile, she would have to be fed and cared for – Kitty too if she came back as weak and poorly as her daughter.

'I saw that John Sharples, and I told him he should do something,' Aileen whispered to Michael later when the children were asleep. 'He gave me a shilling, but it's nothing, is it? We'll all starve if someone doesn't step in to help.'

23

Peggy was pleased to see that it was John when she hurried down the stairs, summoned by the shop bell. She'd been upstairs preparing some lunch and keeping her ears open for customers. It wasn't ideal and she knew John didn't like the shop being left unattended, especially when there were parcels about, but she couldn't be in two places at the same time and she knew he'd expect something to eat when he got back from his postal round.

He looked distracted as he hung up his bag and his hat.

'Is anything wrong?' she asked, wondering if there'd been some problem with the letters.

'I ran into that woman, the rag gatherer called Aileen,' he told her, running his fingers through his hair as he always did when he was unsure of what to say. 'She accosted me in the street, saying we should do something for Kitty Cavanah.' He hesitated and Peggy saw that there was more to come. She waited, watching him as he pretended to busy himself at the post office counter. 'I was wondering if we should,' he told her after a moment.

'No!'

'Hear me out,' he said, ruffling his hair again and making Peggy want to tell him to go and brush it. 'I've had an idea.'

'What?' she asked, wondering what hare-brained scheme he'd come up with now and telling herself that she must be strong. John was a soft touch and it was up to her to stop him being taken advantage of.

'Well, tha's been asking for a bit of help around the house. I thought we could offer her some work.'

'What? The Irish woman?' Peggy shook her head. It had been bad enough having Kitty Cavanah come into the shop; she wasn't going to have her upstairs where she couldn't keep an eye on her. Besides, what about her brood of children? She hoped her husband wasn't proposing that they all came with her.

'Think about it, Peggy,' said John. 'Tha needs some help about the house, and why not Kitty Cavanah?'

'Because . . . because we know nothing about her!'

'Then who dost tha suggest we employ?' he asked.

'I was thinking of a local lass. There are plenty of them. Someone whose family we know,' she told him. She wanted to add that she didn't want any Irish in her house, that they carried diseases and that she didn't trust them, but she knew that it would hurt him and she didn't want to do that. She'd known his mother was Irish when she married him, but it hadn't seemed important then. She certainly hadn't envisaged paupers and tinkers turning up on their doorstep and claiming to be poor relations in need of money.

John didn't reply. He just looked sad and disappointed, and Peggy realized he'd known that she would say no. She wondered why he'd bothered asking.

'I just feel obliged to do something,' he said at last. 'I think she may genuinely be a cousin.'

The shop bell rang again, saving Peggy from having to answer. She put on a smile to greet her customer and John went upstairs. But it bothered her. She knew he could be stubborn, and if he'd got it into his head that this woman and her brood were family, he might insist on doing something to help them, and it wasn't as if they had spare money to be philanthropic. She left that sort of thing to her sister and her sister's wealthy father.

Bessie was in the nursery, putting Julia to bed, when she heard someone at the front door. She presumed it was someone calling to see Joshua on business and was surprised when Dorothy came to tell her that Peggy had arrived. Her sister rarely turned up uninvited.

'Shall I send her up?' asked the maid. 'I'm sure she'll want to see her little niece.'

'Yes. Yes, please,' said Bessie, realizing that it would give her the chance to speak to her sister alone and that Peggy probably wouldn't shout at her in the presence of the baby. Bessie suspected she knew why Peggy was calling so late. It was bound to be concerning Kitty Cavanah and her family.

She sat down to rock the cradle, with a toe on the

end of one of the curved rockers, but she didn't sing to her daughter as she would have done if she'd been alone. She listened to the footsteps as her sister came up the stairs and quietly opened the door.

Bessie put a finger to her lips and Peggy came across the room to see Julia, whose eyelids were fluttering as sleep overcame her.

'I need to talk to you,' said Peggy. 'Can we go to the parlour?'

'Let's just sit here awhile, until I'm sure she's gone off,' said Bessie, watching her daughter.

Peggy sat down on the upright chair and fidgeted with her gloves. She was wearing one of the Jenny Lind straw hats, Bessie noticed. She never came out without making sure she looked well-dressed, no matter how informal the errand. It made Bessie smile.

'John wants me to employ that Kitty Cavanah as a charwoman,' Peggy burst out after a moment, unable to contain herself.

Bessie looked up. 'Does he?' She wondered why she hadn't thought of it as a solution herself. It made perfect sense. Peggy had been moaning about needing help for a long time.

'Well, it's out of the question, isn't it?' demanded Peggy, and Bessie tried not to sigh as she realized her sister had come to try to involve her in a dispute between herself and John.

'Is it?' she asked gently.

'Of course it is. I'll not have that Irish woman in my home. Besides, what about her brood of childer?'

'The older ones could find work,' said Bessie. 'Or maybe the elder lass could take care of the little ones?'

'No.' Peggy was shaking her head emphatically. 'I'll not have it. She's a troublemaker, I'm sure. I don't believe she's any relation to John, but he's starting to say she might be, just because she said the name of some town in Ireland. It proves nothing.'

'Would it matter? If she wasn't related?' asked Bessie. 'If she's down on her luck – and from what I've heard, she is – why not help her anyway if it benefits thee?'

'I might have known you'd take their side!' Peggy spat furiously. 'I shouldn't have come.'

Bessie watched as her sister stood up, realizing that she'd failed to be as tactful as she'd hoped she could be. 'Don't go,' she implored. 'Look, Julia's sleeping now. Let's go downstairs and Dorothy will make us some tea.'

Grudgingly, Peggy agreed, and when they were sitting comfortably in the parlour, Bessie tried to persuade her sister that the best way they could help this family was to find paid work for them.

'It's up to you; of course it is,' she told Peggy. 'But is it worth falling out with John over it? You've been asking him to find you some help for ages, and criticizing him for not listening, and now when he's found someone you're telling him no. What's he to think?'

'I do need some help,' Peggy agreed. 'Just not Kitty Cavanah.'

'But she might be all right. Why not give her a chance?'

'It's all right for you to talk. She's not going to be in your house,' argued Peggy with a sour face. 'I wanted a nice local lass. Maybe one that I used to teach at the school. One that would be glad to help me out instead of having to go into the mill. I've Emily and Becky to think of too,' she went on. 'I don't want them taking on an Irish accent!'

'But it would help our mam if she didn't have to mind them every day. She's not getting any younger,' Bessie pointed out, knowing that although their mother loved her granddaughters she found them very tiring.

'I knew you wouldn't understand,' Peggy complained. 'I'm sorry I came.'

'Don't say that,' Bessie pleaded.

There was a knock at the parlour door, and Bessie hoped they hadn't been shouting so loud that Dorothy had come to tell them that they'd woken Julia or disturbed Joshua who was working in his office.

'What is it?' she asked when Dorothy opened the door a crack and peered in.

'I'm sorry to disturb you,' she said, 'but that lad's back. I thought you'd want to know.'

Bessie jumped up from the chair, her sister forgotten, and almost pushed Dorothy out of the way as she clutched her skirts in her hands to run down the stairs to the kitchen. Sure enough, the lad was coming warily down the outside steps.

Bessie fumbled with the lock, hoping that he wouldn't run away again. 'Don't go!' she called to him as he turned in alarm when she wrenched open the door. 'Aileen is looking for you!'

She saw that the lad recognized the name and he hesitated.

'No one means you any harm. We just want to help you,' she told him. 'Come inside. Please,' she added, hoping that Mrs Briggs from next door wasn't watching.

The lad looked at her guardedly, but didn't come any nearer.

'Would you like something to eat?' she asked, thinking that it was much like when she'd put out a saucer of milk for a stray cat. The cat, Tiddles, was now curled up on a chair by the warmth of the kitchen range. She hoped it would be as easy to tempt this lad inside, but somehow she doubted it.

She heard Dorothy and her sister come into the kitchen behind her and she turned to warn them to keep back. She didn't want the lad overwhelmed.

'Pour a glass of milk and fetch a slice of bread and butter,' she told Dorothy before turning her attention back to the waif who seemed frozen halfway up the back steps. 'Don't go just yet,' she called to hm. 'Have something to eat.'

Bessie held out the food and he came slowly towards

her and snatched a piece of bread from the plate she was holding out.

'I spoke to Aileen,' Bessie told him. 'She says you're to go to her home.' She hesitated to call it a cellar. 'Your brother and sister are there.'

The lad pushed the food into his mouth and chewed, eyeing the other slice that was still on the plate. Bessie held it out. It was clear that he wasn't going to risk coming inside again, but if she could persuade him to trust Aileen, at least he would be safe.

She could sense Peggy behind her, bristling with disapproval, so she set the plate and cup down on the doorstep and began to close the door.

'My mam's not there,' said the lad. 'She took ill with the fever and they took her to the workhouse. They want to send her back. They want to send us all back.'

'Is that why you ran away?' she asked. 'So you couldn't be sent back to Ireland?' The lad's behaviour suddenly made sense to her, and she was reminded of her husband Joshua and how he'd told her that he'd hidden at her father's farm, afraid of being sent back to the cotton plantation.

He nodded. 'But there's nothing for us there,' he said. 'They pulled down our house.'

She longed to bring him inside and care for him, but she knew that he would never agree to it.

'Go to Aileen,' she told him, and he nodded briefly, took his sack and stick and bounded up the steps and away.

Bessie closed the door and turned to face her maid and her sister. Dorothy looked worried and Peggy was furious.

'I don't know what John was thinking about!' she said. 'I had no idea the woman was ill with the fever.'

'Perhaps he didn't know,' said Bessie.

'No wonder they're keeping it a secret,' said Dorothy as she went to pick up the plate and the cup. She wrinkled her nose as she carried them in at arm's length. 'Shall I wash these, or throw them away?' she asked.

Bessie was about to say wash them, but a foreboding overcame her. 'Throw them away,' she agreed, only feeling slightly guilty that it would spoil her full set of crockery.

'I'm going to tell John,' announced Peggy as Bessie followed her back up the stairs. 'He can't argue with me now. It's doubtful the woman will live, and even if she does she's not coming near my daughters!'

Bessie decided not to tell her sister that John already knew. It was clear that Peggy wasn't going to relent. She would need to find some other way to help Kitty Cavanah and her family.

24

It was the middle of the night when Aileen heard someone in the court outside the door. She shook Michael's arm to wake him.

'Go and see who's there,' she told him, anxious about who might be prowling around at this time.

Michael grumbled but got up from the mattress and stepped over the sleeping bodies of Kitty's children to light a candle and unbar the door. Aileen watched him peer out into the darkness and heard him speak to someone. Moments later the boy, Timothy, came down the steps and paused on the threshold. There was barely a place for him to stand, never mind sit.

'Thank you, Lord!' said Aileen, offering a prayer of thanks to St Anthony for finding him. She moved on the mattress to make more room as Michael rebolted the door and told Timothy to sit down.

'We've been so worried about you. Why did you run away?' demanded Aileen in a ferocious whisper that she hoped wouldn't wake the other children.

'So that they wouldn't send me back,' he replied, as if the answer was obvious.

'No one is being sent back,' Aileen reassured him. 'Peter and Maria are here, and Agnes too. She says your mother is getting better and she'll come out soon. But she'll be too sick to work for a while. She'll need you,' Aileen told him fiercely. 'Are you hungry?'

'No. That woman on King Street gave me some bread and butter. She told me to come here.'

Thank goodness for that, thought Aileen, glad the woman who'd come to visit her had heeded her words. She meant well, she realized. She would thank her if she saw her again.

'Get down on the mattress between me and Michael,' she told him, 'and get some sleep.'

'Where will my mam sleep when she comes?' he asked as they huddled down together.

'We managed before and we'll manage again,' said Aileen. 'Don't you worry.' But the truth was that she was worried. Agnes was still very poorly, and even though the girl had said she was keen to go back to her work, Aileen thought it might be weeks before she was fit. Kitty, if she did come, would be similarly weakened by the fever and unable to work. It would be impossible for her and Michael to feed them all until they could fend for themselves again. She needed to get help from somewhere, and as she lay on the edge of sleep she thought that maybe she should seek out the young woman from King Street. She'd come to offer help, and although Aileen had been too proud to accept it, she realized that now they needed assistance from somebody, because it seemed that John

Sharples and his family weren't willing to shoulder their responsibilities.

'You can go home,' the doctor told Kitty next morning after he'd taken her pulse and looked down her throat.

'Do you have somewhere to go?' asked the nurse who had accompanied him on his ward round. 'We could arrange for you to be admitted to the workhouse as a pauper.'

'I have a place to go. And I have work,' Kitty told them, remembering the advice she'd been given by the family she'd travelled with from Liverpool.

'Good.' The nurse nodded before she moved on, and Kitty reached for her clothing before anyone could change their mind.

Her legs were shaky and she felt as if she was floating when she walked out through the gate. It was colder than she'd expected and she was momentarily confused when she reached the road and tried to remember the way she had to take to find Aileen and Michael's place.

She stood for a while as carts rolled past, their wheels squeaking and the horses that pulled them throwing up mud from their hooves. It was early and the sun had barely risen over the high roofs of the mill buildings all around her. The smell of refuse and human effluent wafted on the wind that was tunnelled through the narrow streets, and she almost laughed at the idea that it was the Irish who brought the fever when there was so much filth around the town.

In a gap between the carts, she crossed the road and began to walk in the shadow of the walls. She recognized the buildings as she approached the junction with Mincing Lane. She could find her way to Aileen's now, and once there she could rest and check that her children were well. Then she would have to decide what to do next. She was already aware that they couldn't stay with Aileen and Michael for long. Her friends had already done far more for her than she could ever have expected, and she wouldn't take advantage for a moment more than was absolutely necessary.

When Kitty turned into Butcher's Court, she felt her heart beating wildly through weakness and anxiety. She prayed that Agnes had got here safely and that the rest of her children had been spared the fever. She picked her way across the filth towards the steps that led down to Aileen's door, pleased to see that there were rags fluttering on the washing line. Her friend must have found time to go gathering.

The door stood open, and when Kitty bent to peer inside she saw Agnes sitting on the straw mattress sorting some odds and ends from a sack into Aileen's baskets.

'Mam!' her daughter cried and she got up to help Kitty down.

'Where are the others?' asked Kitty, peering into the gloomy corners of the underground room.

'Timothy's taken the little ones to look for rags.'

'Are they all well?' she asked anxiously.

Agnes nodded. 'They're fine. But Maria will be pleased to see you. She keeps asking when you're coming back.'

'And how are you?' Kitty asked her daughter as she sat down on the chair by the fire.

'I'm all right,' said Agnes. 'I wanted to go back to work but Aileen said not to just yet. So I'm sorting some finds out for her here.'

Kitty watched as Agnes continued her work – nails into one basket, bits of string into another, and odd buttons and bits of bone in a pile at her feet. Her daughter still looked pale and she was thankful that Aileen had kept her off from the tiring work at Mr Reynold's. She could easily have insisted that Agnes go and earn some money, and Kitty was grateful for the consideration.

'I'll go back in a day or two,' said Agnes. 'I know we need the money.' She paused to unknot some string. 'Where we will sleep?' she asked. 'There's no room here.'

'I don't know,' Kitty admitted wearily. It suddenly all seemed too much for her and she bit back the tears that were threatening. 'I wish your father were here,' she said, feeling desperately lonely and not knowing how much longer she could cope alone. She didn't know when she would feel strong enough to go gathering rags again, and even if she could make some money, the dosshouse was no solution. She was certain it was where they'd caught the fever. She couldn't risk her children's lives by taking them there again.

*

Aileen walked past the house on King Street for the third time, still gathering the courage to climb the steps and rap the shiny knocker at the centre of the smartly painted black door. As she passed again she saw the net curtains of the neighbouring house move and realized that she was being watched. She hoped no one would send for the constable. It was what they usually did when they saw the Irish in what they called *their part of town*.

Knowing that if she didn't do it now she would be forced to go back to Butcher's Court without completing her errand, Aileen took a determined breath and knocked. She waited, and was on the brink of turning away when she heard footsteps and the lock being turned. The door was opened, but it wasn't the young woman she'd come to see, but a stout older lady in a plain dress and apron.

'Can I help you?' she asked, sounding polite but looking at Aileen in what seemed a rather suspicious way.

'I was looking for somebody. I thought she lived here,' Aileen explained, wondering if Timothy had described the wrong house. 'I'm not sure of her name, but I think she has a baby and she sews garments,' she added, hoping that the woman might direct her to the right door. 'She's young.'

'Mrs Anderton?' asked the woman.

'I don't know,' Aileen confessed. 'She came to see me a few days ago and I sent her away, but now . . .' She hesitated under the woman's quizzical gaze. 'I thought she might be able to help my friend,' Aileen ended. She knew that she sounded unsure of herself and was on the point of turning away when the woman stood back and opened the door wider.

'I think you'd better step inside,' she said, glaring at the window where the curtain was still twitching. 'I'll tell Mrs Anderton you're here. What name shall I say?'

'Aileen Walsh,' she told her as she stepped inside and took in the hallway with its black and white tiled floor and the wooden bannisters that disappeared towards the ceiling from where a crystal chandelier hung. It was all very splendid, thought Aileen, wondering how the young couple had come by the money to buy a house like this.

The woman tapped on an oak door and Aileen heard a voice call her to go in. She opened it and slipped through, closing it after her whilst she spoke to whoever was in there. Aileen stood tapping her foot nervously, wondering if the only reason she'd been invited inside was so that the neighbours wouldn't see her.

Then the door was opened and the maid came back out, closely followed by the young woman who'd been to visit her.

'Aileen, isn't it?' she asked. 'I'm Mrs Anderton.'

'Forgive me for calling,' began Aileen. 'I didn't know what else to do.'

'How can I help you?' she asked kindly.

'I'm here about Kitty Cavanah,' she told them.

'Has she died?' asked the younger woman, sounding

distressed. Her face was filled with sympathy and Aileen warmed to her.

'No. She's getting better,' she explained. 'But I have her and her four little ones at my home now – and you saw it,' she appealed. 'We can't manage, but I can't just turn them out on to the street. And you did come to offer help.'

Mrs Anderton nodded. 'I did,' she said. 'And I will help. Will you accept some money?'

'It wouldn't go amiss, to feed the little ones, but it isn't a long-term solution,' Aileen told her. 'What they really need is a place to live, and work. They don't want to take charity. No matter what people think, none of us do.'

'I know,' said Mrs Anderton. 'I will help,' she promised again. 'I'll speak to my husband and see if there's a house they could have.' She paused for a moment. 'You gather rags?' she said. 'Is it possible to make a living from it?'

'It is if we work hard, my husband and myself,' Aileen told her. 'And I know that Kitty will work hard as soon as she feels better. The older ones will work as well. If she had somewhere to live it would really help her, but she won't be able to afford much rent.'

'Let me speak with my husband,' Mrs Anderton said. 'I'm sure we can come to some arrangement. You can tell Mrs Cavanah to call in a day or two. But . . .' She glanced at her maid who had stayed to hear the conversation, or to protect her mistress, Aileen wasn't sure which. 'Tell her to come to the back,' Mrs Anderton concluded.

Aileen nodded. She knew the reason for it and was surprised that she was shown to the front door herself, rather than being ushered through the kitchen and out into the alley.

'Can we do anything more to help them?' Bessie asked Joshua that evening as they sat together in the parlour. 'I know it should be up to John and Peggy really, but Peggy's so stubborn.' She sighed at the thought. She loved her sister but she tried her patience at times. 'John suggested they could employ Kitty Cavanah to help about the house, but Peggy won't hear of it, even though she's always complaining that John won't get anyone to help her. I despair. I really do.' She looked up to see Joshua chuckling. 'It's not funny.'

'Sure. It isn't,' he agreed, trying to compose his face. 'But your sister is so perverse sometimes all I can do is laugh.'

'She's prejudiced,' said Bessie. 'She's only refusing to employ the woman because she's Irish.'

Joshua's face became serious. Bessie knew that he'd been the victim of prejudice all his life, and even now there were businessmen who looked at him in horror when he walked into a meeting with them because they hadn't realized he was black. But it was easier for Joshua now that he was making a good living. His standing in the town had increased with his wealth and they had

Bessie's father to thank for that – the man who'd taken Joshua in when he had nothing. Unlike her sister, Bessie was confident that her husband wouldn't turn his back on the needs of the impoverished Irish family.

'It sure would help if Mrs Cavanah had a job,' he agreed. 'I shouldn't really be considering renting a property to someone without paid work.'

'Do you mean my father wouldn't approve?' asked Bessie.

'You know he'd want to help,' Joshua said, 'but it makes me feel uncomfortable. I'm employed to over-look his assets, not give them away.'

'I could write to him,' suggested Bessie. She could see that her husband was conflicted, that he wanted to find a home for this family but that he didn't want to let her father down.

'It would be months before a reply came back all the way from Wisconsin. Time is not on our side,' he told her.

'I could pay the rent out of the money I earn from my dressmaking,' suggested Bessie. She knew that legally the money wasn't hers and that she needed her husband's permission before she spent it, but she doubted Joshua would disagree.

However, he was shaking his head. 'You shouldn't have to do that,' he told her.

Bessie shrugged. 'It isn't as if I need it. I do the work because I enjoy it, not because I have to feed and clothe a family, and I want to help.'

'But it's for you and Julia.'

'To spend as I choose. You said that when I asked about beginning the business,' she reminded him.

He shook his head again. 'It's John Sharples who should be offering,' he said. 'The woman is his family.'

'Can he afford it?' asked Bessie.

'He's doing all right,' said Joshua. 'He can well afford a charwoman.'

'Then it's Peggy who's the real problem,' sighed Bessie. 'I need to go and talk some sense into her.'

Peggy hurried into the shop and a moment of disappointment jarred her when she saw that it was her sister and not a customer. Then the feeling was replaced with guilt. She ought to be glad to see her sister. But she suspected the reason Bessie had come, and it wasn't a conversation she was ready to have.

When she'd been to see Bessie, to ask for her support against John's suggestion that the Irish woman come to work for them, she'd felt cross and irritated that her sister hadn't immediately taken her side. It seemed perverse, although she and Bessie hadn't always seen eye to eye in the past. Now that her sister considered herself to be one of the gentry, Peggy wasn't surprised that Bessie suddenly wanted to play the lady bountiful. But it wasn't her house where the Irish woman would be working. Bessie had Dorothy, and Dorothy was lovely and trustworthy.

'Are you busy?' asked Bessie.

'I've no customers, but I've a lot to do,' Peggy replied. 'What do you want?'

'I can come back later.'

'No. Say what you've come to say,' Peggy told her, bracing herself for an onslaught of accusations about her selfishness.

'I've not come to argue,' said Bessie.

'Of course not.'

Peggy locked eyes with her sister's blue gaze. Her father's eyes, she thought. Everyone else in the family was brown-eyed. It should have been clear from the day that Bessie was born that she wasn't really Titus's daughter. But Peggy would never have believed her mother would carry on with another man, not until it had all come out.

'You'd best sit down,' she conceded after a moment. 'I'll put the kettle on. Call if anyone comes in.'

Peggy hurried up the stairs and stood for a moment on the landing, trying to compose herself. She didn't want to fall out with her sister, and, heaven knows, she didn't want to fall out with her husband, but neither of them seemed capable of seeing things from her point of view. They knew nothing about this Irish woman. It would be madness to have her here, poking about in their home.

She took her time brewing the tea, but when she carried the cups carefully down and set Bessie's beside her on the counter, her sister smiled warmly and thanked her.

'Mind the gloves,' warned Peggy, knowing she sounded rude.

Bessie didn't reply. She picked up the cup and took a drink then set it back down carefully.

'I had a visit from Aileen Walsh,' she told Peggy.

'Aye? And who's she when she's at home?'

'She's looking after Kitty Cavanah and her children. Some of them have been unwell.'

'Fever?' asked Peggy. 'It's a good job I told John I'd not have the woman near Becky and Emily.' Peggy felt goosebumps rise on her arms at the thought that if she hadn't been so certain that the idea was a bad one, her own daughters might have contracted the Irish Fever.

'I don't know for certain. But probably, yes. It's not surprising,' Bessie went on. 'Nobody should have to live like they do. It's a hundred times worse than Paradise Lane. At least we were above the ground and there wasn't filth swilling down the street.'

'I don't know why they come here when there's no work,' said Peggy. She tended to agree with the parish guardians that the immigrants should all be sent back. Blackburn had its own poor to support and charity had to begin at home.

'There would be work if the mill owners would employ them,' Bessie told her. 'But the locals refuse to work with them. It isn't their fault. This family saw their home destroyed in front of their eyes. The landlord did give them tickets for the New World, but they were lost when her husband drowned on the voyage over. None of it is her fault,' Bessie insisted. 'She came here because she thought her family would help her, but it's been left to strangers to take them in.'

Peggy saw that her sister meant to have her say, so she didn't interrupt her, but none of it was changing her mind very much. She still didn't believe the woman was related to John. She still believed she was a charlatan.

'Joshua says he'll try to find them a house, but they need to be earning something to pay towards the rent. It would cause too much resentment amongst the other tenants if they thought the newcomers had been given a house when they had no jobs. The daughter was working for the rag merchant and she'll go back when she's better. If you would only be reasonable and give Mrs Cavanah a chance, then I'm sure they would be able to scrape by. The lad could continue the rag gathering until something better came along, and maybe he could watch the younger ones as well.'

'You've got it all sorted out,' Peggy replied, fidgeting with her display of lace collars and handkerchiefs.

'I'm just trying to help,' said her sister. 'And I know John wants to help them as well.'

'So it's just me being stubborn?' Peggy felt her temper rising. Why could none of them see reason?

Bessie didn't reply straight away, which made Peggy certain that her sister did think she was being deliberately difficult.

'Why not give her a chance?' she asked.

'You know why.'

'I'm surprised at you, our Peggy,' her sister told her. She sounded disappointed and it pricked Peggy's conscience. But it wasn't that she was an unkind person, she told herself. She liked to think that she would help anyone in need, but she was sure that this Irish woman was just trying to take advantage of them. She was sure that if they stood firm she would take herself and her children off to try their luck in some other town, telling the same sob story.

'Why don't you employ her thyself?' she snapped back.

'I might,' replied Bessie. 'But don't expect John to find you a maid or a charwoman in the future. He'll be right to think you can manage without if you say no to his suggestion. And don't keep expecting our mam to mind your children. She's not getting any younger and you can't keep taking advantage of her.'

'I'm not taking advantage! She wants to do it!' protested Peggy, thinking that her sister was hitting very low now, even though deep down she knew that her mother was struggling.

'She'll tell you that. But take a step back, Peggy, and try not to see things just from your own point of view all the time. Mam's looking tired and your lasses can be a handful.'

'I think you'd better go,' Peggy muttered. She suddenly wanted her sister out of her shop. She was so angry that she was almost tempted to slap her, and it wouldn't look very professional if anyone passing the window witnessed it.

'Aye, I'll go,' said Bessie. 'Thanks for the tea.' She got up and went to the door. Peggy thought she was going to leave without another word, but she turned back before closing it behind her.

'Think about it, Peggy,' she pleaded. 'It would solve a lot of problems – a lot of your problems, not just Mrs Cavanah's.'

Peggy remained stubbornly silent and stared at the countertop. She didn't look up until she was sure that her sister had passed the window and was well on her way up the street.

'What's up with thee?' asked her mother later that afternoon when she brought Peggy's daughters home.

Emily was trying to teach Becky to count the fish in the aquarium, but she couldn't keep up with them herself and was telling them off for swimming around.

'Keep still, you fishes!' she berated them.

Normally it would have made Peggy laugh, but she was still cross about her exchange with her sister because she knew that what Bessie had said was true. Her mother did look tired.

'John wants us to employ the Irish woman and our Bessie agrees with him. It makes me so cross that they won't see the woman is just out to trick them.'

'Dost tha think she is?' asked her mother as she sat down.

'Of course. She must be. It makes no sense her suddenly appearing out of nowhere and telling some tale about being a cousin. No one ever talked about any cousins before. And her story about her husband being drowned is just ridiculous.'

'I wouldn't know,' said her mother. 'But I've heard that boats do go down sometimes.'

'You don't mind looking after the lasses, do you?' Peggy asked her mother, changing the subject.

'Of course not. Tha knows I'll have them anytime. Why that look?' she asked her.

'I'm worried it might be getting too much for you.'

'Well, I'm not as young as I once was,' her mother admitted. 'But I'm not so decrepit yet that I can't help out.'

Peggy was distracted by her daughters who had now begun to argue about the fish. 'Go and hang up your hats and jackets!' she told them. 'Do you want some tea?' she asked, turning back to her mother.

'No.' She shook her head. 'Best get back.' She kissed Peggy's cheek and pulled her shawl around her shoulders as she went to the top of the stairs, then she paused. 'I wouldn't mind a day off now and again,' she admitted. 'And tha's been pestering John about some help for a while. He's only tryin' to do what's right. Don't be too quick to judge, Peggy. We used to be poor. There's no shame in it.'

25

Kitty approached the back door of the Andertons' house on King Street warily. Aileen had told her that Mrs Anderton was keen to help her, but Kitty could see no reason why she would want to and it made her suspicious. She had hoped help would have been forthcoming from her own family, and although Aileen had told her that she'd discovered Mrs Anderton was Mrs Sharples's sister, it still didn't seem quite right. Mrs Sharples had made it quite clear that she and her husband would do nothing for them. So why did the sister want to help?

It wasn't until she reached the top of the steps that she saw the baby carriage. It had been left outside the back door, possibly because it was too big to fit inside. But as she approached it, she heard a whimpering sound that almost overwhelmed her. There was a baby inside it!

Kitty felt every nerve in her body sparking as she reached down into the carriage and moved aside the blanket. The crumpled little face inside made her want to weep.

Not able to help herself, she tucked her hands under the warm, solid body and picked the baby up, feeling the weight that her empty arms had been aching for, for so long now. She pressed the child against her breasts, rocking it and holding it close.

'Hush, hush. You're safe now. I have you. I have you,' she soothed.

Kitty pressed her lips to the child's bonneted head, drawing in the mixed aromas of soap and starch, and the unmistakeable baby smell that all her children had shared. Her breasts felt as if they were afire and she longed to feel the tiny pink mouth suckling from her, but Kitty knew that her milk had dried up long since and that it would be impossible for her to feed the baby.

'Hush, hush,' she said again as she raised the baby to her shoulder, cradling its head with a hand and gently jogging it up and down. 'I know you're hungry. I'll get you some food. I promise I will.'

She closed her eyes and joy flooded through her. The child in her arms made her feel that the part of her that had been ripped away had now been made whole again. She felt complete as she kissed the soft skin of the baby's cheek and began to sing the old Irish lullaby that had sent all her children to sleep.

But the baby wouldn't settle and Kitty decided that she must find some milk to make the child feel better. There was a place that she'd passed on her way here, where she'd seen women going in with their kits to be filled. So, with the baby clutched in her arms, she hurriedly retraced her steps.

*

The knocking on the front door had been so loud and so insistent that Bessie lost her concentration and the sharp needle she was sewing with pierced the skin of her thumb, making her give a sharp little cry. She dropped the gown to her lap and sucked the edge of her thumb to prevent any drops of blood reaching her work. The gown was cream silk. It was almost finished and a stain at this stage would be a disaster when she'd promised Mrs Dewhurst that it would be ready by Friday.

Alarmed by such insistent knocking in the middle of the morning – a time that visitors never called and when there were no appointments for fittings – Bessie put her work carefully aside and opened the door of her workroom to lean over the bannister rail as she heard Dorothy's footsteps crossing the hallway from the breakfast room to answer the door.

The person on the doorstep sounded agitated. For a moment, Bessie wondered if it was Kitty Cavanah, but the strident tone sounded more like her neighbour Mrs Briggs. Perhaps she'd seen the rag gatherers in the back again and had come to blame her, thought Bessie with an inward sigh.

She was surprised when Dorothy drew the woman inside and shut the door. It was indeed Mrs Briggs and the woman appeared wild-eyed and distraught. She'd better go down and see if she could pacify her.

As she came down the stairs she heard her neighbour gabbling something about a baby as Dorothy tried to calm her and make sense of what she was saying.

'Where's Julia?' Bessie demanded as she ran down the last steps. Ignoring Mrs Briggs, she took hold of Dorothy by the arm to get her attention. 'Where's Julia?' she repeated as her heart rate soared and panic filled her.

'She's at the back door. I put her outside to get some fresh air. It's such a lovely sunny morning . . .'

'That woman took her!' interrupted Mrs Briggs. 'I saw her with my own eyes. I knew no good would come of encouraging those Irish women!'

'Took her?'

Bessie stared at Mrs Briggs, not sure what the woman was talking about.

'Your baby. She took your baby!' Mrs Briggs shouted at her as if she thought Bessie was an imbecile.

Bessie met Dorothy's glance for less than a second before they both turned and Bessie followed her maid down the steps to the kitchen, wishing that she would be quicker. The need to check that Julia was safe overpowered her. When they reached the bottom she pushed past Dorothy and yanked open the door.

The first thing that Bessie saw was the baby carriage. Relief swept over her but was quickly replaced by disbelief when she went to lift her daughter and found the pram empty. It was still warm. Bessie's hand rested on the cotton sheet where her daughter had been lying until moments ago. She looked around the small yard. It was empty. She looked up into the back alley. There was nobody there.

'I told you!' announced Mrs Briggs, who had followed them down the stairs. 'I saw her. I saw her from my window.' She pointed up to the back windows of the house next door, swathed in transparent net curtains where she seemed to spend much of her time watching the comings and goings in the alley.

'Where is she? Where's Julia?' Bessie heard the cry come from her own mouth. But it didn't sound like her. The voice was that of a demented banshee.

'I . . . I . . .' Dorothy seemed bewildered and lost for words as she looked into the empty baby carriage and then at the yard. 'I don't understand.'

'You need to fetch the constable,' announced Mrs Briggs as if she was proud to be the bearer of such awful news. 'He needs to search those Irish dwellings before something bad happens to the child.'

'No. No. We'll find her,' replied Bessie. 'Dorothy, help me look for her. She can't be far away.'

'I think we should get the constable,' Dorothy agreed. All the colour had drained from her face and she looked white and ten years older as she stared at Bessie. 'I'm sorry,' she said, beginning to cry. 'I'm sorry, Mrs Anderton. I shouldn't have left her unattended. I only went upstairs to fetch down the breakfast pots to be washed.'

'What did you see?' Bessie demanded of Mrs Briggs. 'Did you see who took her?'

'I saw one of those Irish women in your yard. I saw her lift the baby from the carriage. I could see she was intent on stealing her. That's why I came to warn you.'

Bessie ran up the yard steps and looked up and down the back. There was no sign of anyone. She ran down to the end of the alley and out on to King Street, searching for any sign of a woman carrying a baby.

'Mrs Anderton!' She felt Dorothy touch her arm and turned, hoping to see Julia in her arms. But Dorothy's arms were empty. 'Mrs Anderton, you can't go out on to the street with no bonnet or jacket,' her maid insisted.

'Go back to the house!' replied Bessie as she pulled her arm away, gathered her skirts and began to run towards the centre of the town. She didn't care what she looked like, or what people thought of her. She had to find her daughter.

Kitty joined the end of the queue of women outside the milk shop. The baby was quieter now and she cradled it gently as she waited. Some of the other women smiled at her and the child, admiring the blanket it was wrapped in and the quality of its little bonnet. The approbation made Kitty feel proud. For the first time since she'd arrived in Blackburn she felt as if she fitted in.

But as she neared the front of the queue and watched the woman behind the counter dip her ladle into the buckets of milk and pour the liquid carefully into the kits that were handed over to hold it, Kitty realized she had no container with her – and, worse, no money.

When it was her turn to be served, she approached with some trepidation.

'I just need some milk for the baby,' she said, hoping that the woman would be kind.

'Where's thy kit then?' asked the woman, eyeing her suspiciously.

'I haven't brought one. I only need a few drops. Could you lend me something to hold it?'

The woman pursed her lips and put a hand on her hip.

'I've nowt,' she said. 'Tha'll have to come back.'

'But the baby's hungry,' replied Kitty. 'I only need a cupful.'

'Give her a cup, tha stingy cow,' said the woman behind her. 'It'll not break thee.'

'No, but I'd soon be shuttin' up shop if I gave stuff away to every Tom, Dick and Harry who came in unprepared.'

'I'd bring the cup back,' said Kitty. 'I promise.'

The woman looked her up and down. 'Tha's Irish,' she accused as if it were a sin. 'Dost tha not feed thine own brats?'

'My milk dried up. I've been ill.'

Kitty heard the swift intakes of breath all around her as the women tried to step away from her without it being obvious.

'Give her a cup of milk and send her on her way,' said one as she covered her mouth and nose with the edge of her shawl.

Kitty watched as the shopkeeper reached up for a cup from the shelf behind her. It was chipped, and had a black crack running down one side. Kitty suspected it hadn't been washed in a long time, but she knew better than to complain. The woman dipped her ladle into a bucket and filled the cup before pushing it across the counter.

'That'll be a ha'penny,' she said.

'I've no money.'

'Oh ye gods and little fishes!' burst out the exasperated woman. 'Why doesn't that surprise me? Get on out o' my shop!' she told Kitty, glaring at her with undisguised animosity.

'But the baby . . .' Kitty shifted the weight of the child from one shoulder to the other as it began to whimper again. 'It's hungry.'

'Give her the cup of milk and then she can be gone,' advised the woman who was still holding her shawl across her face.

Her plea was greeted with murmurs of agreement and the cup was pushed further towards Kitty.

'Tek it and get out,' said the shopkeeper. 'And don't come back!' she added as Kitty gratefully picked up the milk. 'Don't even bother to bring back that cup. I'd only smash it after it's been in thy filthy hands!'

Kitty walked out, past the curious onlookers who were queuing behind her. She could feel her cheeks burning with shame and anger. She held the milk carefully as she crossed the cobbled street, searching for somewhere to sit down away from any crowd that might jostle the precious liquid from her grasp.

There was a bridge nearby that spanned the lazy river that flowed below. Several people had already taken advantage of the low stone wall on either side of it and Kitty saw a place near another woman but away from two men who already had beer in their hands, despite it being so early in the morning.

She sat down and put the cup beside her before arranging the child in her arms. The baby's eyes were a liquid brown as they stared up at her, and its hair almost jet black, and curly too, noticed Kitty as she tucked a stray strand back under the embroidered bonnet. Not sure how to get the milk to the baby's mouth, she first dipped her finger into the cup and offered it to the child. She felt the warm gums close firmly around her finger and thought she could feel the edge of a sharp tooth coming through at the bottom as the baby sucked fiercely. The pressure pleased her and after a moment she pulled her finger free and dipped it into the milk again. Kitty knew that it would take a long time to finish the feed in this way, but she couldn't think how else it might be done.

Bessie ran up King Street, ignoring the stares of the businessmen going to their offices and the morning vendors carrying trays of pies. As she ran, her eyes scanned both sides of the street for a woman with a baby. There was no sign of her. It must have been Kitty Cavanah, she thought. Who else could it have been at her back door? And why had Dorothy left Julia unattended? She'd trusted her maid to mind the child whilst she worked, and she'd let her down. And what was she going to say to Joshua? He'd caught the early coach into Manchester. She had to find Julia before he came home. She didn't know how she would face him otherwise.

She paused to catch her breath as a cart went by and then she crossed the road by the Sun Inn and began to walk down Church Street, towards the parish church. She wondered whether to call at Peggy's shop and ask her to come out and help, but she knew her sister would try to blame her for encouraging the Irish woman, and Peggy proved correct was something she didn't feel she could face right now.

Bessie crossed the churchyard and made her way towards Salford Bridge. She had no idea what led her in that direction. It didn't even seem a choice. She simply felt compelled to keep walking.

Men stared at her uncovered hair and a few women with baskets over their arms, on the way to market, gave her dark looks. Bessie paid them no heed. Anyone who wasn't carrying a baby held no interest for her.

She saw a woman with a child, walking away from her, and she broke into a run to catch her up.

'Stop! Stop!' she called as people on the street paused to turn and look, and a couple of shopkeepers came to their doors, wiping their hands on their long white aprons, to see what was going on. 'Stop!' called Bessie again and the woman with the baby turned to face her.

It wasn't Kitty Cavanah, and the baby wasn't Julia. Her hopes plummeted and she apologized. 'I thought you were someone else,' she explained. 'Have you seen anyone else carrying a baby?' she pleaded.

'No.' The woman shook her head and she held her own child closer, obviously unsure of Bessie and why she was running down the streets only half dressed.

'My child is missing,' she explained. 'Are you sure you haven't seen anyone?'

The other mother's face softened as if she suddenly understood and would have done the same if it were her child.

'There was a woman sitting on Salford Bridge with a baby,' she told Bessie. 'She was trying to give it milk from a cup. That's why I noticed. It seemed such a strange thing to do.'

Without waiting to thank her, Bessie began to run again, praying that the woman would still be there and that the child would be Julia.

Kitty was mostly unaware of the people going by. Every now and again there was a cart and the wheels seemed very close, but she didn't move because the milk wasn't finished and she thought she might not find anywhere better to sit.

Having decided that dipping her finger into the milk was fairly useless, she was now lifting the cup to the baby's mouth and letting a few drops dribble in at a time, but the child was refusing to drink and most of the milk was being spilled on her lovely little gown. Kitty wondered if Aileen would allow her to wash it. The child would be all right, wrapped in the blanket until it dried, she thought.

'She's not yours! Give her to me!'

Kitty held the baby closer as someone tried to prise the child from her grasp.

'No!' she protested. She wouldn't let go again. She wouldn't!

'Give me my baby!' insisted the voice.

Kitty put down the milk and wrapped her arms protectively round the child. She felt the sharp fingernails on the bare skin of her hands as the girl dug them in. 'Let her go! Help me,' she appealed to passers-by. 'This woman has stolen my child.'

'I haven't stolen her,' protested Kitty as a crowd gathered around.

'She's Irish,' said someone as if that proved her guilt.

'Get the constable. He'll sort it out,' advised someone else.

Bessie stared at Julia, clasped in the arms of Kitty Cavanah. The Irish woman was strong and was holding the child tightly, too tightly, thought Bessie, thinking that the woman might smother Julia under her dirty shawl. All she wanted was her daughter in her own arms, but nobody seemed willing to help her. There was a crowd growing around her and a lot of talking and whispering, but it seemed that people had only come to watch what was happening and were unwilling to get involved.

'She's stolen my child! Please help me!' begged Bessie, but the women who had stopped on their journey back home from the market, with their filled baskets over their arms, shook their heads and advised her to wait for the constable to come. It was clear they didn't want to get into trouble by taking sides, and Bessie realized that with her bare head and no jacket the townsfolk took her for a girl whose reputation was somewhat questionable and didn't recognize her as the respectable wife of a businessman.

She turned back to Kitty Cavanah, whose eyes were downcast as she held Julia tightly. Bessie knew that she ought to think carefully and use some tact to retrieve her daughter, but all she wanted to do was get Julia from the woman, whatever it took.

She was aware of the crowd being pushed aside behind her and glanced around to see if it was the constable. But relief almost overwhelmed her when she recognized her brother-in-law, John Sharples, carrying his post bag.

'What's going on?' he asked, looking bewildered by the scene that met him.

'She's stolen Julia!' Bessie told him, hoping that he could do something. 'She won't give her back to me!'

Kitty flinched when she felt the hand on her arm. She heard someone say her name but she didn't look up.

'Mrs Cavanah! Kitty!' insisted the voice as someone crouched down beside her. 'Give me the baby.'

'No. I have to keep the child safe,' she replied.

'Give her to me!' Kitty heard a woman scream, but the man put out a hand to hold whoever it was back.

'Leave this to me,' he said. 'I don't think she means Julia any harm. Kitty!' He spoke to her again. 'Do you know me? It's John Sharples.'

Kitty looked up and saw the face of the man who was her cousin looming close to her. Had he come to help her at last? She looked beyond him to the woman who was on her knees in the middle of the road, sobbing. Her face was contorted and her nose was running and she was wiping it on her sleeve as if she had no rag to use.

The baby in her arms began to cry in unison. The child's screams reached a piercing level that could be heard over all the other hubbub, and Kitty wondered why there were so many people standing around watching her.

'Kitty,' said John Sharples again. 'Give me the baby.'

It was what the man on the boat had said. He'd tried to prise the baby from her arms, but she'd clung on to him. She'd been afraid they were going to throw him across the raging sea, as they had done with Maria. Maria had been lucky. Someone had caught her, but she wasn't going to risk anyone dropping her youngest child.

'No!' she said, reliving the shipwreck. 'I can hold on to him.'

Kitty struggled to get it clear in her mind. The man had told her to jump and she hadn't wanted to. The man had shouted at her that the ship was sinking and she needed to get off. She hadn't been ready when he'd pushed her and suddenly everything had been black. Sound had been muffled. There had been bubbles. Then she'd been gasping to get her breath and someone had pulled her hair. Then she was on the deck of the ship and her arms had been empty.

As the awful truth of what had happened became clear to her, Kitty heard herself let out a wail of despair. She'd let go of her child. The waves had pulled and sucked him from her grasp. She'd let him go. She was his mother and she'd let him go.

Now people were trying to take this child away from her. She was shaking her head. She mustn't let this child go. She needed to protect it. It was Mrs Anderton's child. She knew that. But someone had abandoned it in the back alley with all the other rubbish, waiting to be taken away. She'd saved it. She mustn't let it go now. She had to keep it safe.

'No!' she wailed again as strong arms pulled hers apart and someone lifted the baby from her. 'No!'

'It's all right. It's all right,' said someone. Kitty thought it must be John Sharples. He was pulling her to her feet. He had an arm around her as the crowd jostled her and she felt the spittle on her cheek as someone spat at her.

Then there was a booming voice and she could hear people saying the word *constable*. And some were saying *prison* and Kitty cowered into the protection of John Sharples's arms and wished that they would all go away.

Bessie ran forward as Julia was taken from Kitty Cavanah's arms. John Sharples handed her daughter to her and she hugged her tightly, burrowing her face against the baby's and kissing her over and over again as she wept with relief. Julia was still screaming and Bessie tried to soothe her.

'Shush, shush,' she sobbed. 'You're safe now. You're safe now.'

The crowd around her began to say that the constable was here, and Mr Lewis pushed his way through.

'What's going on here?' he demanded, frightening both Bessie and Julia with his loud, booming voice.

'It's nothing,' she heard John tell him. 'Just a misunderstanding. It's all been sorted out now.'

'I was told there was a kidnapping,' he said, sounding disappointed that he might not be needed after all.

'No. Just a misunderstanding,' John reassured him.

'Who are you?' demanded the constable and it was a moment before Bessie realized he was speaking to her.

'I'm Mrs Anderton.'

'Whose is that child?'

'She's my daughter, Julia.'

'It's true,' Bessie heard John tell him. 'Mrs Anderton is my sister-in-law. The child is hers.'

'So who's that?

'This is Mrs Cavanah. She's my cousin. She's unwell, but I'll take care of her.'

The constable seemed satisfied with the explanation, even though many in the crowd were shouting various versions of the events at him and demanding that he arrest one or both of the women.

'Come on,' said John as he came to Bessie with his arm still around Kitty Cavanah. 'Let's get away from here before things turn nasty.'

26

Peggy knew that it couldn't be John back from his rounds so soon and she hurried to take her place behind the shop counter with a ready smile to greet a customer. But the sight that met her rendered her speechless with both disbelief and horror. John was ushering two distraught and dishevelled women into her shop, and it was a moment before she recognized one of them as her sister.

'Bessie,' she gasped. 'What's happened?'

'Take her upstairs,' said John. 'Make her a cup of tea. She's had a bit of a fright.'

Peggy reached for her sister and ushered her towards the stairs. She had Julia in her arms and the little girl was red in the face and crying. But it was Bessie's appearance that shocked her most. She had no hat and coat on and she was gasping for breath as she sobbed uncontrollably. It was clear that something was very wrong.

'What happened?' she asked again as she turned back at the door that led to the stairs and saw John sitting the woman she now saw was Kitty Cavanah on her customers' chair. 'You can't leave her there. What if someone comes in?'

'I'm closing the shop for a while,' replied John, going

to the door. Peggy watched as he dropped the latch and drew down the blind. John never shut the shop. Whatever had happened, it must be something serious.

'Have you delivered the letters?' she asked him, looking at the bag that was still slung across his shoulder.

'No. They can wait. See to thy sister,' he told her.

Peggy ran up the stairs and found Bessie standing in the middle of her sitting room, holding Julia tightly.

'What happened?' she asked again as she guided her to a chair, not even able to imagine what might have caused so much upset. 'Why are you and Julia not at home? Why's John brought that Irish woman in here?'

'She stole my baby,' said Bessie as she sat down. She looked white and shocked and her voice was shaking. Peggy couldn't recall ever having seen her sister upset like this.

'No!' Peggy sat down opposite her sister and her niece and stared at them. It didn't seem possible. 'What did you do?'

'I chased after her,' said Bessie. Her bright eyes filled with fresh tears as she explained to her sister what had happened.

'Oh, Bessie.' Peggy knelt beside her sister and hugged her. 'That's terrible,' she said. But it was only a moment before her concern turned to anger. 'So why has John brought that woman here?' she demanded. 'She should be in the lock-up!'

Peggy stormed back down to the shop to tell John that the Irish woman had to go. She couldn't even bear the thought of her sitting on the chair. She would have to clean it, or burn it. Aye, she thought, she'd burn it and buy a new one.

She stopped as she saw John holding the woman's hands. He was on his knees beside her and was talking to her gently. The sight incensed Peggy.

'Get her out of here!' she shouted at him.

John glanced up and shook his head slightly. 'She's not well.'

'All the more reason to get her out. You don't want Emily and Becky to catch the fever, do you? And I hope she's passed nothing on to little Julia. Bessie says she stole her from their back yard. You'll have to fetch the constable. She'll have to go to prison. She can't go round stealing children!'

'Peggy. Calm down,' said John.

'Calm down?' she raged at him. 'What do you mean, *calm down*? I don't know what you're thinking of bringing that woman in here after what she's done. Our Bessie's beside herself. Do you not care about her at all?'

'Of course I care about her,' John protested. 'But Julia is safe now and Kitty's unwell. I can't let the constable take her. She needs help.'

'She needs no such thing. She needs to be locked up! Get her out!' Peggy repeated. 'I don't want to see her in here when I come back down,' she warned John as she headed for the stairs to go back up and comfort her sister.

*

Kitty was only vaguely aware of the talk going on around her. All she knew was that her arms were empty again. The baby was gone. And it was her own fault. She should have held him tighter.

'Come on,' said John Sharples. 'I'll take you to Aileen and then we'll decide what can be done.'

Kitty stood up and made no protest as he led her to the door and out on to the street. They walked. Kitty wasn't sure of the way. She could hear people shouting, but she didn't know why. At last they turned into Butcher's Court and she saw the rags drying on the line and she remembered that she'd collected nothing that morning and she began to cry again because she didn't know how she was going to feed her other children.

'What's wrong?' she heard Aileen ask. 'What's happened to her? She looks terrible.'

Kitty heard John Sharples speaking to Aileen about the baby. 'Take care of her for now,' she heard him say. 'I promise I'll do something to help.'

'Come inside,' said Aileen when John had gone.

Kitty followed her friend down the steps and Aileen told her to sit in the chair whilst she added some more sticks to the fire and set some water to boil in the kettle.

'Where are my children?' Kitty asked after a few moments, realizing that there was no sign of them.

'Timothy and Maria have gone to help Michael. They've taken little Peter with them. And Agnes has gone to speak to Mr Reynolds about starting work for him again.'

'She's still not well,' said Kitty.

'She's getting stronger every day,' replied Aileen. 'And she's keen to work.'

'I wish she didn't have to,' said Kitty.

'Well, it'll do her no good to sit about moping. She's young and strong. She'll be all right.' Aileen poured the boiling water on to a spoonful of tea leaves. 'What on earth made you do it?' she asked as she set it to brew.

'Do what?'

'Take Mrs Anderton's baby.'

'I didn't take the baby. The poor mite had been left in the back alley,' explained Kitty. 'I just went to get it some milk.'

Her friend looked unconvinced.

'Mrs Anderton had offered to help you. I'm not sure she will now,' said Aileen. 'It was a stupid thing to do.'

As Aileen poured the tea into two cups, Kitty saw that her friend's hands were trembling and realized that she was angry with her.

'I didn't mean any harm,' she said.

Aileen handed her a cup. 'Mrs Anderton was your best hope of getting help,' she told her. 'But now you've ruined it. And I'm not sure how much longer you can stay here. There isn't really room, and whilst I didn't mind helping out . . . well, you can't stay here for ever.'

Kitty sipped the weak tea. 'I know,' she said. 'I'm grateful for everything you and Michael have done for us since we arrived.'

Aileen nodded. It was obvious that she didn't like having to tell the truth about the situation to Kitty.

'If we had more room it might be different,' she said.

'I know. I understand,' replied Kitty. 'I don't want to be a burden.'

'What will you do?' asked Aileen after a moment.

Kitty shrugged. 'Perhaps I should move on,' she said. 'As soon as I'm properly well. Perhaps I should go to Stockport or a place where there might be more work. I don't think it was a good idea to come here after all.' She wiped a tear on the back of her hand and took another sip of the tea. 'I don't think my husband will come looking for us,' she admitted. 'I don't think he survived.'

Kitty gave an involuntary shudder as she forced herself to face the truth. Her baby had been lost in the sea and it was probable that her husband had been drowned as well, because surely he would have found her by now if he was still alive.

'I'm sorry,' said Aileen, putting a hand on her shoulder. 'Believe me, I'm really sorry for what's happened to you and your children. But we can't go on like this.'

'I know,' said Kitty.

'Mrs Anderton was keen to help you,' said Aileen again with a sigh. 'It's such a shame that it had to end like this,' she added. Then she put her cup on the table and went outside.

Kitty was sorry that her friend was so upset about what had happened, but she'd been so distracted by the baby that she hadn't been able to think of anything else. She'd been wrong to intervene. But it had been alone and hungry. And Kitty wasn't convinced that Mrs Anderton had ever really intended to do anything for her anyway. Why would she? She wasn't even a cousin. And even though John Sharples had come to help her when the locals had turned nasty, he'd brought her back to Butcher's Court and left her here.

Kitty took another sip of her tea. It became clear to her that she must leave Blackburn. There was nothing for her here. As soon as she was strong enough to walk, she would set off with the children and they would go to Stockport and try to find the friends whom she'd met at the asylum shelter in Liverpool. She would do everything possible to find work and a place to live. And if by some miracle her husband did come, Kitty hoped that Aileen would be good enough to tell him where he could find them.

27

Peggy sighed as the insistent knocking came again. 'Can't they see we're closed?' she demanded.

'Perhaps you'd better go down. It might be important,' said Bessie, who was cradling her daughter to her as the child suckled hungrily.

Peggy stomped down the stairs and shouted across the shop. 'We're closed! You'll have to come back later!' She didn't even care if she was offending her customers. She didn't feel able to put on a bright smile and deal with anyone at the moment.

But the knocking came again, furiously this time.

'Peggy? It's thy mother!'

Peggy rushed to the door and opened it to find her mother on the doorstep. She looked white and shocked.

'Where's our Bessie? Has she got Julia? Is she all right?'

'Aye. She's upstairs. She's got the baby,' responded Peggy, letting her mother in and relocking the door. 'Where's Emily and Becky?' she asked, suddenly feeling a frisson of the fear that must have beset her sister.

'They're with thy father. I just slipped out to buy some milk and the whole town's afire with some tale about our Bessie's child being taken by an Irish woman.'

'It's true. It was Kitty Cavanah,' Peggy told her.

'But Bessie's got her now, hasn't she? Julia's safe? Where are they? They weren't at home and Dorothy's frantic.'

'They're here. Upstairs.'

Her mother hurried to the steps and climbed as quickly as she could, but she was very breathless by the time she reached the top step, Peggy noticed, and she could hear her chest wheezing with the effort.

'Let me see her,' she gasped as she went to where Bessie was sitting. 'Is she all right?'

'There's no real harm done,' Bessie reassured her mother. 'It was frightening, but she's safe now.'

'I still think that woman should have been handed over to the constable,' said Peggy.

'How would that have helped?' asked Bessie. 'The woman's obviously deranged, but putting her in the prison when she has childer of her own wouldn't be right.'

'But she stole Julia!' protested Peggy. 'What would have happened if you hadn't found her?'

She saw a shudder run through her sister and Bessie rocked her daughter even closer to her.

Peggy's mother shook her head. 'We don't need to talk about that,' she warned. 'Thy sister's upset enough as it is. And what's done is done.'

'So are we just going to let her get away with it?' demanded Peggy.

'No,' said her mother. 'I daresay that the parish will send her back to Ireland now.'

The bell rang on the shop door again and a moment later John came up the stairs.

'I've taken her back to Aileen Walsh,' he told them. 'She's very upset. I don't think she meant any harm. She lost a baby of her own, and I think it's turned her mind. She was only trying to help. It seems when she heard the child crying she thought it was hungry and she wanted to feed it.'

'That's nonsense!' burst out Peggy.

'Don't judge her too harshly,' replied John. 'She's been through a lot.'

'She told Dorothy about her baby,' said Bessie. 'I think she lost it in a shipwreck. It doesn't bear thinking about. Poor woman.'

'Don't tell me you have some sympathy for her?' Peggy demanded.

'It was bad enough not knowing where Julia was for such a short time,' said Bessie. 'It must be unbearable to lose a child as she did and never know what happened to it.'

'I can't believe you're all making excuses for her!' exclaimed Peggy.

'Make some tea, our Peggy,' said her mother. It had always been her response to trouble. 'Then I'll take them both home. Dorothy was frantic and we need to put the woman's mind at peace. Where's Joshua today?' she asked Bessie.

'In Manchester,' said Bessie. She lifted her daughter from her breast.

'Will tha tell him what happened?'

'Of course,' said Bessie. 'Why would I keep it from him?'

'Aye, well, he's not one for revenge. I'm sure he'll see reason,' said her mother.

'I'll lend you my hairbrush,' Peggy told her sister. 'And a jacket and hat to walk home. You can't go like that.

'You see. I was right,' Peggy told John when her mother and sister had gone. 'The woman's not to be trusted. It's a good job I refused to have her working for us. Don't pull your face,' she added when she saw that he disagreed with her. 'You can't possibly think that you owe her anything now. Not after this.'

'I need to get the post delivered,' he sighed, picking up his bag. 'People will be complaining that it's late.'

He hurried out of the door, leaving Peggy alone. She sat down on the chair, then remembered that Kitty Cavanah had sat on it. She jumped up as if stung and went up the stairs to fetch some hot water and a scrubbing brush. Halfway up she heard the shop bell and contemplated leaving whoever had come in waiting. But there were parcels down there, waiting to be put on to the evening train, and there was money in the till, and the way Peggy felt today, she didn't trust anyone, so she turned and went back down to find a clerk from the rope works' offices with letters in his hand.

'I want to send these, please,' he said. 'I'm paying for stamps.'

Peggy almost snatched them from him and spread

them across the counter before looking in a drawer for the stamps that needed to be attached.

'Two shillings and fourpence,' she demanded and felt cross when she was handed a half-crown because they were short of change and she knew she was going to struggle to find the tuppence and might even have to run up the stairs to find her own purse to settle the transaction.

It really was too selfish of John to expect her to cope with everything. They needed some help.

Later that evening, after her father had brought her daughters home because her mother was still with Bessie, and after they'd had their tea and the little lasses had been put to bed, Peggy raised the subject of John employing a postboy once more.

'It means I wouldn't be left minding the post office as well as the hat shop when you go out,' she told him, watching as he fussed over the fish in his aquarium.

'I'll make some enquiries,' he promised.

Peggy sighed. It was what he always said.

She also wanted to talk about having a woman to help with the household chores, but having refused to allow Kitty Cavanah to come, she doubted he would want to hear her complaints about that again. But it wasn't just about her. She was worried about how breathless her mother had been when she'd come upstairs. She knew Bessie was right when she said that their mother was finding it hard to mind her granddaughters.

*

Dorothy had been sobbing when Bessie and her mother arrived back at the house on King Street. She took their coats and hats to hang them up and asked if Bessie would allow her to hold Julia.

'I'll understand if you don't,' she told them. 'I'll understand if you don't want me here any more. I've started to pack my things. I can be gone by tomorrow.'

'What are you talking about?' asked Bessie. She placed her daughter into the maid's arms and watched as Dorothy wept even more at the sight of her tiny face.

'It was all my fault,' wept Dorothy. 'I should never have left her unattended.'

'Of course it wasn't thy fault,' said Bessie's mother, taking Julia back into her own arms. 'Go and make us some tea. I'm sure my daughter has no intention of sending thee away. I know how she relies on thee.'

'It's true,' agreed Bessie. 'I never thought of asking you to leave. And Julia's safe now. Do as my mother says and make some tea. I'll go and put Julia to bed.'

Bessie took her daughter from her mother and went up the stairs. Her mother followed her up, but she was breathing hard by the time she reached the nursery.

'You sound very chesty,' Bessie observed as she lay Julia down to change her before settling her to sleep.

'Aye. I am a bit.'

Bessie glanced up at her mother, who'd sat down on the nursing chair. She'd had a hard life, taking in folks' washing for years and years, and it had taken its toll on her. She deserved to rest now and Bessie felt that her sister was taking advantage of her by expecting her to mind Emily and Becky all day long. She felt cross that Peggy had refused to have Kitty Cavanah to help out. None of this would have happened if she'd been more amenable to the solution, she thought.

Downstairs, the front door slammed and just a few moments later Joshua burst into the nursery.

'Is she all right?' he wanted to know as he came to check on his child.

'She's fine,' Bessie reassured him as he picked up Julia and clutched her to him.

'Miss Dorothy's just told me what happened – well, a version of it anyway. She can't stop weeping and telling me it was her fault and that she's packed her bags. What happened?' he asked.

Bessie gave him the bare details. 'Kitty Cavanah meant her no harm,' she said. 'Losing her own child must have affected her mind. When she saw Julia I don't think she could resist picking her up.'

'It was more than that. Dorothy says she took her away.'

'Not far,' Bessie told him. 'I soon found her. It was all a fuss about nothing.'

'Are you sure?' Joshua looked at her searchingly.

'I'm sure,' she replied, not wanting to make more of the events of the day than was necessary. She still felt that she ought to do something for Kitty Cavanah, despite what had happened, and she didn't want her husband to turn against the woman. 'Give her to me,' she said, gently prising their daughter from her father's grasp. 'She's tired. Let me put her in the crib and then we'll go downstairs. Dorothy should have the tea brewed by now.'

Back in the parlour they talked some more about Kitty and her family.

'I'll never be able to persuade our Peggy to employ her now,' said Bessie. 'And it seemed such a good idea.'

'Tha can't blame thy sister for having concerns, especially not after today,' said her mother.

'I know,' replied Bessie. 'But I thought that it would benefit you as well. I know you're finding it hard work to look after the lasses and I know you won't say so to Peggy.'

'I can manage,' said her mother.

'No.' Bessie shook her head. 'She's expecting too much from you. You should be able to take things easy at your time of life.'

'My time of life?' replied her mother, sounding indignant at the suggestion she was growing old. 'I've a good few years left yet, I'll have thee know, our Bessie!'

'I know,' Bessie soothed her. 'And you should be able to enjoy them.'

'So what's going to happen to the Cavanah family now?' asked Joshua.

'I don't know,' said Bessie. 'But the woman needs help. I still think we should do something.'

'Tha's thy father's daughter all right,' smiled her

mother as she set her cup and saucer down on a side table. 'Tha reminds me of him so much.'

Bessie was surprised at her words. She rarely spoke of George Anderton these days, and Bessie sometimes wondered if she'd forgotten him.

'George would help anyone who was in trouble.'

'I know that, for sure,' said Joshua. 'I owe him my life.'

'What do you think he would say if he was here?' Bessie asked her husband. 'Do you think he would want Kitty Cavanah to be sent back to Ireland?'

'I doubt it,' Joshua said. 'Maybe we can find work for her in another house?'

'Who would take her on after today?' asked Bessie's mother. 'What she did is all over the town. She'll find it hard to stay here now.'

28

Kitty lay awake for most of the night going over the events of the day in her head and trying to make sense of them. Everyone else was sleeping. Her children close by, Aileen at the far end of the mattress and Michael snoring softly in the chair by the fire with a blanket spread over him. He'd barely spoken to her since he returned earlier that evening. He'd heard what she'd done and it was clear that he was angry, and Kitty felt so much remorse that she'd let down the friends who had helped her so selflessly. Even though she still felt weak, Kitty knew she couldn't stay here for another night. In the morning she would gather her few belongings and her children and go.

It was impossible to tell when dawn came, but Michael seemed to wake instinctively with the first light. Kitty kept her eyes closed and pretended that she was sleeping as he moved around, collecting his sack and stick ready to go out to work.

Kitty heard Michael climb the steps up to the yard. A cold draught filled the cellar as the door closed behind him and smoke from the freshly lit fire wafted across the room. Aileen stirred, then eased herself out of bed and collected up the pails to fetch some water. Agnes woke, coughing. She was supposed to be starting work again for Mr Reynolds today, but Kitty didn't think she was well enough. Not that it made any difference now, she thought. They would have to set off for Stockport right away. She was left with no choice.

'Stockport?' repeated Agnes when Kitty told her of the change in their plans.

'We'll try to find those people we walked with when we left Liverpool. They said they would help us to find work. It was a mistake to come here,' she added. Kitty hugged her elder daughter to her. 'Say nothing to the others,' she whispered, 'but it seems that our family don't want to know us. They think they're too important now that they've made something of themselves. They don't want poor Irish relations like us dragging them down. We'll make our own way in the world from now on.'

'What about my dada?' asked Agnes.

Kitty was silent for a moment before she replied. It was one of the things she'd been wrestling with in her mind, all night long.

'I think we've lost him,' she said at last. 'I think we've lost him to the sea – the baby too.'

Agnes hugged her tightly. 'I know,' she whispered in her ear. 'Oh, Mam. I'm so sorry.'

They sat and held one another until they heard Aileen coming back from the pump with her two buckets of water.

'Wake the others,' Kitty told Agnes. 'It's time for us to leave.'

Aileen was kind enough to send them off with a hot drink, but she had no food in the house and Kitty knew she couldn't expect any more charity from the friend who had already done so much for them.

Aileen looked sad when the moment came for them to leave and Kitty was relieved that she was no longer angry with her. She owed Aileen so much and she didn't want to part from her on bad terms.

'I'm sorry things didn't turn out better for you,' Aileen said as she hugged Kitty and held her close for a moment. 'I'm sorry I couldn't do more to help.'

'But you've done so much!' Kitty told her. 'Far more than we could ever have expected. I don't know what would have happened to us if it hadn't been for you.'

'I'll miss you,' said Aileen. 'And these little ones.'

She clutched Maria and little Peter to her and kissed them. It was clear that she'd grown fond of them.

'May the road rise up to meet you,' she said.

They left the cellar and made their way across the filth of Butcher's Court. Kitty had tears in her eyes, but she didn't look back because she was afraid it would break her determination to go. Only Timothy and Agnes turned to wave a last farewell.

Timothy carried Peter on his back and Kitty held Maria by the hand. Agnes carried the sack with the few possessions they'd accumulated since they'd arrived in

Liverpool – mostly things that had been found whilst they were gathering rags that they'd kept back for their own use. There were a few items of clothing, a towel that was thin but still serviceable to dry themselves on, a comb with some of the teeth missing, a few pins for their hair and two chipped cups. In her purse, Kitty had a penny ha'penny. It wouldn't take them far or buy them much. Back on the road they would have to rely on what they could find, or beg for, or even steal. The nights that they didn't spend in a hedgerow might be spent in one of the asylums, although Kitty hated the prospect of the oakum picking, or the possibility that they might be rounded up and put on a boat back to Ireland, or the depths of the sea. She wasn't sure which was the worse prospect.

'We'll be better off in Stockport. We have friends there,' she told the children. 'We should have gone with them in the first place.' What she didn't say was how hurt she was that her family had treated them so shabbily. Back at home, family was everything, but here it seemed it counted for nothing.

'I'm going to see Kitty Cavanah,' announced Bessie at breakfast.

'Are you sure?' Joshua asked her. 'Do you think it's a good idea?'

'I do,' she said firmly. 'I can't let things lie as they are. I want to talk to her. If she realizes that what she did was wrong and she's sorry, then I want to give her another chance. Did you find a house that would be suitable for them?'

Joshua folded his newspaper and gave her his full attention. 'There's a little one-up one-down on Mary Ellen Street,' he said. 'There's no running water, but there's a fireplace and the chimney's clean and the roof is in good order. If I rented it out at full price it would fetch three shillings a week, but I could reduce it to two shillings for the first six months. It would give them time to get on their feet.'

Bessie reached across the table and put her hand over his. 'You're a good man,' she told him. 'I'll pay the rent from my sewing money for now. You'll agree to that, won't you?'

'It's your money as far as I'm concerned,' he replied. 'But remember to have a care.'

'Julia's safe, if that's what troubles you,' Bessie told him. 'Dorothy will never let her out of her sight again, not even for a moment. She's that grateful we haven't sent her away, I think she'd work for free if you would let her.'

Joshua laughed. 'I daresay that's true,' he replied. You have a good instinct for seeing what's good and bad in people. You remind me of your father. I just hope you're right about Kitty Cavanah.'

Bessie hoped that she was right about Kitty too. After Joshua had left for his work she once again put on her oldest jacket and a plain bonnet. The hat that Peggy had lent her to walk home in the day before was on her dressing table. Her sister had taken it from the window of her shop and Bessie thought that she must return it later. The fashion suited Peggy but she still felt more comfortable in something traditional.

Dorothy looked aghast when she told her where she was going, but she didn't argue. She was still contrite from the day before and not willing to say a word that might change the Andertons' minds about keeping her on.

'Keep an eye on Julia,' Bessie said.

'I will! I will! I won't take my eyes off her. I'm just grateful that you can still find it in you to trust me!'

Bessie brushed her assurances aside. This wasn't the Dorothy she knew and she would be glad when her maid returned to her old habit of speaking her mind.

Bessie knew what to expect when she reached Butcher's Court, not that it made the place any more salubrious. The yard was still swilling with filth and she picked her way across it to Aileen's door.

'She's gone,' Aileen told her when she enquired after Kitty.

'What? Out gathering rags?' asked Bessie.

Aileen shook her head. 'No. Gone for good. To Stockport, she said.'

'Stockport?' Bessie couldn't master her surprise.

'She said she had friends there. Seeing as her family don't want to know her, she thought she'd be better off with them.' The barbed remark struck home and Bessie felt its sting, even though Kitty wasn't her relative.

'Though I'm surprised you want anything to do with her after what happened yesterday,' Aileen added.

'I still want to help her, if I can,' Bessie replied.

'That surprises me,' said Aileen. 'But, as I said, she's gone.'

Bessie thanked her and picked her way back to the street where she stood wondering what to do. The easiest thing would be to put it all behind her and go home. But when she pictured the children who had trailed after Kitty down the back alley, looking so frail and hungry, she couldn't help wondering if they would ever get to Stockport before they fell by the roadside. Part of her could understand why Kitty Cavanah had fled, but she still felt an obligation to bring things to a better conclusion than allowing a family to starve.

Peggy took the hat from her sister. 'You can keep it if you like,' she offered.

'No,' said Bessie. 'I don't think I'd wear it.'

'How's Julia today?' Peggy asked as she returned the hat to her window display.

'She's well. She's taken no harm. Dorothy looks terrible, though. She's taken it badly, even though Joshua and I have both told her we don't blame her.'

'I've never heard of anything like it,' remarked Peggy as she stepped back from the window. 'A child should be safe enough outside its own back door. I'm sure it never happened before these Irish came.' She gave a sniff of disapproval.

'Your own husband is Irish – or half Irish at least,' Bessie reminded her.

'That's different,' she replied. 'And anyway, he's distanced himself from his mother. She was always trouble,' Peggy went on. 'This family doesn't owe her a thing. I know she's grown old and confused, but it doesn't change the way she treated our mam!'

'That's all in the past,' said Bessie.

'Well, you would say that,' Peggy told her. 'You're too young to remember what it was like.'

'I still want to do something to help the Cavanahs,' said Bessie.

'What?' Peggy stared at her sister. 'After what happened?' she demanded. 'Are you mad?'

'No,' protested Bessie. 'But I feel sorry for them. And I don't think Kitty meant any harm. She was just confused.'

'Don't ask me again to take her on as a charwoman!' Peggy declared. 'The answer is no. I'll not have her anywhere near my children. And if you have any sense you'll keep Julia well away from her as well. You haven't been to see her, have you?' she asked. She'd noticed that her sister was wearing her oldest clothes when she came in and she'd wondered why.

'I did go to Butcher's Court,' Bessie confessed. 'But Aileen Walsh told me that Kitty and her family had gone. They're on their way to Stockport.'

'Well, thank goodness for that,' said Peggy. 'Let's hope it's the last we see of them.'

'Don't you feel guilty? Not even a little bit?' asked Bessie.

'Why should I feel guilty?' Peggy was puzzled by the question.

'The woman is a cousin of your husband and John was keen to do something for her. Does it not worry you that you prevented it?'

Peggy was about to reply that it didn't worry her in the slightest, but the truth was that there was a tiny grain of guilt that pricked her conscience. Had she been wrong? She'd only wanted to save her husband from being fleeced by the Irish woman.

'Perhaps she'll have better luck in Stockport,' Peggy told her sister. 'There might be somebody there who believes her story about being a cousin.'

She saw Bessie shake her head and knew she didn't agree. 'Are you stopping?' she asked. 'You'll have to mind the shop for me if you expect me to go upstairs and put the kettle on.'

'No,' said Bessie. 'I just wanted to return the hat.' She turned and reached for the door handle. 'I'm not going to let her go,' she said to Peggy. 'Kitty, I mean. I'm going to fetch her back. Joshua has a house she can live in and I'm going to pay the rent.'

Peggy stared at her sister. 'No,' she told her. 'That's not a good idea. Let the woman go, then we can forget about all the trouble she's caused.'

'I'll not have it on my conscience if she's found dead at the roadside!' declared Bessie, and she swept out of the shop on a cloud of righteousness. Peggy stared after her. Bessie never failed to amaze her.

Kitty and her family took the road that led out of Blackburn towards Darwen. She hoped she would recall the crossroads where she'd parted from her Liverpool friends so that she could follow their route to Stockport. She had no idea how many days it would take them to reach the town. She knew that neither she nor Agnes would be able to walk far each day and that they would need to rest along the way. But there was no choice, she told herself again, as she had when they'd passed by the warehouse where Mr Reynolds sorted the rags, and then the workhouse in whose grubby hospital she and Agnes had lain so ill.

They climbed the steep brow which left her breathless and panting, then headed out over the moors where a strong wind from the north threatened flurries of early snow as November approached.

'I'm hungry,' said Timothy when they sat down to rest on a stone wall surrounding a small inn.

'I know. We'll get some food soon,' she told him. 'We might meet the pieman,' she said, even though she half hoped that they wouldn't, because once she'd spent her money she knew there was little prospect of getting any more. The thought of begging on the streets again as they'd been forced to do in Liverpool filled her with dismay.

When they'd regained their breath, Kitty stood up

and said they must go on. She'd been watching the door of the inn, afraid that someone would come out and tell them to go away. The bucket of cold water was still not forgotten and Kitty knew that the hardships of the road would be even more punishing this time.

She glanced back at Blackburn in the valley behind her. She'd had such high hopes when they'd arrived here. She'd been certain that cousin Nan would help them. But what she'd found was not what she'd expected. Help and kindness had come mostly from those who weren't her family – Aileen and Michael, and from Mrs Anderton – but she'd ruined it all by picking up the baby.

The baby, she thought, as she turned away and began to walk. Why had she done it? It made no sense to her now. Of course the baby hadn't been hers. She'd always known that. But the urge to hold it in her arms had been overwhelming and somehow one thing had led to another. Kitty wondered if she was sinking into madness. She wasn't sure, but she hoped not. She had her living children to care for and she must keep a clear head. They were relying on her, and she was forced to acknowledge that what Agnes had always tried to tell her was true – she would never see her husband or her youngest child again. They were gone. They were in God's care now, she told herself. They were safe in His arms.

*

Bessie waited impatiently for Joshua to come home for his dinner. There was nothing she could do about Kitty and her family until he came, and even when he did she wasn't sure he would agree to her request. Peggy had thought it was madness. She'd made that very clear. And she didn't even dare to ask Dorothy for her opinion because she knew what it would be.

At last she heard the front door and she rushed down from her sewing room where she'd been unable to settle to her work stitching the delicate lace trimming to Mrs Dewhurst's gown.

Dorothy was in the hall taking Joshua's hat and gloves.

'Where's Julia?' Bessie heard him ask.

'Sound asleep in the kitchen. I'll fetch the dinner up straight away,' said Dorothy, hurrying back down the steps.

Joshua looked at Bessie, seeing that she had something important to say, but Bessie waited until Dorothy had gone before she spoke. She didn't want the maid to overhear.

'Kitty Cavanah and her children have set off to walk to Stockport,' she told her husband. 'We have to find them and bring them back!'

'Maybe she won't want to come back,' he reasoned.

'But we can't just let them go. They have nothing. They probably won't even get to Stockport. I just can't bear to think of them starving in a ditch by the roadside.'

Joshua was nodding and looking thoughtful. Bessie knew that when he'd first come to this country he'd been shocked by the numbers of destitute people who walked the roads with no homes of their own, subsisting on what seasonal work they could find, supplemented by begging. 'It's not what I expected,' he'd said after an early excursion with Bessie's father to look at the route of a new railway line.

'The poor will always be with us,' her father had told him. 'And those of us who are fortunate to rise in the world would be wise to remember that and try to do what we can to help them.'

'What can we do?' Joshua asked Bessie now. 'I have a meeting this afternoon and I can't let the investors down. It's important.'

'I could go after them,' said Bessie. 'But I need transport – a chaise or a cart.'

'Not a cart!' he replied. 'I'll not see my wife on the back of a cart!'

'Will you hire a chaise for me then?' she pleaded. 'Before you go to your meeting? Will you have time?'

They both looked towards the kitchen stairs as they heard Dorothy coming up with the dishes.

'Let's eat,' suggested Joshua. 'Then we'll decide what's for the best.'

'I'm not sure going on my own would be a good idea,' said Bessie presently, as they ate their dinner. Her earlier enthusiasm had been replaced by the worry that a driver might not be amenable to her errand.

There were few people in Blackburn this morning who hadn't heard the story of the stolen baby, Joshua had told her. 'Are you sure you can't come with me?'

'Not until after my meeting,' said Joshua. 'And I'm not sure how long it will take. But we could go later if you'd rather not go alone.'

'I'm wondering if that might be better,' said Bessie. 'Surely we could still catch up with them before darkness falls.'

It was late in the afternoon before Joshua came back from his meeting with a horse and carriage. The driver waited outside the door whilst he came in to collect Bessie.

'We won't be long,' Bessie told Dorothy. She'd been forced to give the maid a brief explanation of their errand and although Dorothy had pursed her lips in disapproval, she'd said nothing.

Julia was fed and settled in her crib. Bessie knew that Dorothy would watch her carefully and she quickly fastened her bonnet, threw her red cloak around her shoulders and hurried out of the door with her husband.

'Head for Bolton,' Joshua instructed the driver. 'We're looking out for someone – a family – walking along the road.'

If the driver thought it was odd, he kept his thoughts to himself and clicked his tongue at the horse to move it off. It was slow-going as they negotiated the carts and wagons all down Darwen Street, but then they burst out of the cobbled streets and on to the dirt road that rose up the steep hill, through Darwen and then out on to the moorland, deserted apart from some isolated homesteads and flocks of sheep.

Bessie and Joshua didn't speak much as they travelled. Each of them was scanning the road ahead for any sign of Kitty and her family.

'What will we do if we can't find them?' asked Bessie at last, hoping that she hadn't brought her husband out on a wild goose chase.

'We'll find them,' Joshua replied.

Bessie wasn't sure if he really believed it or if he was merely saying it to pacify her. But they must be on the road, or at the roadside, she told herself. As long as they caught up with them before it went fully dark, they should find them easily enough.

Carts and wagons rumbled past Kitty at irregular intervals. All were heavily laden and it would have been impossible for the drivers to offer them a lift even if they had been so inclined. In a way, Kitty was glad. She didn't want to be forced to make conversation with anyone, to have to explain herself, or risk being recognized. She was thankful that Mrs Anderton had been prepared to let the matter lie, but she remembered that the crowd around her on the bridge had been hostile, even after the baby had been returned to her mother. She knew that the townsfolk had probably talked of little else and that everyone who passed her surely knew who she was and what she had done.

Kitty plodded on until she felt she couldn't take another step without a rest, and she gathered her children around her to sit on the damp, springy grass a little distance from the road. She wished that she could offer them food, but there had been sign of the pieman and it was too late in the day for them to meet him now.

She was hoping that they could reach Bolton by nightfall, although she remembered it was an unfriendly place when they had passed through before. She knew there was no asylum there and, as she wasn't prepared to knock on the doors of the workhouse, it meant they would have to find shelter somewhere or spend the night in the open.

As they sat, with the little ones on her lap, Kitty heard the sound of more wheels and hooves approaching on the road. This time it wasn't a heavily laden cart but a carriage that was bowling along at a good speed. She wondered who it was carrying and where they were going, envious of those who were privileged to ride in such comfort.

She and the children watched as it went by. The sun had gone down and in the twilight she saw two lamps shining to light the carriage's way. As it passed she caught a glimpse of a face, peering from the window as if desperately seeking something.

A moment later the vehicle slowed and stopped some few hundred yards along the road. Kitty watched, feeling anxious, wondering what was wrong.

'Do you think someone's sent the constable after us?' she asked as two figures got down and began to walk back along the road towards them, lighting their way with a lantern.

Kitty wondered if they ought to run. She stood up, but her legs almost gave way under her and she realized that although her instinct was to flee she wasn't physically capable of getting away.

'Take the little ones,' she said to Timothy urgently. 'If they've come for me then make sure you get away. Go to Stockport. Try to find our friends. They'll take care of you,' she assured the children, though whether it was a false promise she had no idea.

Timothy gripped the hands of his younger siblings, but Agnes stood firm.

'I'm not leaving you,' she told her mother.

They watched as the couple came nearer. Kitty could see that it was a man and a woman, hurrying in their direction. When they came within earshot the man called out to her.

'Mrs Cavanah! Kitty!'

A terrible sense of foreboding filled her as she presumed that he was a constable.

'Run!' she told the children. 'Run away!'

Timothy began to lead the younger ones away from the road. There was no cover for them to hide, but

Kitty thought she could delay the pursuers for long enough to give them a chance to get a head start.

'Go with them!' she urged Agnes. 'It's only me that they want.'

Agnes looked conflicted and moved away a short distance then stopped and turned back to watch her mother.

'Mrs Cavanah! Don't go!' the man called.

Kitty hesitated. The man and the woman had increased their pace and were gaining ground with every stride.

'Go!' Kitty called again to Agnes, flapping a hand at her. 'Go with Timothy!' It was breaking her heart to see her children run from her, but it was the only way that she could keep them safe. She couldn't bear the thought of them all being sent to the prison with her.

'Mrs Cavanah!' The woman was nearer to her now and Kitty could see her cloak and the strings of her bonnet flapping in the fading light as she ran. She was breathless and clutching her skirts up above the ground. The man caught up with her, but when he did he grasped her arm and drew her to a halt. Kitty stood and matched their stance. She was sure that they were glaring at her although it had become too dark to see their faces clearly.

'Mrs Cavanah,' said the man, 'we've been searching for you and your family. We're your friends. We want to help you.'

Kitty wondered if he wasn't a constable after all. She

would have expected a constable to be angry and to seize her without any warning. But she didn't recognize the man.

'Kitty, my husband and I want to help,' called the woman. 'We can offer you a place to live.'

As she came nearer, Kitty recognized her as Mrs Anderton. She didn't know what to do. Why had she come looking for her? Why did they want to help her after what she'd done? She was certain that it was a trick. She watched as the woman began to inch forward, encroaching on her. This must be how deer felt when the hunters had them cornered, she thought as she felt her heart beating wildly and her breathing become rapid, as if she'd been running herself rather than simply standing still.

'Kitty, come with us,' said Mrs Anderton, extending a hand. 'Come back to Blackburn. There's a house waiting for you. You can live rent free until you find work.'

It must be a trick, thought Kitty. They would hand her over to the law if she agreed. And then they would all be sent back to Ireland, to starve to death.

She glanced over her shoulder. Timothy and Agnes were a distance away, but they were watching. She wished they would run.

'Go!' she called out to them.

'No! Mrs Cavanah! Don't send the children away. We're here to help you,' insisted Mrs Anderton.

'Why would you want to help me?' Kitty asked suspiciously, looking at the man who must be Mr Anderton.

His face was dark, she noticed. He was keeping his distance, allowing his wife to approach and speak to her.

'I'm sorry for what happened yesterday. I don't blame you,' Mrs Anderton reassured her.

Kitty thought the whole world had turned on its head.

'You should blame me,' Kitty replied. 'What I did was wrong.'

'It's in the past,' said Mrs Anderton. 'When I asked you to come to see me it was to offer you a place to live. I'd still like to offer it to you, if you'll accept it.'

It made no sense to Kitty. If it had been cousin Nan or John Sharples, she could have understood it, but this woman and her husband owed her nothing.

'Someone helped me once,' said the man as he walked slowly towards her. 'And it's the only reason I'm where I am today. I have so much because of one man's generosity, and the best way I can thank him is to pay his kindness forward and help you in turn.'

'It should be family that helps family,' said Kitty.

'Not always,' Mrs Anderton told her. 'But I know your cousin John does want to help you as well.'

But not his wife, thought Kitty, although she said nothing. She had to remind herself that this woman was Mrs Sharples's sister and it was best not to offend her.

'The carriage is waiting,' said Mrs Anderton. 'Where will you go if you don't come with us?'

'We're on our way to Stockport. We have friends there.'

'You have friends here,' replied Mrs Anderton.

Kitty looked back to where Timothy was standing. Little Peter was crying and he'd picked him up. Maria was sucking her thumb and watching her. Where would they sleep if she refused this offer? How could she find food for them?

After a moment she nodded.

'Thank you,' she said, bewildered by the kindness she was receiving. Although as she called for Timothy to bring the little ones, she felt a moment of dread that it might be some sort of trap after all and that they would be put on a boat back to Ireland.

Kitty and her family followed Mr and Mrs Anderton across the tussocky grass and back on to the road. When they reached the carriage they all climbed aboard. There wasn't much room, but with the younger children perched on the knees of their older siblings, they managed to find space for them all and the carriage began to move, still travelling towards Bolton until the driver found a place to turn around.

'There's a house you can live in,' explained Mrs Anderton. 'I'll take care of the rent until you're earning enough to pay it yourself. It's only small,' she went on, 'and there's no furniture in it yet, but we'll get it sorted out for you. You can sleep at our house tonight. That will be all right, won't it?' she said to her husband.

'We can't leave these children to sleep on a bare floor in a cold house.'

Kitty watched a moment of doubt cross the man's face. She thought he would refuse, but he nodded.

'I don't mind. We have the room. But I'm not sure what Miss Dorothy will say.'

'She'll make no objection,' Mrs Anderton told him. 'And it's only for one night.'

Considering it had taken all day to walk up on to the moors, Kitty was surprised by how quickly they reached Blackburn in the carriage. The street lamps had been lit and she recognized the house on King Street as they drew up outside.

Both Peter and Maria had fallen asleep and she carried her youngest son up the steps as Timothy lifted Maria into his arms. Mrs Anderton ushered them into the hallway where they were met by the older woman Kitty had spoken to before.

'What's this?' she asked, staring at them all.

'The Cavanahs are going to stay the night,' Mrs Anderton told her as she handed the woman her bonnet and cloak. 'It's much too late for them to go to a house that isn't furnished yet.'

'Very well,' she replied, although Kitty could see she was far from pleased, and she felt sad that she'd let down this woman who had previously offered her sympathy.

'I'm sorry,' she burst out. 'Please forgive me.'

The woman, Dorothy, ignored her. 'Where are they to sleep?' she asked Mrs Anderton.

'There are beds in the guest room. Fetch some clean sheets from the laundry cupboard. I'll take them down to the kitchen and see what there is to eat.'

'I've prepared chops for you and Mr Anderton. But there's none to spare.'

'Well, I'm sure we can share out what we have, and there's plenty of bread and milk and vegetables,' said Mrs Anderton. 'Come this way,' she told Kitty and led the way down a flight of carpeted stairs.

They came to a huge kitchen. There was a polished range with a fire burning and some pans with steam escaping from lids that had been left at an angle. The smell of food made Kitty feel sick and hungry at the same time.

'Sit down,' said Mrs Anderton, pointing to the scrubbed wooden table with chairs around it.

Kitty thankfully lowered herself on to one. Although she was tired out, she felt an overwhelming sense of gratitude at this unbelievable kindness that was being shown to her. She knew that she didn't deserve it and she had no idea how she could ever pay these people back.

She watched as Mrs Anderton lifted the lids on the pans and looked into each one. Then she brought a loaf of bread to the table with a sharp knife and began to fill a dish with butter.

'Help yourself,' she said, although Kitty barely had the strength to slice thick wedges and pass them around. Then Mrs Anderton brought cups and saucers, a jug of creamy milk and a teapot. She reached down a tea caddy from a shelf and put four spoonfuls into the pot before filling it with boiling water and setting it to brew.

'There are plenty of vegetables here,' she announced, setting dishes on the table. 'You can mash some for the little ones and I'll pour a jug of gravy.'

To Kitty it seemed like a feast. She'd had no idea that wealthy people could put so much food on a table so easily.

'I don't want to leave you without,' she protested as Mrs Anderton transferred delicious white potatoes into a dish and offered butter, milk, salt and pepper to go with them.

'There's plenty,' replied Mrs Anderton. 'And I know how hungry you must be. Here, you must have one of the chops,' she said.

'No!' protested Kitty. 'I can't accept that. The vegetables and gravy are more than sufficient for us.'

When they'd eaten, Mrs Anderton took them back up to the hallway and then up another flight of stairs. She opened a wooden door and Kitty followed her into a room where there were two feather beds.

'I thought you and your daughters could take one and the boys can go in the other,' she said. 'I'll ask Dorothy to fetch you up some hot water so you can wash. Then I'll see if I can find you some nightclothes.'

'I'm so grateful to you. I don't know how to thank you. Words don't seem enough,' Kitty told her. She wanted to pinch herself to make sure she hadn't fallen asleep under a hedgerow and was dreaming all this luxury. But she was sure she was still awake, and part of her still worried that it might be some sort of a trick. She couldn't understand why the Andertons would take so much trouble to help strangers, especially not a stranger who had tried to steal their child.

Mrs Anderton went out of the door and closed it behind her. Kitty almost expected to hear a key turn in the lock so that they were imprisoned, but no such sound came, and she turned to the beds to fold back the crisp, clean sheets and settle her children to sleep, still not believing that she could possibly deserve any of it.

Bessie went to the nursery and stood for a while watching Julia sleep before she went downstairs to the dining room. Dorothy had brought up their supper and gone back to the kitchen. Joshua was staring at the two pork chops on his plate.

'I'm still waiting for Dorothy to come back with the vegetables and gravy,' he explained.

'I'm sorry,' Bessie told him. 'I gave it all to the Cavanahs. You don't mind, do you?'

He looked up with his serious dark eyes and just for a moment Bessie feared he was going to be angry. Then a smile twitched his lips and he began to laugh.

'I love you, Bessie Anderton,' he told her. 'Apart from your father, you're the most generous person I know.'

'And you meant it, didn't you?' she asked. 'What you said about paying kindness forward?'

'I did,' he agreed. 'I'm a lucky man to have *two* chops for my supper and a wife like you.'

29

Kitty woke to a softness she'd never experienced before. Everything around her was soft – the mattress underneath her, the pillow that cradled her head and the blankets that covered her. For a moment she kept her eyes tightly closed and savoured the sensation. She thought that she would like to live in this moment for ever. But, she told herself as she opened first one eye and then the other, such things came at a price, and as she roused herself and looked around the room at the carpet, the floral curtains, the flocked wallpaper and dark expensive furniture, she began to worry that she would never be able to pay back this kindness.

The children were still sleeping as she forced herself from the warm bed and began to dress herself. She washed her face in the water that was now cold and combed her hair as best she could with the broken comb. Then she crept down the two flights of stairs to the kitchen and tried the back door. It was locked and she felt panic rise in her.

'What's tha doing?'

She turned as the older woman came in.

'I'm not stealing anything!' she protested. 'I was looking for the privy.'

The woman came across with a key and unlocked the door for her. Kitty hurried to the outbuilding, glancing up as she went. There was no sign of Aileen or any of the other rag gatherers, and she was relieved. Heaven alone knew what people would say if they saw her in the Andertons' back yard again.

'I'm so grateful,' she told the woman, Dorothy, when she went back in. 'I've never known kindness like it.' She felt tears threaten as she spoke.

'I was sorry for thee, when tha first came,' Dorothy told her. 'I thought tha deserved a bit of help. But after what tha did . . .' She didn't end her thoughts, but turned back to her pans with a shake of her head. 'I can't forgive it,' she said after a moment.

Kitty wondered what more she could say. She didn't at all blame Dorothy. She must have been responsible for the baby, Kitty realized. Though why she'd left the child alone like that she couldn't understand.

Dorothy pointedly ignored her as she set bacon to fry and whisked eggs in a bowl, so Kitty retreated back up the stairs to the room where she'd slept. She needed to rouse the children. Then maybe they could leave. Where to she wasn't sure. There had been talk of a house but she didn't know where it was or if it even existed.

She had the children dressed and washed as well as she could manage. Peter had slept soundly but thankfully hadn't wet the feather mattress, and she was telling the others to go down to the privy in the yard, and warning them to ask politely before they crossed the kitchen, when there was a knock on the bedroom door.

'I hope you all slept well,' said Mrs Anderton. 'If you go downstairs Dorothy will give you some breakfast and afterwards I'll take you to see the house.'

'Thank you,' said Kitty, feeling that she was running out of words to express her gratitude. She ushered the children to the kitchen and the appetizing smell of the breakfast that Dorothy was preparing.

There was scrambled eggs, toast and butter and tea or milk to drink. She fed Peter first and Agnes helped Maria, though all of them struggled with the fancy cutlery, not quite knowing how to hold it and what it should be used for. But it didn't prevent them eating well and the plates were all cleared before Dorothy came back down.

Kitty helped clear the table and wash up the pots. It was the least she could do whilst she waited. Her heart lurched when Mrs Anderton came down the stairs and she saw that she was carrying her baby. She longed to hold the child again, but only watched as Julia was settled into a crib and Dorothy fussed over her. She hoped that the woman wouldn't make the mistake of leaving the little girl unattended in the yard again.

'Are you all ready?' Mrs Anderton asked after Kitty had thanked her again for the food. 'I have the key.'

Kitty put her shawl over her head and she and the children followed Mrs Anderton back up to the hallway and out of the front door. As they waited at the bottom of the steps for Dorothy to close it behind them, Kitty saw the face of the woman who lived next door looking out. Their eyes met briefly and the woman dropped her curtain hurriedly.

'This way. It isn't far,' said Mrs Anderton and they set off at a brisk walk, following her through the busy morning streets, through the town where Kitty was sure every person they passed stared and then whispered behind their hands to their companions. She hated being the object of such interest, and people must be talking about Mrs Anderton too, she thought, although her host went briskly ahead with her chin held high and spoke a bright *Good Morning* to everyone who caught her eye.

They turned down side street after side street, and Kitty was quite lost when Mrs Anderton eventually stopped in a narrow street that appeared to lead nowhere.

'This is it. Number four,' she told them and drew out the key to fit it to the lock. She pushed open the door and Kitty followed her inside. 'It's only small,' said Mrs Anderton, sounding apologetic, 'but I'm sure you can make it into a home.'

Kitty looked around. There was just one room, but a flight of steep steps rose from the back corner and she presumed there was another room of equal size up above. Against one wall was a rusty grate for a fire with a hook to hang a cooking pot or kettle from. To the front, beside the door, was a window with wooden shutters. It all looked in need of sweeping out and smelt a bit musty as if it hadn't been lived in for a while, but Kitty could barely conceive of her good fortune.

'There are some shared privies at the end of the street and a water pump,' said Mrs Anderton. 'It isn't much, I know,' she said. 'There are plans to knock this row down and build better housing for the workers in the mill, but for the time being I hope you'll take it on.'

'It's more than enough! Thank you!' Kitty replied. Compared with Aileen and Michael's cellar it seemed like a palace to her. Even the single-storey cottage back in Ireland had not been as big as this. 'But I can't allow you to pay our rent,' she added. 'We'll all find work. We'll pay our own way.'

'Well, the first four weeks are already paid,' Mrs Anderton told her, 'because you'll have other expenses until you're settled. After that, we'll see,' she agreed. 'But my father owns this street and my husband collects the rents on his behalf, so you don't need to worry about being turned out.'

'I don't deserve your kindness,' Kitty told her, as tears of gratitude overwhelmed her once again. 'Especially not after what I did.'

'That's in the past,' Mrs Anderton told her kindly. 'We won't speak of it again.'

'You did what?' asked Peggy.

Bessie wasn't surprised by the incredulity on her sister's face. She'd known this was going to be a difficult conversation.

'Why would you do that?'

'They needed help,' Bessie replied.

'I don't understand thee, Bessie. I really don't,' Peggy told her. 'What does Joshua say?'

'He wants to help her too. He wants to repay his debt to my father.'

'By giving a house to an Irish family? That makes no sense.'

'We haven't given them the house. They'll pay rent as soon as they're able.'

Peggy snorted. Bessie saw that her sister didn't believe the family would ever pay a penny.

'She's taking thee for a fool. First John and now you. Both of you are so incredibly gullible!'

Peggy looked up as the door opened and John came in.

'You'll never guess what our Bessie's done!' she said to him. 'She's found a house for that Irish woman!'

'Has tha really?' John asked Bessie. He looked pleased.

Bessie repeated her story to him as Peggy continued to shake her head.

'It'll end badly. Mark my words,' she warned them both.

'I feel a bit guilty,' John confessed to Bessie when Peggy had gone upstairs to put the kettle on. 'It should have been me doing summat for them. They are my cousins.'

'Joshua and I are in a better position to help them,'

Bessie told him. 'And I feel so sorry for the woman. Her life hasn't been easy.'

'I know. But I still wish I'd done more and not left it to others,' he told her. 'I wish Peggy had let her come to work for us. What happened yesterday would never have happened then.'

'Yesterday is in the past. We must forget it.'

'Peggy'll not forget it,' John observed, and Bessie knew that he was right. No one could hold a grudge like her sister. 'But tha's cut from a different cloth,' he told Bessie. 'I'll not say that tha's better than her, but tha's different.'

'I know,' said Bessie. She'd always been different. She knew that and she knew that part of Peggy's problem was her jealousy that Bessie had somehow managed to outstrip her in wealth and status. 'But Peggy'll come round,' she said. 'She always does, given time. And it would be better for our mam if she didn't have to look after the children so often.'

'Aye.' John nodded and Bessie thought he looked even more guilty. 'I've been remiss,' he admitted. 'I've been so busy building up this business that I've never noticed those suffering around me. I will get some help,' he promised. 'If it can't be Kitty Cavanah then it'll have to be another lass.'

'There's the daughter,' Bessie suggested.

'I doubt that would go down well either,' John mused. 'Isn't there a lad as well?'

'Timothy,' Bessie told him. 'He's about ten years old.'

'I was thinking of taking on a lad to deliver the post.'

'You'd need someone who could read,' said Bessie. 'I doubt he can.'

'He could learn.'

'Yes. That's true.'

'I could take him on as an errand lad at first. Maybe Peggy would teach him his letters; she knows how it's done. Or maybe he'd be better off at the Sunday School,' he added as he thought Peggy would probably refuse. 'Either way I could promote him when I was sure he wouldn't mix up the addresses.'

Bessie thought it seemed a good solution. It would mean one of the family would be employed and she knew that John was keen to do his bit to help the Cavanahs – to ease his own conscience if nothing else.

'I'll have to mention it to Peggy first,' he said, sounding gloomy.

'She'll come round,' Bessie told him, hoping that it was true.

'What are you discussing so earnestly?' asked Peggy when she came back downstairs and saw them with their heads together.

'John's telling me he plans to take on a postboy.'

'About time too! I've been telling him for an age that I can't mind the post office and the hat shop at the same time.'

Bessie didn't tell her sister who John planned to employ. She refused the offer of tea, made her excuses and left, expecting the sound of arguing to follow her up the street.

Kitty glanced out of the grubby window when she heard the sound of a cart outside. Agnes had gone to see Mr Reynolds about her job at the warehouse and Timothy had insisted on going out to look for rags even though it was late in the morning. Kitty had found a bucket in the upstairs room and been to the pump to fill it with water, intending to wash the floor – although really it needed a good sweeping first, but she had no brush.

A sudden rapping on her door made her jump and spill a good portion of the water, which trickled downhill towards the bottom step of the stairs. Reaching for Peter to move him out of the way of the wetness, she went to the door cautiously, hoping that it wasn't the constable or some angry neighbour come to tell her that she wasn't welcome here.

'Mrs Cavanah?' asked the wagon driver. Kitty nodded. 'Delivery for thee,' he said and began to unload things from the back of the cart. 'Where dost tha want these?' he asked as he propped a mattress up against the wall by her front door, covering the window and darkening the room. He turned back for another and lifted it down.

Kitty watched as the man carried the mattresses up the steep narrow stairs and let them fall with a thud to the floor, throwing up clouds of dust. If he thought her floors weren't clean he didn't let it show on his face, and when he came back down he carried in a rough wooden table, two chairs, a pile of blankets and a huge box containing some pans, mismatched crockery, a few basic items of cutlery including a good sharp knife and a ladle, a kettle and a teapot.

'Are you sure this is all meant for me?' asked Kitty as he thumped the box down on to the table.

'I were told to fetch it here. That's all I know. Good mornin',' he said and briefly touched the peak of his cap before climbing back on to his cart and flapping the reins at the horse who reluctantly heaved in the shafts to pull it away.

Kitty watched him go and when he'd turned the corner she carried Peter back inside and found Maria looking at the contents of the box with interest.

'We used to have one of these at home,' she said, pointing to one of the pans. 'Is it the same one?'

'No,' said Kitty remembering how they'd had to leave behind the things they hadn't been able to carry when they'd left Ireland. Her husband had promised her new things when they arrived in America – things bought with the honest money he was sure he would be able to earn. Instead, she had these, but she was more thankful for them than she could ever express.

When Peggy had heard her husband say he was thinking of taking on a postboy, she'd been thankful. It would mean he would be able to stay in the shop and she wouldn't be so stretched. All she had to do now was persuade him to take on suitable help for the house and things would be much better. Better for her mother too. She knew that her mother was tired and she felt guilty about expecting her to mind her daughters every day. Still, Emily would be starting at the school soon – the same school where she'd learned to read and write herself and where she'd taught for a while as an assistant teacher. Thank goodness she'd left that job, she thought as she smoothed the feather on a hat that had just been unpacked from a consignment sent all the way from London. She'd hated it.

'So who were you thinking of employing as a post-boy?' she asked John. 'The Slaters have a boy who seems keen. What about him?'

'I was thinking of the Cavanah lad,' he suggested warily.

'What?' The hat fell from her fingers and she bent to retrieve it even though her floor was spotless. 'You can't be serious?'

'He is family.'

'He's an Irish urchin who can't even read and prob-ably has light fingers as well!' she burst out. 'Why even consider him when there must be a dozen lads who're much more suitable?'

'I want to do something to help,' he told her firmly.

'I can't leave it all to Bessie and Joshua. I have a responsibility to do my part.'

Peggy put the hat down, uncertain how to reply. She didn't want to argue with John again. He'd been cross enough when she'd refused to have Kitty Cavanah as a charwoman, and it was most unlike him to lose his temper. They did say that blood was thick, she told herself, and maybe John was more like his mother than she'd ever given him credit for. She hoped it wasn't true. After six years of marriage she hoped that she knew him better than that. She hoped she could trust him. But the arrival of this Irish family had turned his head and she found she was completely bewildered by it. She couldn't understand why he insisted that they were cousins simply on the word of an Irish woman who had proved herself to be so untrustworthy. Goodness knows what she would have done with Julia if Bessie hadn't found her in time. But then her own sister seemed to have fallen equally in thrall to the woman. Why she wanted to help her rather than calling the constable was something Peggy would never understand.

John looked up from the post he was sorting, clearly puzzled by her silence. It was not like Peggy to say nothing, but she felt she'd said every word she could on the subject.

'He seems a bright enough lad. He can start with errands,' John suggested.

'Do as you like,' snapped Peggy. 'Just keep him away

from me and on no account must he be in the shop when I have a customer! My ladies do not want to see Irish when they come in to make their purchases.'

She watched as John packed the letters into the bag, slung it over his shoulder and reached down his cap.

'I'll not be long,' he said.

Peggy sat down on the chair and listened to the echoes of the shop bell. There was nothing she could do to stop this, she realized. Her husband and her sister and her brother-in-law were all set on providing as much as they could for these Cavanahs. She wondered if she was the only one who could see that they were simply storing up trouble ahead. She'd be proved right in the end, she told herself. She stood up, took out a duster and began to furiously polish her countertops.

When the letters had been delivered, John glanced up at the market hall clock and decided there was time to see Kitty Cavanah before he went back to the post office. Bessie had told him that they were on Mary Ellen Street and he headed that way, hoping to catch her at home and make the offer of a job to Timothy.

Kitty answered the door looking anxious. John could see the fear in her eyes and he was quick to reassure her.

'I just came by to ask if there's anything tha needs.'

'Come in,' she invited.

John was surprised to see that she had a few sticks of furniture, although the fireplace was empty and even though she had a kettle there was no way of boiling it.

'Tha could do with a bucket of coal,' he observed.

'I could,' she agreed, 'but I'm keeping the penny ha'penny in my purse for some supper.'

'Where did you get this?' he asked, sitting down on one of the chairs.

'Mrs Anderton sent it. She's been so good to us. I don't know how I'll ever repay her.'

'Here.' John delved into his pocket and brought out a shilling. Kitty began to shake her head, but he left it on the table, knowing that she needed it. 'I've come to talk about Timothy,' he said.

'What's he done?' Kitty sounded alarmed.

'He's not in any trouble,' John reassured her and explained about the errand boy's job.

'Is it all right with your wife?' asked Kitty, sounding unsure.

'She's been nagging me to take on a lad for a while now,' he replied. It was the truth, if not the whole truth.

'I'm sure he'll be keen,' said Kitty. 'He's out collecting rags at the moment, but I know he'll want to come and work for you. He'll work hard. I'll make sure of it,' she added. 'You won't regret taking him on.'

'And where's your other daughter? Agnes, is it?'

Kitty nodded. 'She's gone to ask Mr Reynolds at the warehouse for her job back. And once I'm feeling well I'll go out looking for rags again. I can take the little ones with me.'

John nodded. Maybe Kitty wouldn't have accepted

the charwoman's job if it had been offered, he thought. She couldn't have cared for his daughters when she had no one to care for her own children. Perhaps it would be better if he found somebody else to help Peggy.

'He can't read,' said Kitty. 'My Timothy, I mean. His father could read a bit and he was going to teach him, but there were so many other things to do. He had to go looking for work when the potato harvest failed – though there wasn't any work.'

John felt uncomfortable when he saw her eyes brighten with tears.

'Dost tha still think he'll come? Thy husband?'

'No,' she whispered. 'I hoped he would, but I think he'd have come by now if he was still . . . alive.' She almost choked over the last word and wiped her face on the palms of her hands. John wanted to put an arm around her to comfort her, but he wasn't sure the gesture would be welcome.

'Well, send Timothy to see me when he gets back,' he told her, feeling awkward. 'He can run errands for now and I'll get him a place at the Sunday School as well, so he can learn a bit of reading and writing.'

'I'm so grateful to everyone that's helped me,' Kitty told him, still trying to compose herself. John nodded and got up to go. There was a knot inside him – sympathy and a good feeling that came with assisting someone worse off than himself. He understood now what pleasure that could bring. George Anderton understood it well, as did Joshua and Bessie. If only Peggy would soften a little she would feel it too, he thought as he walked back to the shop. And she would in time. He was sure of that. It always took Peggy a little longer than most to see the good in people, but she usually saw it in the end. Otherwise she'd never have married him.

30

Kitty woke with the sunrise. Whilst it would be nice to have curtains for her window when she could afford them, at least the sun in her eyes roused her early enough to go out and look for the best rags.

She got up from the mattress, still wondering if she would ever get used to such luxury, stretched and began to dress herself.

'Time to get up,' she told the children as she bent to lift Peter, thankful that he'd slept through the night and that he was dry. He'd not wet the bed once since they'd come to live in this house.

She helped her youngest boy down the stairs, trying not to think that there ought to be another child, even younger. The hurt still stung as she thought of the baby. He'd been a poorly scrap of a thing. He might not have lived long anyway, but to lose him to the sea was a terrible thing. She'd been to the church to speak to Father Kaye about him and to say that he'd been baptised at their little church back in Ireland.

'God would never allow such an innocent babe to stay in purgatory,' the priest had reassured her. 'He'll be in the arms of Our Lady and she'll hand him to you when you get to heaven.'

Kitty had been comforted by the words. So much so that she'd started to attend St Alban's regularly on a Sunday – after she'd gathered her rags. For it was all very well for Father Kaye to tell her that Sunday was a day of rest. He didn't have four children to feed and clothe on what little they managed to earn. Though she always kept a ha'penny back for the collection plate. It was her bargain with God that he would care for her baby until she could hold him in her arms again.

As for her husband, common sense decreed that he wouldn't come now. Too much time had passed. Yet she still clung to a fragment of hope that she might be proved wrong and that one day he would find them.

'Hurry!' she called up to her other children. 'The kettle's on!'

She always made them tea before they went out. It was a luxury they could barely afford, but Kitty felt the need to make up for the loss of their father. It had been hard for all of them, but she was proud of the way Timothy and Agnes worked so hard and never grumbled.

Timothy came down first. His shirt was clean and his hair was brushed. She knew that John Sharples expected him to look smart and she tried hard to send him out looking presentable, even though another change of shirt wouldn't go amiss because it wasn't easy to get clothing washed and dried in the little house.

Agnes was pushing her hair into her cap as she came downstairs. Hers was a dirty job and despite the apron she wore, her gown was often smeared in grease and dirt. Kitty wished she could afford to buy her another, and a new bonnet for Sunday best. Perhaps in another month or two, if she was lucky on the streets, she would have managed to save enough for some material from the market, as well as putting some pennies aside to try to pay back those who had been so kind to her.

She left Agnes and Timothy drinking their tea and, with a reminder to close the door behind them when they went out, she picked up her sack and stick and took Maria and Peter to start their rounds.

The day before, she'd scoured the backs of the houses on Richmond Terrace and today she planned to begin on King Street. The alley was empty when she arrived and Kitty hoped she was first to search it that morning. Maria exclaimed over two nails and put them into her sack. She was sharp-eyed and seemed to enjoy her task.

Kitty set Peter down to toddle beside them as she poked her stick into the piles of rubbish, finding some coloured cloth at the back of one house and a discarded copper pan outside another, which she hoped would bring a generous payment from Mr Reynolds.

When she reached the house where the woman who was always complaining about her lived, she hurried past with her head down. She never put anything outside her back gate.

Then she heard a door open, and fearing trouble, she picked up Peter and grasped Maria's hand, ready to flee.

'Mrs Cavanah.'

She turned to see that it was Dorothy quietly calling her name. Kitty approached her cautiously, not sure of her welcome.

'Would the little ones like a cup of milk?' she asked.

Kitty wasn't sure if the offer was being made because Dorothy had forgiven her or if it was because she'd been sent to ask by Mrs Anderton. Kitty suspected the latter, but she accepted gratefully. She knew how much Maria and Peter would enjoy the treat of creamy milk and she hoped there might be a slice of bread on offer as well.

'Step inside,' Dorothy invited, and Kitty knew it was to hide them from the view of the neighbour.

She left the dirty sacks and sticks by the back door, hoping that no one would come along and sneakily steal them. The other gatherers were friendly enough but she wouldn't trust any of them if they saw easy pickings.

The kitchen was warm and clean and Dorothy told Peter and Maria to sit at the table. The chair was too high for Peter to clamber up and Kitty lifted him on to a cushion and watched as Dorothy poured their drinks. There was a loaf of bread on the table and Dorothy cut slices and lavished them with butter before setting them on plates in front of the children.

'Would tha like a cup of tea?' she asked Kitty.

'Yes. Please.'

'Sit down then,' said Dorothy as she put a cup on a

saucer and poured from the teapot before returning it to the hearth to keep warm.

'Mrs Anderton sent these down in case tha came by,' Dorothy said, reaching for a bundle of fabric. To her amazement, Kitty saw that the material was new.

'Is she sure? Does she not need this herself?' she asked.

'She says it's offcuts.' Dorothy sniffed her disapproval, but still pushed the bundle towards Kitty. The material was too good for rags and Kitty realized she was intended to take it home and make clothes for her children.

'Please tell her thank you,' said Kitty as she watched Dorothy sit down and add milk to her own tea. 'She's been so good to me. It's more than I deserve.'

Dorothy didn't reply, but Kitty suspected she agreed.

'I didn't mean any harm,' she said after a moment, feeling uncomfortable in the strained atmosphere of the kitchen where she sensed she wasn't welcome.

'Aye. Happen so,' replied Dorothy.

'You were kind to us when we first came,' Kitty continued. 'I'm grateful.'

Dorothy nodded again but didn't reply. Kitty was sorry. She worried that Dorothy had been blamed for leaving the child alone.

As soon as the children had finished, she stood up to go and Dorothy let them out of the door. Kitty was thankful to see the sacks were still there.

She hurried away from King Street and scoured one

or two other places, but there wasn't much left to find and she decided that she might as well take what she had to Mr Reynolds and then go home. *Home*. It was strange to think of the little house as such. But it was the only one she had now so she must acquaint herself with the idea and do everything she could to make it a proper home for her children.

When she turned into Church Street, she saw Timothy coming towards them. He was hurrying along with eager strides and carrying a parcel under his arm. His face was serious and determined, and pride flooded through her as he suddenly saw them and a smile lit his face.

'Can't stop,' he told her as he passed. 'I'm on a very important errand.'

Kitty watched him for a moment. He was so keen to do well and please Mr Sharples, even if Mrs Sharples was harder to satisfy. She was watching them from the window, Kitty saw. She was tempted to wave, but thought better of it and hurried the younger children on. She wished that she could be on better terms with Mrs Sharples. Her husband and sister had done so much to help them, but her very existence seemed to offend the woman. Still, that wasn't her fault, she reminded herself. She'd only come to Blackburn to seek help from her family and that wouldn't have been necessary if they hadn't fallen on hard times.

Kitty heard the shop door jingle and someone called her name. It was John Sharples on his way out with the post.

'I see tha's found some good stuff this morning,' he greeted her, nodding towards the bundle of cloth she had under her arm.

'It's your sister-in-law being generous again,' she replied, glancing at Mrs Sharples again. Surprisingly the woman gave her a half-smile. Kitty returned it. It was a start, she thought.

When they reached the warehouse, the smell struck her with its pungent force, as it did every morning. How Agnes managed to work in it every day she had no idea, but when she'd suggested to her daughter that she should look for something else, Agnes had said that she was used to the pong and she enjoyed the work. She was laughing now with some of the other girls as they sorted the myriad stuff piled on the table. When she saw them, Agnes waved and smiled, and Maria ran across to watch what her older sister was doing.

Mr Reynolds came and weighed the cloth and counted the nails and paid her sixpence.

'What's tha got there?' he asked. 'I can give thee more for that.'

'I'm keeping this,' Kitty told him. 'I think there's enough to patch together something for Agnes to wear to church on a Sunday.'

He nodded. 'I'll not take it from thee then,' he agreed. 'How's things?' he asked.

'Things are good,' Kitty told him with a smile.

It was true, she thought. With her older two children's wages and the money she was making from gathering rags, they were managing. And even though she'd regretted it at first, she was glad that she'd come here now. It wasn't the new life in America that she'd been looking forward to when she left Ireland with all her family – and nothing would ever compensate for the loss of her husband and baby – but there'd been more blessings than she could ever have imagined when she'd first looked down on the smoking chimneys and sooty mills of Blackburn. She'd found friends who had helped her without any thought of recompense for all their kindness. She'd been given so much more than she had ever expected or deserved. And although there were days when the image of her ruined cottage formed in her mind's eye, Kitty knew she must keep her promise to herself and never look back. Her family's future was here now, and she would strive to make a good life for herself and her children in this northern English town.

Acknowledgements

Thank you to my editor Hannah Smith for all her hard work and input. Also to Clare Bowron, to my copy-editor Sarah Bance, my proofreader Jennie Roman, to Emma Henderson and all the editorial management team, and everyone at Penguin Michael Joseph.

He just wanted a decent book to read ...

Not too much to ask, is it? It was in 1935 when Allen Lane, Managing Director of Bodley Head Publishers, stood on a platform at Exeter railway station looking for something good to read on his journey back to London. His choice was limited to popular magazines and poor-quality paperbacks – the same choice faced every day by the vast majority of readers, few of whom could afford hardbacks. Lane's disappointment and subsequent anger at the range of books generally available led him to found a company – and change the world.

'We believed in the existence in this country of a vast reading public for intelligent books at a low price, and staked everything on it'
Sir Allen Lane, 1902–1970, founder of Penguin Books

The quality paperback had arrived – and not just in bookshops. Lane was adamant that his Penguins should appear in chain stores and tobacconists, and should cost no more than a packet of cigarettes.

Reading habits (and cigarette prices) have changed since 1935, but Penguin still believes in publishing the best books for everybody to enjoy. We still believe that good design costs no more than bad design, and we still believe that quality books published passionately and responsibly make the world a better place.

So wherever you see the little bird – whether it's on a piece of prize-winning literary fiction or a celebrity autobiography, political tour de force or historical masterpiece, a serial-killer thriller, reference book, world classic or a piece of pure escapism – you can bet that it represents the very best that the genre has to offer.

Whatever you like to read – trust Penguin.